The Scrolls of the BONEFAIRY CASTLE

DAVID L. SPIEGEL

THE SCROLLS OF THE BONEFAIRY CASTLE

iUniverse books may be ordered through booksellers or by contacting:

iUniverse
1663 Liberty Drive
Bloomington, IN 47403
www.iuniverse.com
844-349-9409

Because of the dynamic nature of the Internet, any web addresses or links contained in this book may have changed since publication and may no longer be valid. The views expressed in this work are solely those of the author and do not necessarily reflect the views of the publisher, and the publisher hereby disclaims any responsibility for them.

Any people depicted in stock imagery provided by Getty Images are models, and such images are being used for illustrative purposes only.
Certain stock imagery © Getty Images.

ISBN: 978-1-6632-3304-2 (sc)
ISBN: 978-1-6632-3305-9 (hc)
ISBN: 978-1-6632-3306-6 (e)

Library of Congress Control Number: 2021924880

Print information available on the last page.

iUniverse rev. date: 12/10/2021

This book is dedicated to Julie Spiegel.

PROLOGUE

There I stood, frozen like a deer caught in headlights. I didn't know what to say. A shy kid's nightmare. My hands started to sweat as I stood there holding my index card with the topic I was sharing in front of the class. Everything was going great. I was in midstream sharing details about the many trips I took out to my grandparents' farm when my teacher stopped me and asked where my grandparents came from. I looked at her and then at the faces of my classmates. I felt the blood rush to my face. I was so embarrassed because I didn't know. The children pointed and laughed at me because I stood there frozen. I ran out of the classroom, almost tripping over the podium, and found myself running to the nurse's office. I asked the nurse to call my mom.

My mom showed up with a worried look on her face. "Oh, sweetheart, are you okay?" she asked.

"I'm okay, Mom. I just want to go home," I answered.

"I thought you were supposed to share something about yourself in front of the class. What happened? You look so flushed."

I explained, "I was sharing my memories of when I visit Grandpa and Grandma and how much fun I have on the farm, but the teacher gave a surprise question and asked me about where my grandparents came from. I froze, Mom. I really don't know anything about where my family came from."

"Oh, goodness, I thought your dad told you that your ancestors are from Europe," she said.

I was confused. "I don't remember Dad telling me that, but what else don't I know? Like, what nationality are we?" I asked.

"I'll tell you what: you should visit your grandparents. They'd love to see you, and I know how much your grandpa loves to tell stories. I remember your father told me that when he was little, his dad did the same thing. You could spend some time and sit down together, and he'll tell you all about your ancestors and where you came from, answering all your questions," she explained.

"That sounds like a great idea, Mom. Will you take me this weekend?" I asked.

"Oh honey, your dad and I have plans this weekend, but we can drop you off, and you can stay the whole weekend," she said.

When the weekend arrived, we took off to my grandparents' house to see what I could find out. My grandparents lived on a farm about fifty miles away, and it was always fun to go to the farm because it was high in the hills and away from town. I could look down this long driveway and see the cars go by. They were so far away that they looked like little ants. I loved to play in the barn and with the chickens, but this trip would be much different. I was on a mission. I had so many questions and didn't know how or where to begin. I hoped my grandpa would be willing to share everything with me.

Grandpa was sitting on the porch as we drove up, and he gave us a wave. I got out of the car, ran up to him, and gave him a big hug.

"There's my little man Hunter. My goodness, how you've grown since the last time I saw you. Let me take a look at this handsome young man," he said as he shook my hand like an adult. "You've become quite the strapping fella. How much can you lift now?" he asked.

"Oh, Grandpa, I'm only ten years old," I said, giggling.

"Well, that certainly can't be. I bet you could help me with some chores while you're here. You know, I'm not as young as I used to be, and it takes me longer to get things done," he said as he winked.

"Dad, I'm sorry we're not going to be able to stay. Hunter wanted to come see you, and he can stay all weekend. I'm sure Hunter would love to help you. I think you two have some catching up to do," praised Mom.

"That's real grand. I'd love that," Grandpa agreed. "Why don't you go inside and see your grandma? I bet she's got some milk and homemade chocolate chip cookies."

"Oh, yummy! Thanks, Mom, for bringing me here," I said as I ran to hug her goodbye.

"You're welcome, sweetheart. You have fun, but be a good boy for me," she requested.

"I will, Mom," I promised.

My mom got in the car and drove off as I waved. When the car disappeared from sight, I went inside to the kitchen. There was my grandma taking the hot, delicious cookies out of the oven. My grandma made the best cookies. I ran to her to give her a big hug. She smelled just like cookie dough.

"Hi, Grandma. I missed you so much," I said emotionally.

"My little Hunter, you are such a sweet boy. I missed you too. Now, I know you want some cookies, but I just took them out of the oven, so they're very hot," she explained.

"But, Grandma, that's when they're the best. The chocolate is melted and all gooey," I countered.

I got some cookies and a glass of milk and walked back out to the front porch. Grandpa was rocking on his favorite rocking chair. He once told me it was the same chair his mother had sat in while rocking him to sleep when he was a baby. It has been restored several times due to the bad weather. It was one of the big, roomy rockers that could fit two people, but my grandpa was a tall man and needed all the space for his long legs. I sat down on the stoop and started eating my treat.

"Well, little man, what have you been up to? I hope you're keeping up with your studies," says Grandpa.

"I am. We have been doing special projects in the classroom," I replied.

"Your mother told me over the phone that you had a bad day the other day at school. Is that true? What happened, son?" he asked.

"Yes, Grandpa, that's true," I said as I stopped eating my cookie and put my head down. "We normally get to talk about anything we want when we stand in front of the class. The teacher asked about you and Grandma and where my family is from. I was prepared to talk about you and Grandma, but also about this farm—how I have so much fun here. I froze. I can't explain it, Grandpa. I was so embarrassed. The other children laughed at me, so I ran out of the classroom." I started getting all flustered again just thinking about it.

"My little Hunter, you shouldn't worry so much about that. Other children can be cruel, but that's because they're jealous of you. You're such a handsome and smart fella, and they wish they were like you. That is their way of trying to hurt you," Grandpa said with a look of proudness.

"The teacher said I can make it up next week. Please, Grandpa, won't you help me?" I begged.

Grandpa gave me a big smile. He could see how important it was to me to learn. I had so many questions but didn't know what to ask first. Grandpa stood up, patted me on my head, and said, "Wait right here. I'm going to go get a cup of coffee and some of those wonderful cookies. The smell is making me hungry!"

He went in the house and was back in no time. He sat back down on his rocker. I wanted to fire away with my questions, but he looked so solemn. Little did I know he was preparing to tell me the most exciting story.

"Now, this is a good cup of coffee, and these cookies are definitely worth waiting for," he said.

"Grandpa, what was it like when you were my age?" I asked.

Grandpa said, "It was definitely different. I grew up on this very land, as you know. The house was much smaller, and we had a lot more farm animals. I had many chores to do before and after school. It is not like how it is today for you young people. You know how important it is to do your chores and mind your parents, don't you, Hunter?"

"Yes, sir, I do. I clean my room every day. I take out the trash. I set the table for dinner and help clean up after dinner," I proclaimed.

"That's my boy. Chores teach you a lot. One day you will move away and go to college. You will need everything that you've learned as a small lad when that happens, because you will have to take care of yourself. Until that happens, you listen to your mom and always do what she asks of you," Grandpa said.

"I will, sir," I said.

Grandpa asked me to take our dishes to Grandma. I got up off the stoop, gathered the dishes, and took them into the kitchen.

"Oh, thank you, dear," says Grandma.

I replied, "Thank you, Grandma. The cookies were delicious."

"You're quite welcome. I made plenty because I knew you'd be here all weekend."

I went back out to the porch. It looked like Grandpa was asleep. I didn't want to wake him, but I was so anxious to find out our family's history. As I started to walk down the steps, Grandpa spoke up. "Come pull up a chair, son. I'm going to tell you about our ancestors. Now, pay close attention to me."

"I will, Grandpa. I really want to know everything," I announced.

"Your father was told this very same story when he was about your age."

"Then why hasn't Dad shared it with me?" I asked.

"That's a very good question. Your father wanted it to come from me. He said he isn't as good at telling stories as I am. Plus, he knows how I enjoy it. I've waited for you to be the right age so you'd understand. I still remember the look on his face when I told him. Oh, he interrupted me with questions and disbelief. Some of it may be hard for you to believe as well, but it is all true," Grandpa said.

"Please tell me everything," I said.

"A long time ago—and I mean, a long time ago, in the medieval times—over in another part of the world known as Europe, that is where our ancestors came from. The medieval era was the period from the fifth to the fifteenth centuries. Your great, great, great, great-grandfather lived back then. By the way, that is who you got your name from. His name was Hunter, and he was well-known as the royal servant to the queen of Bonefairy Castle. The Bonefairy Castle was where the queen lived, and as far as I know, it is still there. Remember that this is back in medieval times, and things were very different back then. Hunter was very loyal to the queen. He was the leader of the Royalmen, kept everyone in line, and made sure that they all did what the queen wanted."

"Wow, Grandpa, how do you know all of this?" I asked.

"This information was written on scrolls and was kept a secret, but it stayed within our family. However, no one knows where those scrolls are. You might want to write this down so you can remember, for when you share with your classmates," explained Grandpa.

"What's a scroll?" I asked.

"Scrolls were made of special paper. They were used for writing records of events. They were rolled up at each end to protect the written words. When you unrolled it, you hold the left side and open from the right so you can read the events in order," explained Grandpa. "Now, the story goes like this …

★★★

There was a long, brutal battle. The battles during the medieval era were very violent. There were many battles back then because that was the only way people owned any land. Lands were always subject to invasion, and there was the constant threat of war or land disputes. Castles were built to act as a power base. The largest of all castles was the Bonefairy Castle, and it was more than just a castle. It was where the queen of Bonefairy lived. Bonefairy was the name of the land that was just outside of the town of Harbor. It was a very large piece of land, and the Bonefairy Castle was built on the land by the queen's fairies. The queen of Bonefairy had special powers. No one really knew what powers she had, but she was feared and honored at the same time. When you looked at the queen, you would wonder how such a beautiful woman could be so powerful. She looked so young. She had long, flowing blonde hair; very large white wings; and an extremely bright golden hue around her.

Hunter was a large, muscular man. He wore his armor proudly with his broad shoulders and chest. He was six feet five inches and strikingly handsome with dark European complexion, dark long hair and beard, and blue eyes. Hunter visited the queen of Bonefairy on several occasions, and he knew he should always abide by the queen's wishes. The queen liked Hunter and knew he'd always be loyal to her. Hunter had fought many battles and defeated anyone who tried to hurt or take over Bonefairy Castle. The queen ruled Bonefairy Castle and the surrounding land. Hunter led the Royalmen when it came to fighting wars and battles. The queen would rely on him to make the right decisions, and the she knighted Hunter. That is how he became Sir Hunter.

CHAPTER 1

—————◇—————

S ir Hunter couldn't believe how long the battle lasted. He thought it would never end. At one time, he was worried that they wouldn't be able to defeat their enemies. There was so much bloodshed. Everyone wanted to take over Bonefairy Castle. He had a feeling it wouldn't be the last time people would have to safeguard the castle. He knew he and his men could not give up and let others conquer the castle. His men were very vigilant. He hated that he had lost many of his men, but that was a part of being a Royalman. They served and protected at all costs. Many good men died defending the Bonefairy Castle.

Sir Hunter and his men may have won the battle, but the threat wasn't over. Going back home was going to be difficult, and there could still be other enemies threatening their journey back home. Many of the men were wounded, so it would slow down the travel back home, but Sir Hunter knew the men looked forward to being back home. It was his mission to ensure they got back safely.

There were many long days and nights when the fighting was so bad that the men didn't know when one day ended and when the next started; the sun never came out. Eventually it was time for the men to take everything they had left from the battle and start their trip for home. They had many miles to travel.

Sir Hunter and his trusty friend, Wheels, packed up and started their journey home. Wheels was Sir Hunter's big, strong horse, and they'd traveled the lands many times. Sir Hunter had enough water for the journey and should be able to find food along the way. What a day for the return home. Many of the men would not make the trip and had lost their lives in the battle, but Sir Hunter was glad it was over.

The queen would be happy when she learned that they had won, and there should be a great festival in town after everyone got back. Sir Hunter knew that it would take several days to make the journey back, so the news will have to wait. He told the men that they were allowed to head back to their homes and families. He told them that he would be in contact with them later. The battle was very hard for the men, and many families would never see their loved ones again. Sir Hunter wished he could be there to console them, but he had to head toward the castle.

As Sir Hunter started out, he could see that there was an opening in the forest ahead. He knew he must be careful. There could still be enemies out there who did not know the war was over. They could be slightly wounded but still able to attack. He'd have to be on his guard at all times. Enemies could be hidden in bushes, or anywhere. He decided to wait at the edge of the opening for a few minutes, just to be safe. The birds were singing. Birds were always aware of their surroundings and danger, so Sir Hunter guessed that it was all right to move on.

As the morning warmed up, Sir Hunter could see that there was someone ahead of him. It looked like one of his men had made it through the battle and was trying to make it back to his family. He didn't look like he was going to make it without some assistance. Sir Hunter stopped to ask him if he was all right and if he could be of any help with his journey.

Sir Hunter said, "Hello, friend, I see that we are traveling on the same path and going in the same direction. Can I assist you? You don't look like you are going to make it, and your horse is worse for the wear. The battle we survived was very demanding and has taken a great toll on us both, but I have the time to give you a helping hand. Let's rest for the night and continue tomorrow. I will build a fire and find some food for us. We can stay in the opening just ahead of us, if that's all right. I will put our horses over there as well and give them water and food for the night. I know that a good night's sleep will help us both for the rest of the trip. I understand that you know my name as Sir Hunter, and that I am the leader of the queen's Royalmen. What is your name, friend?"

"Yes, I know who you are. My name is Xavier," the man answered.

"It's my great pleasure to know you. I'm heading home and then will meet up with the queen at the Bonefairy Castle to give my report on the battle. Where is home for you, Xavier?" Sir Hunter asked.

"I live just outside the town of Harbor. It's just a few miles from the castle," he explained.

"Yes, I know it well. I have been there many times. I will make sure you get back to your home safely. I will go to my cabin before continuing on to Bonefairy Castle," Sir Hunter responded.

As night came upon them, Sir Hunter felt good that he had met Xavier on the trail so they could look out for each other the rest of the way.

"Do you have any food, Xavier? I don't have much myself. I was going to hunt or fish a little as I headed home. If you don't have anything, we can make do. After all, we just came through a rough battle. If we can make it through that, we can make it the rest of the way home, right? I'll make a fire for the night. That should keep all the animals away. A fire is always something that I enjoy,"

As they settled down, Sir Hunter saw Xavier having trouble. "Let me help you, my friend," Sir Hunter offered. He took some of the old clothing that was attached to Xavier's horse saddle. It was dirty and tattered, but it was better than sleeping on the hard ground. He spread it out next to the fire. "There you go, Xavier. That should be more comfortable."

It didn't take long for Xavier to fall asleep. He looked three times more exhausted than Sir Hunter. Sir Hunter gave the horses some water and food. As Sir Hunter laid down, he looked over at Xavier. He could see the tension drawing away from his face as the flames from the fire made dancing shadows.

"Xavier, it is morning, and we need to get moving. I hope you were able to sleep. We need to put a few miles behind us before we need to stop and rest our horses. Did you get enough rest?" Sir Hunter asked.

"Well, yes, more than I've gotten in a long time," explained Xavier.

"Yeah, I can understand that," Sir Hunter replied.

"Sir Hunter, I do appreciate all that you are doing for me. I will never forget your kindness."

"Well, I didn't see any reason that we couldn't help each other with the journey, if we were going in the same direction."

"I'm glad that you came along when you did. Now I can truly believe that I will see my family again, thanks to you!" Xavier said enthusiastically.

"Glad I can help. Let's get going!" Sir Hunter replied.

Sir Hunter and Xavier packed up their belongings and began their day. "There is a small river a few miles ahead of us, so we can let our horses drink and rest a little before moving on. I'm sure I'll be ready to stop by then myself. I figure that we should be home in a few days—if we still have a home. It's been six months since the battle started, and I know that there must be a lot that needs fixing up. Only time will tell," Sir Hunter said.

Xavier gave a thumbs-up and a big smile. The weather was to their advantage. There was a pleasant breeze, as well as a few clouds so the sun wasn't shining strong upon them. There was debris everywhere, and they had to be careful where to walk the horses. The horses were already beaten up. Without their bravery and endurance, they probably would not have survived the battle. Wheels meant the world to Sir Hunter was the only family he had.

"I see the river ahead of us. I'm ready for a break," Sir Hunter stated.

"Yes, I'm ready also, Sir Hunter."

"Okay, let's stop over there under the trees. It's time for a little food, right?"

"That sounds good to me, Sir Hunter. Let's not make a fire now; we can do that later tonight, when we stop for the night."

"Right! That makes a lot of sense to me. Glad we are thinking alike. Are you doing alright?"

"Yes, just need a little break," Xavier said exhaustingly.

They rested by the river under the trees. The horses were getting their fill of water. Sir Hunter took the opportunity to fill his canteens. The water was cool and refreshing. The river had a steady stream moving that came down from the springs flowing down from the top of the mountains. One couldn't beat the fresh taste.

As a few days passed and their journey seemed to be coming to an end, as they could finally see the town of Harbor in the distance. Harbor was one of the biggest towns in the area. The town grew due to all the vessels and barges shipping goods to other towns or merchant ports. With the town being built near a river, it made it easy for the fishing vessels to come in and out. The river brought plenty of fresh spring water, allowing the townspeople to grow large vegetable gardens and fruit trees. The town of Harbor was also known for having a big shipyard, where they built vessels. The town was surrounded by mountains and forests, which made the town flourish with building materials. Most of the homes were wood cabins, but there were some made of clay, which were for the rich or those of higher standards, such as merchants or specialty craftsmen.

Sir Hunter knew that he and Xavier would part ways. Xavier was glad they made the trip together. It made the trip a lot safer for both of them. Xavier was a good man. It was tremendously comforting to Sir Hunter to have a companion during his travels; he could say I had a true friend. They talked here and there about what their futures held for them. Xavier had a wife and wanted to plan for a family. Sir Hunter didn't have a family to go back to, but that was the life he had chosen as the leader of the Royalmen.

They approached town, and every step felt like a thousand. Sir Hunter saw Xavier's face light up with glee.

"I recognize the church. I can see children running around," Xavier said excitedly. He started to speed up as he became more anxious.

"Easy, my friend. You must be careful, or all your belongings will topple off your horse," Hunter explained.

"You are so right, Sir Hunter. I'm just so eager to see my wife and be home safely," exclaimed Xavier.

They finally arrived into town, and soon after they reached Xavier's cabin. Sir Hunter could tell Xavier's cabin was slightly bigger than his.

"Sir Hunter, it's good to see home again. I have many thanks for your kindness. I hope someday I can repay you," Xavier said with gratitude.

"Maybe that will happen, Xavier, but now that you've made it back home, I'll say goodbye. I have a long trip ahead of me. I hope to see you again in our travels, but not due to war. Good luck to you."

"Good luck to you as well, Sir Hunter. Are you sure you don't want to stay here tonight and start out after you get some rest?" asked Xavier.

"No, but thanks. I want to keep moving for my cabin. I can rest then," Hunter said.

"I understand. Be safe, my friend," Xavier replied.

"Well, Wheels, we have about a half a day's ride before we'll be at the cabin, so I can rest a couple of days before the hard journey to the Bonefairy Castle," Hunter stated.

There were many challenges and obstacles Sir Hunter would encounter before he reached Bonefairy Castle to see the queen. These challenges were not only going through bad weather and overcoming obstacles of debris from the battle. There were also strange creatures that lived in the wilderness on the way to Bonefairy Castle. No one knew what was out there or how they had gotten there, but Sir Hunter had heard many horror stories. There was an ogre, which was inhumanly big with a disproportionately large head. He had unusually colored skin and a voracious appetite for humans, especially infants and children. Sir Hunter had to think about that after he had a couple of days rest. He would have to clean up a few things around the cabin. Sir Hunter hated the thought of how it looked while he had been gone, but it was his home and all he had.

As Sir Hunter continued on his journey, he reminisced about how he had built his cabin. It took him many years and long nights of cutting trees down and clearing a spot to build his cabin. These weren't average trees; the bark was very tough. After he cut down the trees, he had to remove the bark and sand them down so they were smooth.

He had to find the perfect spot that allowed sun to shine in order to keep warm during the winter months, and he left some trees for shade for those sweltering days in the summer. He found the perfect area and cleared a plot of land. It took him forever. He made sure that there was enough space around the cabin for a garden and a barn. He was able to use most of the trees to build the cabin and the barn. The trees had to be just right. He had to cut all the branches off and make sure they were straight and close to the same size. He didn't have any issues with finding trees because the forest had an abundance of them. He built the cabin by himself, so he was restricted on how high he could build it, but he was very pleased and comfortable because it was just him. Building the walls and putting them together was the most difficult part. He didn't have much material, but he daubed them together using mud and clay.

Finally, Sir Hunter could see his cabin in the distance. It had never looked so enticing. He knew Wheels would be content as well. The first thing Sir Hunter had to do was chop some wood for a fire and put on a kettle of water so he could have a delightful hot bath. Boy, that sounded good. While the water got hot, he would feed Wheels and bed him down for the night. It looked like it was going to be a peaceful evening, which was long overdue. He'd wait to clean his sword and other equipment in the morning. He could see Bonefairy Castle in the distance from his window and the sunset that slowly cascaded down around it. It was very beautiful and luminous.

It was time for Sir Hunter's bath and a little food and rest. As he stepped in the tub, he felt the hot water engulf him. It felt so wonderful after not be able to take a bath for so long. He remained there for a while, until the hot water became colder and unbearable. As he laid there thinking about all that he'd been through, he realized how fortunate he was. His body ached all over from riding and fighting. He threw a little more wood in the fireplace. That had to be good enough for the rest of the night. Tomorrow would come, and he'd have to get things ready for his trip to see the queen. She was the ruler of the region and had been for a long time. She controlled Bonefairy Castle. Sir Hunter never knew what to expect when he saw her because of her powers. She could be so beautiful and powerful but then turn on her magical powers and change to being malicious and horrifying. Sir Hunter hoped she would be in the right frame of mind when he arrived. Why wouldn't she be in a good mood? They had just won the fight to protect the land of Bonefairy Castle.

The next day arrived, and it was time to check on the condition of Wheels. A good night's sleep should have done him well. The wagon was in need of a lot of repairs before Sir Hunter could start out on the journey to Bonefairy Castle. He thought it would be a good idea to change the wagon wheels, just to be safe. He remembered some were around back of the cabin—if they hadn't been stolen. Sir Hunter looked around back, and they were where he had left them. It didn't take him too long to throw a couple of wheels on the wagon. That's was ironic:

he changed the wheels on Wheels. That was how Sir Hunter came up with the name for his horse, actually; he had gotten him to pull the wagon. He was the best horse and friend Sir Hunter could ask for.

Sir Hunter thought he'd better check to see whether Wheels needed shoeing. He sure didn't need the horse to come up lame. Sir Hunter wasn't the best farrier, but he'd done it so much that he'd gotten better at it. He'd also have to get extra food and water for the trip.

Sir Hunter had a crate that he filled with many valuable things he took from the dead men in the battle, such as clothes, swords, and personal things for the queen. She demanded that he bring everything when he arrived. Her powers changed the contents of the crate, and she consumed the substance to give her power.

It was time for Sir Hunter to load up the wagon. He was going to need some equipment just in case the wagon had a problem along the way. He also needed some weapons for any trouble that came up. It was going to be harder for Wheels with the wagon being heavier, but he was strong and shouldn't have any trouble. Sir Hunter hoped the wagon held up. He knew it was going to be a rough trip ahead of him. There were going to be threats that he'd experience along the trip, but he had been there before and would endure. Wheels was up and ready to get started.

The road going to Bonefairy Castle was very dangerous because it was so narrow, not to mention all the twists and turns. Sir Hunter never knew what could happen. Plus, there was a lot of the debris from the storm. Sir Hunter had to stop several times to move large branches and poking twigs. Even some of the small rocks could cause damage to the wagon, as well as hurt Wheels. It took longer than he'd expected, going at a slow pace, but he moved on. There could be encounters causing him to fight creatures, as well as rivers and bridges that were almost impossible to cross. The sun was out, and it looked like a nice day.

In a couple of hours, Sir Hunter stopped so Wheels could rest. Sir Hunter came to an area that was very heavy with trees. He had to be ready for surprises. Anything could come out of the woods at any time, so it wasn't going to be easy. Sir Hunter hoped Wheels wouldn't get frightened and run off, or at least go so far off that he couldn't find him.

Sir Hunter came to an area where an ugly ogre was rumored to live. He saw something rustling in the trees. Sir Hunter thought that it must be the ogre by the way the trees moved. It was definitely something big. He had to be prepared to keep it away from him and Wheels. He knew Wheels was brave, but he'd been through a lot, and even after resting, he could still be weak. Sir Hunter felt he may not have all his strength back either. He had a feeling something was going to happen. Sir Hunter thought he'd better tie Wheels to a tree so he'd be all right.

"Come, Wheels, hurry up. I've got to get you tied up before this creature gets here. Now, where's my sword? Here it comes! This creature is gigantic and ferocious looking," Sir Hunter said.

Sir Hunter had to try to keep something between him and the beast. He could thrash his sword at it. Wheels was scared and reared up. Sir Hunter hoped he wouldn't get loose or tumble the wagon over. He couldn't show any fear to intensify the fear in Wheels. The evil thing thrived on fear; it was obvious in its eyes. Sir Hunter had to continue swinging and slashing at it with his sword. It seemed to back off the more he did that. He needed to get closer to it so he could stab it. The beast was hideous, and its arms were mammoth in size. It could definitely squeeze him to death. Its head was huge, and it had no neck. Its teeth were like sharp knifes that protruded from its lower lip. Sir Hunter imagined the ogre could rip something to shreds.

He began throwing some sharp-edged rocks. His aim wasn't like it used to be, but he gave it his best shot. He got it right on its bald head, and the rock made a deep gash. That made it so angry that it lunged at him. Sir Hunter pushed forward and stabbed it. He made contact in the middle of its chest. It lunged again at him and almost grabbed him. It fell to its knees while it grasped at the sword. It pulled it out and threw it at Sir Hunter, possibly thinking it may stab him back with the sword. Then it fell flat on its face. Sir Hunter fetched his sword and ran to Wheels without looking back. He wasn't going to stay around to see if he had killed it.

"Okay, Wheels, let's go before that ugly thing gets up and attacks again. I hope it's dead so I don't have to deal with it ever again. It's time to head on down the road and look for a safe place to stay for the night. That confrontation wore me out. It looks like the road is going to have a big curve in it up ahead, so I need to take it easy so the wagon doesn't tip over. The road is narrow as it is, and now you're pulling a wagon. I know that tomorrow we'll be at the river, and I'm sure there will be a few more dangerous things, but that's tomorrow," Sir Hunter said aloud.

Sir Hunter walked Wheels for a while, who began to settle down. Suddenly there was something dark moving around up ahead.

"Oh, great, now what? Easy, Wheels. I see it."

Sir Hunter slowed Wheels down to walk quieter. As he got closer, he could see that it was a wolf looking for some food. He was surprised to see another creature so soon. He thought that it was unusual for the two creatures to live so close to each other. It wasn't an average wolf. The creature was big and black, about three times the size of a normal wolf, and it seemed more like a werewolf because it moved around more like a human than a wolf. Its eyes were red, its teeth extended much more than a normal wolf, and its claws were like daggers. Sir Hunter hadn't encountered a beast like it before. He hoped he would have been lucky enough not to. He knew that according to some legends, this type of wolf was known as a werewolf, which were part human and were considered bloodthirsty beasts that couldn't control their lust for killing people or animals. Sir Hunter could tell that it sensed them being there. It could probably smell the fear in Wheels. Sir Hunter had to take it slow and easy until he could see what the wolf was going to do. There was no way around the creature.

As they got closer, the werewolf became more restless, and so did Wheels. In fact, Wheels was hesitating at every step. Sir Hunter eased in a little closer. It was obvious that it wasn't going to leave them alone, so he had to get ready. He knew that werewolves liked horse meat and would love to get hold of Wheels, but it was going to have to get by him first. The beat showed its teeth and glared at him. It was definitely predatorial and aggressive, showing no signs of fear or backing down.

"Watch out, Wheels—here it comes!" Sir Hunter said sternly.

Sir Hunter had some meat that that he was going to eat, but maybe if he threw it at the werewolf, it would take it and run away. He didn't want to kill it if he didn't have to, mostly because that would draw attention to him or cause a counterattack if there were any more of them out there and saw it happen. Sir Hunter quickly stopped Wheels, grabbed the meat, and threw it out in the woods. The werewolf ran after it just as he expected it would. He guessed there was still some doglike manners within it. Just like chasing a stick. "We need to move fast, Wheels. That wasn't much meat, and it may come looking for more."

There was a small river ahead. Sir Hunter thought they should walk along the river to cover up their tracks and their smell. A couple of miles from here was where they could stop for the night. He would start a big fire that he knew would protect them until morning and keep away the werewolf.

They came up to a good spot to stop for the night. He set up there to have some large boulders around one side of them. That would help so we didn't have to worry about their backs. A fire had been built there before, so it wouldn't take too much time and effort to get a fire started. Sir Hunter gathered some kindling. He needed to make sure Wheels was calm and got him some water from the river. It smelled like rain, so he had to keep the fire going and slept under the wagon for shelter. He could hear the thunder in the distance and saw the heat lightning. He saw the stars occasionally, so it was just a little rain and nothing too serious. That was good for sleeping! Wheels would let him know if anything came around. All was quiet, just a few crickets, and he heard an owl in the distance. It had been a long day, and Sir Hunter knew the next day would come soon enough. He put a little more wood on the fire. He knew he probably wouldn't sleep very well because of the werewolf that lingered close by. He hoped the rain and the smell of the river had disguised their scents.

CHAPTER 2

"I guess Bonefairy Castle was really valuable if everyone wanted to invade it all the time. Such loyalty the Royalmen had for the queen," I said.

"Yes, Sir Hunter trained his men to be very loyal. The queen made sure of that," Grandpa said.

"You know, I've watched many war movies on TV, as I'm sure you have. The way you describe how Sir Hunter fought in many battles reminds me of what those war movies are like. A lot of men getting killed. It's awful," I said.

"It is unfortunate that there had to be casualties. It could have been worse if Bonefairy Castle was taken over," Grandpa explained.

"Do you know how many battles Sir Hunter had to fight?"

"There is no actual record of how many battles there were. They didn't have the same resources available to them to track everything. In fact, some of the battles were so close together that it seemed to be one big, long battle. More and more men kept trying to invade Bonefairy Castle. They wanted it for themselves. The queen was not selfish, and the land always flourished after each battle. She didn't want it all to fall in the wrong hands and have it all destroyed."

"It seems like the battles back then were very brutal, but they didn't have guns, tanks, or stuff like the way we do today, right?" I asked.

"That's right, Hunter. The battles back then were called medieval warfare and were very brutal. Sir Hunter and his Royalmen fought many cavalries. Their weapons were more like swords, knives, daggers, spears, and bows and arrows. That's why the battles lasted so long."

"What's a cavalry?"

"It means the soldiers or warriors fought mounted on horseback," Grandpa explained.

"Wow, I can't imagine having to fight like that. I feel bad for the horses. They didn't choose to be in the middle of battle. The men had to have some sort of protection, though, right?" I asked.

"Oh, yes, they had armor and shields, and some men had helmets. A lot of the fighting was man-to-man combat. The men that whom Sir Hunter fought off were highly skilled warriors, and their mission was to take over Bonefairy Castle no matter what the consequences were. But the queen's Royalmen were much more skilled, so they always defeated any armies that threatened the land."

"The man that Sir Hunter ran into on his way home, Xavier—did Sir Hunter know him well? I know there were many men in the war, so I'm sure it was hard to know all his men," I said.

"Sir Hunter did know of Xavier. He knew him from when he was recruited. Xavier had served with Sir Hunter through many battles. It was good that they met up on their way back home, because Xavier was wounded, and so was his horse. Xavier may not have made it home on his own," Grandpa said.

"It sure was good that they ran into each other. I wonder if they ever kept in touch?"

"I am not sure. There weren't any other stories of them meeting up later in their lives," Grandpa responded.

"Sir Hunter's trip back home seemed pretty challenging. Did he really have to fight off those creatures?" I asked.

Grandpa said, "He sure did. He was so brave and knew what he had to do to stay alive and get back to the queen at Bonefairy Castle. Sir Hunter was a warrior and feared nothing."

"What does Sir Hunter's sword look like?" I asked.

"Well, I never saw it, of course, but I heard about it. There are a few different kinds. Thrusting swords have a pointed tip on the blade and tend to be straighter; slashing swords have a sharpened cutting edge on one or both sites of the blade, and they are more likely to be curved. I do know Sir Hunter's was straight. Many swords are designed for both thrusting and slashing," answered Grandpa.

"You said that Sir Hunter did both, right? So he has a special one," I said excitedly.

"I suppose so. Sir Hunter became known as the best swordsman. That was why the queen made him the leader of the Royalmen. He was able to impale his target quickly and inflict deep stab wounds. The sword is long and straight with a good hilt for gripping. It was light in weight and well balanced, allowing Sir Hunter to maneuver in a deadly duel. A well-aimed lung and thrust could end a fight in seconds with just the sword's point. I want you to know that Sir Hunter killed men only because they were trying to take away the land of Bonefairy Castle. He was not a man who killed for no reason. He was a good man. I don't want you to tell your mother all the details I have shared with you; I don't think she'd like it. But I want you to really understand how brave Sir Hunter was. In today's time, they call it fencing, but it is more of a sport."

"I've heard of fencing, Grandpa. Do you think I can learn fencing?" I asked as I stood up and pretended to fence.

"A fencing sword is much different. It is long and very narrow and not meant for fighting in battle. It is better known for being a martial art. It relies on the use of tactics and strategy, as well as speed and skill while facing your opponent. There is definitely the need to think quickly and adapt. In fact, the modern sport of fencing has been described as trying to play chess while running the hundred-yard dash. The sport may be too complex for you because although the fencing sword is not like Sir Hunter's sword, you could get hurt. Maybe when you get older, we can look into you taking fencing lessons," Grandpa replied with a smile.

"I think it would be neat to learn," I said, still posed in the fencing position.

"They didn't have fencing school like we do today. Sir Hunter was a self-taught swordsman. Today, you kids have the privilege of someone to teach you."

"How can those creatures exist out in the wilderness? Where did they come from?" I asked.

"No one really ever knew. Many creatures existed back then. You've heard of dinosaurs, right? Look how many different ones there were back then. Like the tyrannosaurus—that was a carnivorous one with powerful jaws and small, claw-like front legs. You probably know it as the T-Rex. Then there's the brontosaurus. That one wasn't a threat to humans, though; it ate plants and leaves off the trees. There were so many different kinds because different species would mate with others. I imagine that is what happened back then as well regarding how the odd creatures came to life," said Grandpa.

"I want to know more, Grandpa. Sir Hunter does sounds like a great man. I can't believe I'm related to him. Did you ever go to Europe, where he was from?" I asked.

"No, I never did go there. I wish I had. I would have loved to have gotten to see that homeland. You know what, though? With these stories that I'm sharing with you, I have always been able to envision what it was like there and what Sir Hunter was like, especially living in a cabin. He really roughed it out in the woods. It wasn't like it is nowadays, where you can go to a store and buy anything you need. Sir Hunter had to grow his own vegetables and kill for his meat. He didn't have electricity, so he had to cook his food by fire in a big potbelly stove," answered Grandpa.

"I bet I would like living in a cabin in the forest. I could climb trees and make a treehouse," I replied.

"I suppose you could." Grandpa laughed.

"Tell me more. You said Sir Hunter ran into other creatures. What other kind of creatures? I can't believe Sir Hunter saw a wolf that big. Did it really look like a werewolf? I love werewolf movies. I can't wait to tell this part to my class, but they'll probably laugh at me," I said.

"Yes, Sir Hunter did encounter other creatures. I'll get to those parts. You may not want to say it was a werewolf. Just describe it has a very big wolf. A lot of people don't believe they ever existed. Now, where did I leave off? Oh, yes. The next day, Sir Hunter began another day of his travel to Bonefairy Castle.

CHAPTER 3

It was a new day, and Sir Hunter got some needed rest, even though it wasn't the best of sleep because he had to stay alert. The rain wasn't so bad while he slept; it was just enough that it kept the animals away. A steady beating of raindrops on the wagon continued as he lay underneath. He watched Wheels for a while and tried to get comfortable. It was funny how the rain didn't bother Wheels. He was a bit restless, but his nerves began to settle down. Several times he tried to move, but Sir Hunter blocked the back wagon wheels so the horse couldn't move the wagon. That was the best way to keep him from moving and trampling on the fire.

The next morning, Sir Hunter relived what had happened the day before. He was surprised he had gotten any sleep. It didn't seem real when he woke up, but then he could feel the aches and pains in his muscles. As he slowly rolled out from under the wagon, he felt even more of the pain, but he had to keep moving. Sir Hunter saw that Wheels was already up and ready to take on the new day. He simply needed to get him fed and get him some water.

"There, how's that, big fella? Are you ready?" Sir Hunter asked Wheels.

Wheels looked at him and blinked. Sir Hunter took that to be a yes.

"All right, we'll get going here in a minute," he said to Wheels, trying to keep a positive attitude.

He put the fire out so it wouldn't spread in case a high wind blew through and caused a big fire. He heard the sound of the river, which wasn't too far down the road, so he could get more water for them. As he got closer to the river, he saw something moving along the river bank.

"Great! Something else I have to deal with, and so soon. I've just started the day," Sir Hunter said aloud.

It looked like some kind of eight-legged crab with two huge claws, but it was also part man. It didn't look too friendly. No one really ever knew what one would run into when making the trip to Bonefairy Castle. It started to move toward them. He saw that it meant them harm with its big, pinching claws. It sure wasn't the average-size crab that Sir Hunter was used to seeing. It looked at him with its stalked eyes and antennae. It couldn't move very fast, so Sir Hunter thought they could get by it by staying away from the bank of the river and going farther down to cross. He picked up a thick stick and jabbed at it. It didn't like that and went back into the water. He thought it would have wanted to fight, especially with it rearing up with its claws clacking together. The claws looked like they could crush every bone in his body.

"Well, that did the trick. That's a good thing," Sir Hunter said.

He moved on down the river a little and found a good place to cross. The water wasn't as deep there, and it wouldn't be as hard to pull the wagon across there. They continued to move forward along the path. The sound of the river was soothing. Once in a while, it became louder than the clunking of Wheels' hooves. It was amazing how the shoes stayed on his hooves. He was so glad he wasn't in pain while wearing them too. Sir Hunter had to learn all this because he did the shoeing himself.

"Woah, okay, wait. What's the matter, Wheels? Why are you backing up? Let's go! Oh, I see in the water there's a piranha. Good boy," Sir Hunter said calmly.

There was a big school of them. He knew they have very sharp teeth and attacked all at once. They were very dangerous and attacked quickly, and there was no stopping them. Sir Hunter didn't want them to come anywhere near Wheels. He would have to look for another place to cross. He sure didn't need to mess with piranhas. Up ahead, he saw a better place to cross. As they got closer, it didn't look like there were any other dangers. The water was already a little bit higher and deeper here, but he knew they'd make it.

Sir Hunter thought it was a good idea to stop now that they were on the other side of the river. The sun felt good. It would dry everything, especially on the path. With the rain they had had, there was mud on the path. It made it more difficult to keep the wheels moving on the wagon. The mud also got stuck within the wooden spokes of the wheels, which built up on the wheels and made them heavier. It would dry as they sat in the sun, and Sir Hunter would be able to knock off the dry mud. They rested a little before moving on. Sir Hunter imagined he'd have more threatening events coming yet. He simply wanted to make sure he got to Bonefairy Castle. He still had a long way to go yet. The road looked pretty dry and clear for a while. It didn't look like he'd have to worry about any rain. The birds sounded pretty happy. The chirping of birds was always a pleasant sound. Any type of bird that sang its own language was very comforting. It had been quite a long time since he'd heard birds singing, with the battle that had gone on for so long. There were definitely no birds around during that time. They had flown away when they had sensed the danger.

Sir Hunter saw a clearing up ahead where he had run into a wild creature the last time he had come to Bonefairy Castle. He wondered whether it was still around. With his luck, he'd run into it.

"Yeah, I was right. There it is!" Sir Hunter yelled.

Its eyes protruded with a glowing hue, and it came right at him. He guessed he was going to have to fight the creature, so he stopped to wait for it. The creature looked like an overgrown, ugly toad with horns on top of its head and spikes down its body. It was huge, almost twenty feet tall. It had a horrendous odor coming out of its skin and poisonous glands that were highly toxic if ingested. Its toxic skin could kill anything in an instant. It seemed like it couldn't move very fast; it was just a big fat green blob. It also had a long tongue that came out for capturing its food or prey. If he didn't get near it, he could probably miss having an encounter. It looked like one of its horns had blood on it, maybe from its last prey.

"Uh oh, I was wrong! It can move pretty well," Sir Hunter yelled.

The big, ugly toad leaped in the air and landed close to him—too close. He swung his sword back and forth as fast as he could. The creature tried to sting him with its long tongue, and it sprayed some of its toxic liquid. It jetted out with a powerful stream that just missed him. Sir Hunter pulled on the reins to steer Wheels out of danger. He had to be careful where he stepped. Then he lunged forward to stab the ugly beast.

"Oh, I think I got him that time. I see some yucky, gooey blood coming out," Sir Hunter said aloud.

The creature acted hurt and leaped back into the woods. That was Sir Hunter's chance to get out of there. He had to move faster down the road for a while, and he hoped the wagon held up before they stopped to rest. He remembered there was a spectacular waterfall coming up. It sounded good, but the clearing up ahead of him would work too, because it was closer, so he could stop there. He was going to have to let Wheels cool down and rest. A little food was also overdue.

"Over there, Wheels. Let's go. Okay, that's a good boy. Hold it right here. The rest will do us well," Sir Hunter said.

He leaned against the wheels of the wagon. He needed to catch my breath. He started thinking of the glorious waterfall ahead. It was known to be the largest in Europe. The waterfall began at the top of the mountain and plunged downward. The flow was a glacial stream as the snow melted from the top of the mountain. During the spring and summer months, the flow was extreme with a lot of fresh, ice-cold water. It felt good to rinse off and refill his water canteens.

A couple of hours passed, and Sir Hunter got some rest, so it was time to move on. He had another half a day ahead of him before he could stop for the night. The queen wondered where he was and when he'd show up. The Royalmen were always in demand, and he'd been gone for a long time. The road was getting worse with all the rocks and holes. That was never good for the wagon wheels. He would have to have to be careful until the road got better.

"Oh, wow! That hole was huge and could have really done some damage. Easy does it, Wheels, not so fast. That's better," Sir Hunter said gently.

Sir Hunter could see something up ahead. It was the Grim Reaper standing the middle of the road. He had appeared many centuries ago during a time that Europe was dealing with what was then the world's worst pandemic, the Black Death. It was estimated that about one-third of Europe's population had perished. Sir Hunter wondered what it wanted to allow him to pass. He knew it looked for souls, but that was of the dead, so he was probably very busy gathering souls from the dead men from the battle. There was a big bend in the road, so it was going to be hard not to stop. If he went too fast, he wouldn't make the turn.

"All right, take it easy, Wheels. Yes, that's it! It's the Grim Reaper, and he shouldn't be much of a problem," Sir Hunter concluded.

Death is a fundamental part of life, and it is the Grim Reaper's duty to claim souls of the deceased to maintain the balance of nature. All Sir Hunter knew was he was not a friendly looking character, with his skeletal face, glowing red eyes, a large black hooded cloak, and a scythe, which is a long stick with a curved blade.

"Let's go nice and easy by, and maybe that will be good enough. That's right, Wheels, easy. He is allowing us to go by. I guess it is not my time to die yet," Sir Hunter said.

The road was rough, but he was going to have to pick it up a little anyway. The waterfall was coming up soon. That would do it for the night.

"There it is just ahead. Wheels, it's been a long day. We've overcome some challenges that weren't so bad. It was nothing that we haven't been through before," Sir Hunter said soothingly to his trusty steed.

Sir Hunter built a little fire. The water ran down the waterfall. The sound made it for a good night for sleep. He thought maybe he could do some fishing for extra food for the rest of the trip. He needed to unhitch Wheels from the wagon and take him down to the waterfall for some good water. He was definitely ready for it.

"There you go, Wheels. Some nice, fresh water," Sir Hunter said.

Sir Hunter thought that it looked like he'd be able to cross over from the area where he slept. He could see something out in the water that looked like large, poisonous pods. He'd have to worry about that tomorrow. Hopefully they would be gone by tomorrow.

"Wheels, let's go back to the wagon and get something to eat," Sir Hunter said.

The night was quiet, and the waterfall sounded just the way he thought it would. The fire popped and crackled and looked like fireflies rising up into the air. It was a good night. Many different thoughts went through his head during his journey to Bonefairy Castle, and he anticipated meeting with the queen again. He always wondered what the queen was doing and what she would say to him. He knew that she was the queen of the country and had done a great job, but he had always wondered how she got her powers. He remembered one day when she had resolved a problem that none of the people understood. It was as if she knew what was going to happen before it did and stopped it. It seemed that her powers were always greater after a battle, when Sir Hunter brought her back some of the things that belonged to the dead Royalmen. The only thing that he knew for sure was that the queen took everything that he brought back into Bonefairy Castle and disappeared behind the walls. What she did with the things, no one knew, but it was never seen again by anyone. It was like they vanished forever. She used these things to create more power somehow. There was always a large cloud of smoke that came from Bonefairy Castle during that time, which made Sir Hunter think that the queen made some kind of magical potion that strengthened her powers. The queen had many servants and Royalmen that she relied on, but none of them left with her when she went to her private quarters. It was like she was two different people. Maybe he would learn the secret someday, but until then he had to continue his trip toward Bonefairy Castle.

The next morning produced a nice sunrise, and the weather was perfect for the day. As Sir Hunter hooked Wheels back up to the wagon and headed back toward the river, he looked for the pods that had been in the water the night before, but they were gone. He didn't have to worry about getting any poison on him or Wheels. He got a little water for Wheels, and then he would cross the river.

"Oh, well, now what do we have here? I can't be dreaming. It's a mermaid," Sir Hunter said as he rubbed his eyes to clear them.

He had heard that mermaids had been seen, but this was his first time. She didn't seem to be afraid of him and Wheels. That was good, but he wondered what she was doing out there. He also wondered whether there were any more of them. He guessed not, and that was all right too, but she was so beautiful while stretched out, with the sunlight shining off her long, thick dark hair. Her tail had a fin on top, and she had multicolored skin that shimmered in the sun. He knew that there were severe storms, and it was known that mermaids were forced onto the land. That happened because the high waves were so extreme and caused havoc, so they came onto land for safety. He thought he should keep moving on, or he would never get to Bonefairy Castle. He now knew that mermaids were real and where he could find them again. He couldn't let her beauty distract him from making his journey to Bonefairy Castle.

The road was starting to get covered with leaves, and the trees surrounded him as he went through the woods. It was almost like the trees were coming to life.

"I don't believe it. That tree right there is coming to life. It's moving and talking to me," Sir Hunter said to Wheels.

The tree said that he needed to be careful because there was danger on the other side of the woods, so he should cross the river back to the other side. Sir Hunter could see the edge of the woods, so the river must be coming up soon. He was really curious as to what the danger was on the other side of the river.

"Well, I didn't have to wait very long. There it is! These challenges that I'm having to deal with are starting to get harder as my trip to Bonefairy Castle continues," Sir Hunter concluded.

The creature was huge, green, and manlike. It was at least fifteen feet tall.

"Wheels, you'd better be ready to do some fast moving if that green giant starts coming toward us."

It didn't look like it saw them yet, so he thought he should wait a little bit and watch. He wondered why it was green. Its skin and clothes were green. It looked the size of at least five men. It stood alert with its axe, ready for anything. It had two horns sticking out of its head. As long as it moved on and he didn't have to deal with it, he would be happy. It looked like it was definitely territorial. It wanted to protect itself and its surroundings. He had heard it liked to challenge people to fights, but only if they got too close to it. If he moved a little off the path, and moved really fast, it may understand that he didn't want to fight and did not want to hurt it or its living area. It wouldn't be easy.

The creature watched him go by. It looked very fierce as its eyes glared at him, waiting for any possible sign of threat.

"Okay, good, it's moving on, and we can get passed it," Sir Hunter said to Wheels.

Sir Hunter could see that there was a lake coming up. He would be able to relax as he crossed over. His friend Sepp Lehmann, whom he called Skipper, would be there with his barge, so he wouldn't have to go all the way around the lake. Skipper had been a great friend for a long time. He had been a bargeman for many years. Sir Hunter didn't think Skipper had any family, but he seemed to enjoy what he did. He imagined it would be lonely if he didn't have any passengers for a long period of time. He charged a little bit for the trip across, but it was worth it. He hoped that he was on this side of the lake and not on the other side. That would make his trip delayed if he had to wait for him to come back across to get him. As Sir Hunter got closer, he could see he was there on this side.

"Hello, Skipper. It is so good to see you again. I didn't know whether you'd be here," Sir Hunter said gleefully.

"Well, my goodness, Sir Hunter. How have you been? I was hoping you'd made it through that terrible battle," replied Skipper.

Sir Hunter asked Skipper if he could take him across the lake. He also asked if his fee had changed at all, because he knew that some days, he didn't get anyone who wanted to cross, so business was slow. But then, what else did Skipper have to do? Skipper informed him that he had a pretty big load that he was taking to the queen, and he would be happy to take him across. His fee was the same for him as always. Sir Hunter let Skipper know that he was just about ready and had to tighten up Wheels so he didn't get afraid when they started moving.

"Okay, we're ready when you are," Sir Hunter said.

Now he could relax and enjoy the hour it took to cross the lake. He could even put his feet in the water. He thought that was a good idea. He could wash off all the dirt.

"Hey, Skipper, it looks like a good day ahead of us, don't you think?" Sir Hunter noted.

"It sure does, Sir Hunter. Thank goodness. We've had quite a bit of bad storms lately."

Sir Hunter asked Skipper if he had any extra hay he could buy so Wheels could eat while they had the time. Skipper told him he had a little bit under the tarp. Sir Hunter lifted up the tarp, and sure enough there was some there, so he pulled some out, put in a bucket that was nearby, and placed it in front of Wheels.

"Skipper, have you ever done any fishing here as you go back and forth? I've seen quite a few fish when I look down in the water, and they look like they're a pretty good size. Maybe I'll remember to bring a pole next time and try my luck. What do you think?" Sir Hunter asked.

"I don't get to do much fishing while maneuvering the barge. I've got to keep an eye on it and concentrate," answered Skipper.

Sir Hunter and Wheels were relaxed now, thanks to Skipper for being available with his barge to help him save a lot of time.

"It looks like you may have a few people waiting on the other side. Well, at least your day will be busy, and you'll be able to make a little money for you," Sir Hunter said.

"Yes indeed. I do like to keep busy," Skipper said.

They were almost across the lake, so Sir Hunter needed to get everything ready to get off the barge. He had always wondered why the barge was so big, and now he understood after he saw all the people waiting. Maybe they went out to fish.

"Hello, everyone. It would be great if you can let me get my horse off and out of your way," Sir Hunter said graciously to the crowd of people. He slowly took Wheels off the barge, while being careful not to tip over the wagon.

"I truly appreciate your kindness in helping me across the lake. Here is your fee and a little more for your friendship. I wish you well," Sir Hunter said while shaking Skipper's hand.

"It was such a pleasure seeing you again. I hope to see you soon, and I wish you safe travels," Skipper replied.

Sir Hunter could see Bonefairy Castle in the distance, but it was much closer than from his cabin's window. It was still going to take a while. He wanted to stop for spirits of course on the way. He wanted to see his lovely lady friends and take a hot bath.

CHAPTER 4

"I can't believe all Sir Hunter had to go through to get to Bonefairy Castle, Grandpa. You mentioned a couple of times that Sir Hunter brought items to the queen from the dead men from the battle. Why is that? I mean, what's so important about the clothing from a dead man?" I asked.

"Now, Hunter, don't be disrespectful. Those men were important and gave up their lives to save the land, the queen, and Bonefairy Castle," replied Grandpa.

"I'm sorry. I didn't mean to be disrespectful. I am just wondering the queen did with the men's belongings."

"All anyone knew was the queen somehow melted everything down to keep her powers strong. No one knew how," Grandpa answered.

"What about the crab-man creature? How could it be part human and part crab? I can't even imagine what that would have looked like," I said.

"I know what you mean. There were so many creatures back then. I'm sure there were many more that we don't even know about or have any stories about," replied Grandpa.

"Have you ever seen piranhas, Grandpa? Do they live just anywhere?"

"No, I have never been around any piranhas. They tend to live in freshwater rivers or lakes. They have one of the strongest bites found in bony fishes. The extremely powerful and dangerous bite is generated by large jaw muscles that are attached closely to the tip of the jaw and the finely serrated teeth, making it easy to tear at flesh. There aren't many stories of attacks on humans, only if the piranhas are in a stressed situation, or when the water is lower during the dry season and food is relatively scarce. So you would never really have to worry about piranhas attacking you. But Sir Hunter had to be careful not to get in a situation for the piranhas to attack Wheels."

"Yeah, I don't think I'll ever see piranhas, and I never want to. I like the part about the toad. I like to try to catch them all the time in the yard. I've never seen any with horns, though. Where did the horns come from? Was it really one hundred pounds? That's more than I weigh, Grandpa!" I said.

"Remember, Hunter, everything I'm saying really happened. I know it is hard to believe, but it's true. It is a fact that toads don't have horns, and they don't grow as big as one hundred pounds. Sir Hunter was lucky, though, that because this toad was so big, it couldn't move very quickly. However, it could leap and attack with its sharp horns that could puncture right through bone and flesh. It could have been very deadly for either Sir Hunter or Wheels."

"Now, Grandpa, the Grim Reaper is totally awesome. I wanted to dress like him for Halloween, but Mom wouldn't let me. She says it represents death. He's very scary looking to me. I would love to have a long, hooded cloak and his scythe. He's like a walking skeleton man. Why did he kill people for their souls, though?" I asked.

"Well, he didn't actually kill. He simply took their souls. He had a unique skill to separate the soul from the body. He collected the soul when a human reached the end of his or her time on earth. He ended any suffering for people who are old or sick, and he prevented overpopulation," responded Grandpa.

"Oh, so he is a good guy. Wait till I tell Mom. Maybe she will let me wear a Grim Reaper costume next year for Halloween," I replied anxiously while rubbing my hands together.

"I don't think that's a good idea to bring that up again, Hunter. You do what your mother says," Grandpa answered as he stopped Hunter from rubbing his hands together.

"What's a barge, Grandpa? Is that like a boat? How does it move?" I asked.

"A barge is a flat-bottomed boat used for transporting people or goods. The story is that the barge had a large rudder that could be manually moved back and forth, which made the barge move. Sir Hunter's friend, Skipper, was able to move the barge at the helm, which you know today as the wheel on a sailboat. He also used a long pole to push the barge in the water," Grandpa said.

"So all he did all day long was go back and forth across the lake?" I asked.

"Yes, that was his job, and he charged a fee. Sometimes he'd be very busy, and other times there'd be very little work. It especially depended on the weather," replied Grandpa.

"Why didn't that green giant attack Sir Hunter?" I asked.

"The story goes that if you don't bother the green giant, he won't attack you. He was very territorial but loved challenges. He would easily accept a challenge if anyone approached him. He would dare anyone to strike him first, because then he would be able to strike back with his axe, and he would usually behead his challenger."

"What's a mermaid? Is it a real woman?"

"A mermaid is part woman and part fish. The upper part is the body of a woman with a tail of a fish. The word *mermaid* simply means *girl with tail.* They live in freshwater and can survive on land, but only for a short period of time. Otherwise, they dehydrate."

"What do they eat? Are they harmful to humans? Can mermaids have babies?" I inquired.

Grandpa replied, "Hold on, Hunter. Ask one question at a time. The mermaids do eat fish, but some are vegetarians. They eat the seaweed or algae deep down in the water. Mermaids are not harmful to humans. In fact, their life goal was to find their true love, and only then would their soul bind with a human's and become everlasting. The mermaid can find a human mate and have a baby, which would also be a mermaid. They can live in water or land. When they are on land, their fish tail transforms into human legs."

"Wow! I wish I could do that. I love to swim. Just think how fast I could swim if I had a fish tail with fins."

"Indeed, you'd be a much faster swimmer. You would beat all your classmates. Now, unless you don't have any more questions, I'd like to continue before I forget where I left off," Grandpa said.

"I can't promise I won't have any more questions, but go ahead and continue. I really want to know more!" I said.

CHAPTER 5

The queen wondered where her faithful leader was and when he would be coming to see her. She was always very busy with her fairies and making sure that the things that they did and the places that they had gone to were for the good of Bonefairy Castle and her people. Fairies usually traveled at night, and that was why most people didn't see them. There were always a few of them at Bonefairy Castle to welcome any Royalmen who came to see the queen. Royalmen were allowed to see the queen only after the fairies had checked each of them to make sure that they were who they say they were and their loyalty wasn't compromised.

Fairies also took care of the queen every day. They washed and combed her long hair. The queen must always look very royal when in the presence of any townspeople. The queen could fly from place to place, like the fairies. That was just one of her many powers. Once her Royalmen brought her the many things that she had asked for, the queen would disappear to her personal quarters behind the wall and not be seen for many days. She would then reappear more vibrant and with more energy to continue keeping her people safe and happy.

The queen had received word that Sir Hunter was on his way from the battle with many things that she had requested. She was very grateful to hear that he'd won. She would then take what Sir Hunter brought back to her, use her powers to melt everything, and consume it to increase her strength.

★★★

Back on the road, Sir Hunter was moving along with Wheels and getting closer to one of the main bridges that they would have to cross. The bridge was old but that was the only way to get across to Bonefairy Castle. Sir Hunter had crossed the bridge many times, but the bridge had taken a toll over the years with all the battles and the bad weather.

★★★

Back at Bonefairy Castle, the queen continued to wait for Sir Hunter to return. There were always many things that were required to be done by the fairies around Bonefairy Castle, which were controlled by the queen. The queen was very powerful and would always seek the best from the fairies as her servants. Only the fairies were aware of what the queen could do.

The land of Bonefairy Castle was hidden and protected with high trees and a high wall that surrounded the grounds. Guards were at the entrance at all times that led into Bonefairy Castle, which stopped anyone from entering. Only the fairies were allowed to come and go without being questioned. Every month there was an event that allowed the townspeople to come to Bonefairy Castle's grounds. The fairies performed a spell on all the people who attended to keep the queen's powers a secret. The queen didn't want to take any chances.

There was a great event planned for when Sir Hunter returned to Bonefairy Castle. Sir Hunter would be rewarded for his long, treacherous journey to bring all the items to the queen. He would be granted some time off from his duties as the leader of the Royalmen. Some of the men had already returned from the battle and were home safe with their families. Word got out that there would be a celebration soon. It would be a celebration with drunken men and wild parties on the town's streets. Many of the women in town also looked forward to the event, because drunken men had a way of throwing their money around. The celebration would go on for days, or until everyone was no longer able to function.

Sir Hunter had many friends in town, and half of them were his lady friends. He couldn't wait to see them. There was one very special lady whom Sir Hunter had been seeing over the years, and he spent most of his time with her. She would always stop whatever she was doing to be with Sir Hunter, and they would go off together by themselves. One of their favorite places was just outside of the town, along a river where they had first met. They planned on going there after Sir Hunter got back, but the queen had rules when it came to her Royalmen. She always came first when it came to loyalty. Sir Hunter's lady, Lady Isabella, knew that the queen always asked Sir Hunter to do things for her, so Lady Isabella kept trying to take Sir Hunter away, out of reach from the queen. Lady Isabella knew that if Sir Hunter would ever settle down with her and get married, he could no longer be one of the queen's Royalmen. Lady Isabella wanted to have a family, but she would have to wait for now, because Sir Hunter was the leader of the Royalmen.

Sir Hunter spent most of his time with Lady Isabella when he wasn't busy doing what the queen asked of him. Lady Isabella liked to cook up some of Sir Hunter's favorite meals, which were usually from the wild meat that he brought back with him from hunting. That would also make the storytelling come out after the meal had been completed. Sometimes his stories would be unbelievable, and he always made her laugh when he told them.

★★★

There were still many challenges that Sir Hunter would have to go through before he could make it to Bonefairy Castle. The biggest one of all was the dragon that guarded one of the bridges that he needed to cross in order to get to Bonefairy Castle. The dragon was very large and known as the fiercest one ever. Many men were killed by it. There was a cave that was high above the bridge on the side of one of the mountains, and that was where the dragon lived. There were only a few mountains and valleys that he would have to cross before getting into town, and that meant even more challenges. Wheels would also want to rest. Sir Hunter could hardly wait to get to town. It sounded good, and he looked forward to excellent food and great times.

It started to rain a little, and that would make the road muddy for Wheels again. Sir Hunter could see lightning in the distance and he heard the thunder. He knew he had better look for a place to hole up until the bad weather passed. He spotted a good spot by some trees, and it looked like someone had been there before. An old firepit and extra wood was there.

"Time for a rest, Wheels," Sir Hunter said.

He needed to start a fire before the rain got everything wet. He also needed to put a blanket on Wheels for the night to keep him dry. He didn't have much to eat, but Wheels could eat the grass. He still had a little dry food that he had brought from home in the back of the wagon.

"There you go, Wheels. That should feel good with the blanket on," Sir Hunter said comfortingly.

The lightning kept hitting nearby. He realized he'd better tie up Wheels by a tree so he wouldn't run away. He got under the wagon to stay safe. It started to rain and got very dark, with more lightning. There were sharp, jagged strikes across the sky that lit up as if someone had turned on the lights. He wished he was already in town with Lady Isabella. She hated bad weather, but at least they would be together, along with some good food. The rain started to let up, so he would have to make a fire again for the night. It was a good thing he had put some of the wood he had found under a tarp to keep it dry.

The next morning came fast, and Wheels was ready to go. Sir Hunter hooked Wheels back up to the wagon. He had just got started out onto the road when he saw a problem ahead on the road. A tree had fallen across the road from the storm last night and blocked his travel. He could see other people on the other side of the tree having the same problem. As Sir Hunter greeted the people, he discussed with them an idea for them to use their horses to move the tree. Sir Hunter had just hooked Wheels up to the wagon, but he had to unhook him again.

"Okay, Wheels, I know you are a little confused right now, but we can do this," Sir Hunter explained.

Sir Hunter and the people got their horses ready to pull the tree out of the way. Luckily, they had enough rope to tie around the tree and connect it to their horses. They could see the road was muddy, and the tree could be moved very easily and with no problem. The tree was soon out of their way, and they laughed a little and thanked each other.

Sir Hunter hooked Wheels back up to the wagon so he could continue. He said good bye to everyone and started on down the road. The road was still a little muddy from the rain last night, but with the heat of the day, it would not take very long to dry out. He would have to keep an eye on it so it didn't cake on the wheels.

★★★

While Sir Hunter continued on his journey, back at Bonefairy Castle, the fairies were busy flying around and doing all that was demanded of them by the queen to prepare for Sir Hunter's return. Many things needed to be ready for the queen so when Sir Hunter arrived with all the materials, it wouldn't take very long for the queen to do what she needed to do to strengthen her powers. After every battle, Sir Hunter had to go around to all of the men who had been killed and remove a piece of clothing, a piece of their hair, or something else that they owned. That was what the queen demanded because she needed the possessions to create the substance that was would strengthen her powers.

★★★

Sir Hunter and the people who had helped move the tree in the road arrived at their village. He came upon a camp just outside the town where some of the men were sitting around. As Sir Hunter came closer, he could see that many of the men were hurt and taking care of their wounds. Sir Hunter stopped to ask who was in charge. One of the men said that the captain was in charge, and he pointed to where the captain was standing. Sir Hunter started walking over to the captain. Some of the men recognized Sir Hunter as he approached and were very happy to see him. One of the men went to give the captain a heads-up that Sir Hunter was coming over. The captain stopped what he was doing to welcome Sir Hunter.

"Sir Hunter, welcome to our camp. We are glad to see you. The queen sent us out to look for you because you have been gone for so long," explained the captain.

"Well, Captain, you know very well that when you are fighting in a battle, you can't just stop whenever you want. It has taken longer than I wanted, but now that it is over, I'm on my way back, as you can see. Captain, as I rode up to the camp here, I could see that some of the men were taking care of their wounds. What happened?"

"They got wounded when they came to the bridge where the dragon lives. The dragon was on the bridge, and we couldn't cross over, so we had to fight it off. We had more men than we have now. Some of the men fell off the bridge when the dragon came toward them. We tried to push a wagon that we had set on fire toward the dragon. That was when the dragon moved off the bridge and flew off back to its cave. Sir Hunter, you haven't seen the dragon since you left. It has grown much bigger and fiercer."

Sir Hunter smiled and said, "We will have to take care of it the next time that it comes around."

"Yes, that's true," the captain agreed.

"Captain, have you got some food for me and my horse?" pleaded Sir Hunter.

"Yes, sir, right away," the captain said assuredly.

"Good, thank you, Captain. Can you have some of the men take Wheels and bed him down for the night? We will rest and talk some more tomorrow. How's everything going back at Bonefairy Castle with the queen?" Sir Hunter asked.

"The queen sent us out looking to see if we could find you, and that is when we came upon the dragon," repeated the captain.

"Captain, I understand. We may have to deal with the dragon again when we go back across the bridge. Okay, so where's some of that food you said you had?"

"Over here, Sir Hunter."

"Good, and I will want some wine too."

"Sir Hunter, we are glad to have found you," the captain said gleefully.

"Well, I'm glad to be found. A battle is never something you want to go through. Anything can happen to your men or yourself. Captain, I'm going to relax here with what I have, so why don't you go out, check with the men, and make sure they all have fires going, with plenty of food and water for the horses?" Sir Hunter concluded.

"Yes, sir, right away."

Sir Hunter took off some of his clothes and laid down on his blanket in front of the fire for a long, much-awaited rest.

33

CHAPTER 6

Grandpa stopped talking because the look on my face indicated I wanted to ask a question.

"Let me have it. What is your question?" Grandpa asked.

"Well, about the fairies. Really, Grandpa? Fairies? I find that hard to believe. So how many were there of these so-called fairies who worked for the queen?" I asked.

"There are twelve, with one being the leader, and her name is Galaxy," Grandpa responded.

"Wait, did you say *is*, as in present? How can that be?" I speculated.

"Well, yeah. People say they're still around. No one can see them, though. The queen created them as her frolic of fairies to be her servants. They don't have the same powers as the queen, but they do have powers. They never age, they're all female, they're all the same size, and they look alike, with the exception of Galaxy. She has bigger wings because she was crowned the leader of the frolic of fairies by the queen," explained Grandpa.

"Wow, wouldn't that be great to never die?" I said excitingly.

"I imagine so. Fairy magic is mysterious, but fairies of royal blood have much stronger magic than the average fairy. As ruler of the frolic of fairies, the queen can be ruthless and often merciless. The queen is intelligent and cunning and can easily manipulate those around her. The queen is a visionary."

"What is a visionary?" I asked.

"It means she tends to see people for what they can be in the future, rather than what they are currently. Despite the queen's cold attitude toward people, she is very nurturing toward her fairies," Grandpa said.

"So, when the town people go to Bonefairy Castle, they don't get

34

to see the fairies? I mean, what's the point? That would be why I would go there," I claimed.

"I agree with you there. It would be important to me too. I'd want to see the fairies too. The townspeople couldn't see the fairies because the queen made it that way for a reason. If the people were allowed to see the fairies, they'd lose their powers," explained Grandpa.

"Well, that's not fair. How come the Royalmen got to see the fairies?" I asked.

"The queen allowed the Royalmen to see the fairies only temporarily. When the men came into Bonefairy Castle, the fairies checked out the Royalmen to make sure they were who they said they were."

"What do the fairies do to make sure the Royalmen were who they say they were?"

"The fairies took their wands and touched them on the men's heads before they could come into Bonefairy Castle. If it didn't spark a flash, the man was not one of the queen's Royalmen. It didn't happen often because the Royalmen made sure no one attempted this. Some people were so curious about what happened in Bonefairy Castle. If someone tried to impersonate a Royalmen, the queen punished them."

"Oh, boy, I can imagine the punishment would be really bad. What kind of events happened in Bonefairy Castle?" I asked.

Grandpa replied, "Oh, they had festivities such as to celebrate their religion. Food was such a vital resource that many of the festivities were around harvest time. The townspeople knew how important it was to keep the farms thriving because all the people relied on them. Sometimes they had a big gala or a ball, where everyone got dressed up in their finest of clothes. That was the type of event that occurred when Sir Hunter came home from the battles. It was a big celebration to show everyone's gratitude for winning the battle to save the land and Bonefairy Castle."

"So, Sir Hunter has a girlfriend. Woo-hoo. I bet he was glad to see her." I chuckled.

"Yes, Sir Hunter liked Lady Isabella a lot," confirmed Grandpa.

"How come Sir Hunter couldn't be with Lady Isabella all the time?" I asked.

"The queen had rules and had total control over all her Royalmen.

None of them were allowed to marry or have families until they completed their services to the queen. They had to be completely devoted to her every request. It is like they were on call all the time. Like say how a doctor is these days," Grandpa responded.

I grimaced. "That doesn't sound like something I would want to be. How can some of the stories that Sir Hunter brought back be funny? They don't sound funny to me. The stories are real and are scary to me."

"Well, Sir Hunter told his adventures was in a way that wasn't too scary to Lady Isabella. He didn't want to frighten or worry her," noted Grandpa.

"Did Sir Hunter see the dragon?"

"Oh, yes, the dragon came around, but I'll get to that. Let's take a break for now. You're probably getting bored with me rambling on, or you're antsy to get outside to play. Plus, I don't want to take up all your time while you're here. Your grandma would like to see you and talk with you too. Why don't you go back in the house for some lunch? I think I'd like to take a nap after lunch. We can start up again after that," Grandpa offered.

"Oh, Grandpa, I want to know more," I said.

"Not to worry.. We'll get back to it in a little while," Grandpa said while patting Hunter on the head.

I scoffed off into the house. went into the kitchen, where Grandma was making homemade vegetable soup.

"Something sure smells good, Grandma," I praised.

"I'm making vegetable soup. I got the vegetables from our garden," replied Grandma.

"Grandpa wants to sleep after lunch, but I want to hear more of the stories," I said.

"You'll have plenty of time to hear the rest, sweetheart. You know your grandpa needs his rest. He isn't as young as he used to be. He was up early tending to chickens and the garden."

"I know. I'm just really enjoying it."

We all sat down at the kitchen table for lunch. The vegetable soup was really good. Fresh vegetables were the best, and I had two big bowls full. We finished eating. As much as my grandpa liked to talk, he sure didn't like to talk while eating. I helped Grandma clear the table, and

Grandpa went upstairs to take a nap. Grandma did the dishes. I asked if I could go out to the barn and play in the loft. Grandma said I could after I helped her with some chores. I took out the trash, fed the chickens, and gathered some eggs for breakfast tomorrow. I finished the chores that Grandma wanted me to do and went running out to the barn. The barn was very old, but I loved it. I liked to climb the ladder like a fireman. But now I want to pretend to be a Royalman. I found a long stick and acted as if it was my mighty sword. There were many barn cats around, and they scurried away as I made noises like I was defending myself in a battle. I also made a fort out of some the bales of hay. I eventually wore myself out with all the dueling and plopped down on the hay. As I lay there thinking of Sir Hunter fighting that ferocious dragon, I dozed off.

I woke up in the loft in the barn and forgot where I was. I didn't know how long I had been asleep, but I climbed down the latter to go back in the house and see if Grandpa was awake.

"Well, there you are," said Grandma.

"I can't believe I fell asleep. I was playing in the loft, and I guess I wore myself out. I suppose kids don't admit to that, but that's what happened," I explained.

"Your grandpa is up now and will be down shortly. I think he's going to ask you to help him with a small project," Grandma replied.

"Oh, ok," I responded obediently.

Grandpa came down the stairs. I could hear the stairs creek—the sound of an old home with character. I loved that sound. All the sounds I ever heard at home were from the city, like busy traffic sirens of police or fire trucks all the time. It is so peaceful here on the farm.

"Hi, Grandpa. I hope you had a good nap. I even fell asleep out in the barn," I admitted.

"That is easy to do here with the fresh country air, and the birds singing and bathing in the birdbath or eating from the feeder. It drives all the cats nuts, though," Grandpa commented.

"Grandma said you had a project you needed help with," I reported.

"I sure do. I almost forgot about that. Getting old is not pleasant. I seem to forget a lot, but your grandma helps keep me in check."

"What do you need help with?"

"Let's go on out to the barn. I have a chair that needs fixing, but I can't do it by myself. Someone needs to hold it while I work on it. You think you're up for that?" Grandpa asked.

"Oh, yes, I can help you with that," I remarked.

Grandpa and I went out to the barn. Grandpa brought out an old wooden rocker. It was smaller than Grandpa's, so I assumed it was Grandma's. It definitely needed working on. The leg was hanging on by an old, rusted hinge. Grandpa asked me to help him pick up the chair and put it on the working table. Grandpa's working table had seen many projects and repairs. I remember when I was younger, I was allowed only to watch off to the side. Many of the projects Grandpa worked on involved dangerous equipment or tools. Now that I was older, I was excited to help Grandpa. Maybe one day he would let me build something.

"Okay, what I'll need to do is replace the hinges on this leg. They're not easy to get to or easy to get off. Do you think you can hold the chair like this?" Grandpa asked while demonstrating.

I put my hands on the locations he described to me and said, "Like this?"

"Perfect. Now, this will take a spell, so I need you to hold steady the best you can," reiterated Grandpa.

I held on to the chair as he began using his tools to remove the hinges. I didn't know if Grandpa would be willing to continue with his stories, but I thought I'd give it a try. "Can you share more about Sir Hunter?" I asked.

"I will try. Sometimes it is hard for me to do two things at the same time, but sure," grandpa said.

CHAPTER 7

As the next morning began, the Royalmen started to move around, made their fires, cooked something to eat to build their strength, and prepared the horses for the trip back to Bonefairy Castle. The men were honored to have Sir Hunter as their leader. They were afraid something bad had happened to him, and they were thankful he was still alive and that the battle had been won.

"Captain, it's time to get the men ready, so let's break up camp and move out," Sir Hunter commanded.

"Yes, Sir Hunter," replied the captain.

"Bring me Wheels and get him hooked back up to my wagon. I can't wait to see this dragon that everyone is talking about."

"Sir Hunter, I hope we don't run into him again," clarified the captain.

"Captain, we are going to have to deal with it sooner or later," Sir Hunter countered.

"Yes, sir, you're probably right," confessed the captain.

"Okay, let's get going. Captain, I want you to send one of your men ahead to the bridge to check whether the dragon is back."

"Yes, Sir Hunter, I agree that's a good idea," the captain said.

"Then tell him to come back and report back to me with what he saw."

"I'll make sure he reports immediately what he sees."

As the rider took off, Sir Hunter knew that it would be about a half a day before he would make it back—if he made it back at all. All the fires were put out, and the rest of the men headed out on their journey back to Bonefairy Castle.

"Captain, how many men did you have when you left the castle?" Sir Hunter inquired.

"Fifty men, Sir Hunter," the captain replied.

"How many do we have now, Captain?"

"Thirty-Eight, sir."

"All right. When we get back to the bridge, if the dragon is there, this is what we are going to do. First off, we need to find where its cave is and see whether it is the only one. If it is on the bridge when we arrive, we'll have a chance to go into the cave. We should have some of the men at the bridge for the dragon to watch and keep it occupied. The rest of the men can then go into the cave and set a trap so when it goes back into the cave, we can try to close it off when it is in there. At least that will make it safe for crossing the bridge until it figures a way to get back out. If this dragon is as big as you say it is, when we get back to Bonefairy Castle, we will have to talk to the queen. Maybe she will be able to give us the answer about how to take care of the dragon."

As the day went on, it wasn't long before the rider was on his way back. One of the men saw him coming and told the captain, who told Sir Hunter.

"Sir Hunter, our rider is back," declared the captain.

"What did he see?" Sir Hunter asked impatiently.

"He saw the dragon hovering in the distance, but it wasn't at the bridge, and he couldn't say that the dragon wouldn't be there by the time we arrived at the bridge."

"I understand, Captain. We will have to be careful, and maybe we will get lucky," Sir Hunter said uneasily.

They could see the bridge in the distance, and as they approached the bridge, they could see the dragon flying away.

"All right, Captain, have the men move out faster to get over the bridge before the dragon comes back," Sir Hunter commanded.

"Yes, sir, right away," replied the captain.

Sir Hunter could see that wasn't going to be a problem to get the men to move out across the bridge because off in the distance, it looked like the dragon was returning to its cave.

The men quickly moved across the bridge.

"That sure worked out. We made it across the bridge, Sir Hunter," the captain said.

"Now, let's move out and get down the road and back into the woods again, where that big, overgrown thing won't see us," Sir Hunter emphasized.

"Yes, sir. Let's go, men! We need to move quickly," yelled the captain.

The bridge they had just crossed was really high up and a long way down, but that was the only way to get across when traveling out of town. Sir Hunter's wagon was the last to cross the bridge and move under cover of the forest.

"Captain, have one of the men fall back and watch to make sure that we are safe and do not get a surprise," Sir Hunter said.

"Yes, Sir Hunter. You two, fall back and keep your eyes open," demanded the captain.

As the rest of the men moved into the forest with Sir Hunter, the feeling started to ease up about the dragon. Sir Hunter was tired but wanted to move on to the town and Bonefairy Castle. He thought of some good food that Isabella would make and the nice, relaxing time he would have with her. It would take a little more time to get back now that there were more of them travelling together. Sir Hunter knew that just on the other side of the forest, they could see the town and Bonefairy Castle.

They traveled through the trees and down the road, and the men started to laugh and enjoy themselves as they got closer to the clearing that was on the other side of the forest. The clearing was coming up just ahead of them, and the town was in sight. One more bridge to cross before getting into town. There were always some of the queen's Royalmen standing by the bridge and checking to see who wanted to cross.

As Sir Hunter rode up to the bridge, the Royalmen greeted him and congratulated him on winning the battle for the queen. The men made room for Sir Hunter to cross the bridge and cheered his name. Sir Hunter was crossing the bridge when one of the wheels on the wagon broke off. The wheel blocked the way for everyone else to be able cross. Sir Hunter called for his men to help replace the wheel. It took only a few minutes because the men moved quickly. Sir Hunter then thanked his men, and they continued across the bridge and headed into town.

The people in town were very busy because they were getting ready for a big festival to celebrate the return of Sir Hunter and the news of the battle. This was something that happened when a battle was won and the townspeople could relax, knowing that things were going to be better for them. People started to cheer as he rode into town, but Sir Hunter was tired and wanted only to get to Isabella. His celebrating was going to have to wait, because it would be going on for several days. He wanted some quiet time and couldn't wait to eat some of Isabella's good food.

Isabella wasn't home when Sir Hunter rode up to where she lived. Sir Hunter didn't care because he had to take care of Wheels. He needed to get the horse food and some water, and then he had to unload the wagon. Word that Sir Hunter had returned spread throughout the town, and it wasn't long before Isabella was on her way back home. She had been in town helping the rest of the townspeople prepare for the festival.

As Isabella got closer to her home, she could see Sir Hunter unloading the wagon, and he called out his name as she ran toward home. "Oh, Sir Hunter, I've been waiting and was wondering when you'd arrive."

"Well, my lady, it has been a while, but you know that I can't predict how long I will be gone. So, what do you have to eat? I'm tired and hungry," Sir Hunter begged.

Isabella said, "Sir Hunter, I don't have anything made or prepared. I didn't know when you were going to show up. What do you want? I'll see if I have it."

"My lady, I don't really care at this point. Just something quick. Oh, and some wine. I'm going to go out back and wash off some of the dirt from the trip. I'll be back in a few minutes and then tell you about the battle, or anything else that you may want to know."

Isabella was happy that her man was back safe, and she hurried to make some food for him. The wine would also make things better because it helped him relax. Sir Hunter finished washing up and returned to the front porch. Isabella was cooking. She took some of the wine out to Sir Hunter as she finished cooking. Some of the townspeople waved to him as they passed by while Sir Hunter waited for the food. Sir

Hunter didn't really want to be friendly right now. He simply wanted to relax with some wine, some good food, and his woman.

Isabella called to Sir Hunter. "Come in and close the door. You know if you stay out there on the porch, all those people are going to keep waving at you. They're ready for the festival to start so they can get drunk."

Sir Hunter came in and said, "Well, I'm ready to get drunk too. It's been so long. Let's eat! What'd you make?"

Isabella didn't have too much food, but she was able to put something together, and it would have to do. Tomorrow she'd go into town and get some more food now that Hunter was back. Sir Hunter and Isabella could hear the noise from the town as the festival started, but they wanted to stay home by themselves. They sat and enjoyed each other's company. Sir Hunter was so hungry and felt like he couldn't get enough.

"While you go into town tomorrow for more food, I will to see some of my men," Sir Hunter said.

The next day came, and Isabella left for town to get more food. Sir Hunter got himself cleaned up and went to join some of his friends to enjoy some spirits together. One of his close friends, Agenda, was usually there and was usually drunk. And of course, he always had a lady on each knee. As Sir Hunter went from place to place, it wouldn't take too long for him to start feeling anxious to see his friends. It had been so long since Sir Hunter had had a lot of spirits, and he wasn't used to it. Sir Hunter didn't care, and then he saw Agenda sitting over in the corner. Sir Hunter walked over, and Agenda stood up.

With spirits in his hand, Agenda yelled out, "I want everyone to know that this man, Sir Hunter, is back from the battle, and we are now going to celebrate his return today, right here in this tavern. So, everyone stop what you are doing, and let's raise our cups and honor him and what he has done for all of us."

"Agenda, you're drunk!" Sir Hunter yelled over the cheering crowd.

Agenda laughed and said, "Well, my friend, you need to join me."

Sir Hunter laughed too. "I guess I'll just do that."

The festival was really going now, with everyone having a good time. The word of Sir Hunter's return had now gotten back to Bonefairy

Castle. The queen sent word that she wanted to see Hunter by the next morning.

Agenda laughed and said, "Well, Hunter, you'd better make sure you keep that appointment."

Sir Hunter replied, "You know I will. I just hope she simply wants to know is about the battle and does not want me to leave again."

"She also is going to want all that you brought back from the battle, right?" Agenda asked.

"Yes, that is true, but for now let's have some more spirits. I'll see the queen tomorrow. More drinks over here," Sir Hunter demanded.

Sir Hunter was very happy to be home. He always enjoyed hanging out with his men to have a few laughs and spirits. There wasn't much talk about all that Sir Hunter had gone through; there would be time for that later. The men always gave Sir Hunter a hard time after battle, teasing him that he exaggerated his experiences. The men did that for fun, though, because they all knew too well that it was true. They thanked God that they hadn't experienced as much as Sir Hunter had. The night got rowdier and turned into the early morning. Sir Hunter knew he had to stop to be at his best for when he saw the queen. The men tried to keep him from leaving and asked him to party some more and celebrate with more spirits and the pretty women, but Sir Hunter declined and said he must leave.

Sir Hunter stumbled back to Isabella's cabin. She had a nice fire going and some hot coffee to relax him before going to bed. Sir Hunter was very grateful to sleep in a real bed. As he sat in front of the fire with the crackling sound of the dancing flames, he reminisced a little of the quiet moments he had with his trusty friend Wheels. He may have taken Wheels for granted sometimes, but he knew he would not have been able to get out of some of his dilemmas without him. Sir Hunter was almost falling asleep as he brought the cup of coffee to his mouth. Isabella helped him, took the cup, and set it on the table. She helped him out of the chair and walked him to bed. He fell flat on his face. Isabella struggled to get off his boots. She didn't dare try to take off any of his clothes. At least he was able to take off his coat when he returned from drinking. As soon as Sir Hunter hit the bed, he was in a deep sleep, snoring. Isabella tiptoed back to the fire, sat down in the chair, and watched him sleep. As she rested her head on the back of the chair, a big smile grew on her face, and she prayed to the Lord to thank him for Sir Hunter's safe return.

The next morning came faster than Sir Hunter wanted. As he got Wheels ready to go to Bonefairy Castle, Isabella asked with sad eyes, "Do you know when you'll be back?"

"No, I'm not sure. I haven't talked to the queen yet. I should be back before the festival is over in town," Sir Hunter said encouragingly.

"I hope so. I'd like to do a little celebrating with you myself," Isabella confessed.

"I know. And we will! The queen needs the things I brought back from the battle."

Isabella knew that almost anything could happen or change now that Sir Hunter was back. Hunter said goodbye to Isabella and promised that he would try to get back as soon as he could.

"Okay, Wheels, let's take all the stuff to the queen. I hope we don't have to be there long," Sir Hunter said.

He climbed up on the wagon, looked back at Isabella, and waved. Sir Hunter was expected at Bonefairy Castle that morning because the queen wanted to see him. Sir Hunter had his wagon full of things from the battle and knew that it was what the queen really wanted.

Thank goodness the trip to Bonefairy Castle wasn't too far. As he pulled the wagon up to the gate, he was greeted by the Royalmen. They took Wheels and unhooked him from the wagon. Sir Hunter was going into Bonefairy Castle when he looked back and saw the queen's fairies carrying the things from the wagon high up into Bonefairy Castle. When Sir Hunter entered the castle, he could see the queen and immediately kneeled down. It was something that Hunter hadn't done in a while, but he knew it was expected from everyone. Plus, it showed respect.

The queen told Sir Hunter to rise and come forward. "Sir Hunter, welcome back. You must be glad to be back," the queen stated with grace.

"Yes, I am, Your Highness. I know you wanted me to report in," Sir Hunter said.

"That is true. Do you need to talk to your men? We will be talking for a long time, so if you need to see them first, then you should go now before we start."

"No, Your Highness. They have been without me for this long, so I believe they can wait. I know you have many questions and things to talk about," Sir Hunter said calmly.

"Indeed, I do. One of the fairies will take you up in Bonefairy Castle, and I will meet you there."

"Yes, Your Highness."

None of the Royalmen, including Sir Hunter, was allowed into the upper part of Bonefairy Castle, where the queen's private quarters were. Only the queen's fairies were allowed, and they were controlled by the queen. No one knew how the queen did the things that she did. Sir Hunter only knew that the things that he brought back from the battle, such as hair, bones, or any other possessions of the dead men, were taken to the queen's private quarters. She consumed the molecules of life from these things that were taken from the dead, men with the key component of white blood cells, which were part of the body's immune system. The queen was advanced with knowledge of the future. She knew that several hundred years from now, a mysterious substance called nucleon came from the cell nucleus, and that the discovery of the molecular basis of life would be known as deoxyribonucleic acid (DNA) and be used throughout the world. It would be very helpful in identifying individual humans. The queen and her fairies would still be around, but no one that was around now would be. Many things happened from time to time that couldn't be explained by the people, but they knew that these unexplainable things came from the queen's fairies.

★★★

While Sir Hunter was spending time at Bonefairy Castle with the queen, Isabella decided to go into town to participate in some of the festival activities. Everyone was having a great time, and many taverns were full as Isabella arrived. Isabella had made many friends over time while Sir Hunter was gone. One of her favorite taverns was called Bonefairy House, which she had purchased with one of her best friends. Isabella would help her friend there from time to time while Sir Hunter was gone, just to keep busy and not think about him. As people came in, Isabella would greet them and put men with different ladies around the tavern. Many nights Bonefairy House would get wild, and many men would get drunk and fight, but that was what brought in everyone, and that was how Bonefairy House got the name. After each night when Bonefairy House closed, the fairies would come in and clean up the mess, which usually meant men laid around drunk with broken bones. If there was anything that the fairies cleaned up and thought would be something the queen would want for DNA, they would take those bones and other things back to Bonefairy Castle. After the queen got the DNA, she would have the fairies burn everything. That was when people would see smoke coming from the top of Bonefairy Castle.

One night long ago, when Isabella was at Bonefairy House, a man came in with a few of the Royalmen for some spirits. That was when she met Sir Hunter. He was a large, handsome man and looked like he was important. She wanted to get to know him right away when she saw him. There was something that she liked about him. After that night, Isabella would always be seen with him whenever he was back in town. Unfortunately, she was not with him now. Sir Hunter was at Bonefairy Castle, and she was busy cooking and serving patrons at Bonefairy House.

Isabella didn't know how the night was going to go when she got there because every night was different. The night was wilder than most because of the festival, and there were many new faces in town. She greeted the men as they that came in. One of them was already drunk from having too much from another tavern, and he started bothering her. Isabella told the man that he was drunk but could stay as long as he did not start anything. The man smelled from dirty clothes and spirits that had been spilled all over him. People didn't want to be around him, but the festival was going strong now and getting wilder.

About that time, Agenda came in from the street and saw Isabella trying to get the drunk to sit in a corner and not bother anybody, but she was having a little trouble with him. Agenda went over to help Isabella and told the drunk to sit down and stay quiet. The drunk didn't think that Agenda had the right to tell him anything, and he told Agenda to keep out of it, or he was going to put Agenda in a corner.

Agenda smiled and said, "I don't think you can even stand up, let alone do anything."

The drunk stood up and took a swing at Agenda. Isabella tried to stop what was about to start by telling Agenda to get back, and she would take care of it. Agenda was a good friend of Isabella. He came into Bonefairy House often and didn't want to make trouble for Isabella. Agenda agreed and went over to the bar, but he still watched Isabella and the drunk. As she sat down the drunk, he was trying to kiss her. Isabella finally left the drunk and returned to the bar, where Agenda was sitting.

Agenda said, "You know if Sir Hunter was here right now, he would have thrown out that drunk."

Isabella smiled and said, "I know, but he isn't, and that drunk will pass out sitting over there. The fairies will remove him later and take him to Bonefairy Castle, and that will probably be the last time we see the guy. In the meantime, let me get you another bottle of spirits, and maybe you can find a lady here and see if you can get a kiss from one of them."

Agenda laughed and said, "That is something I just might try before I leave."

More people from town came in, and Isabella was getting busy, so Agenda decided to move on and check out the rest of the festival. As Agenda moved out into the street, he could see Bonefairy Castle in the distance and noted the black smoke that was coming out of the tower. He knew that Sir Hunter was there with the queen and would be there for a while. Sir Hunter had promised that if he could get away later from the queen, he would meet Agenda for some spirits. The days were long at Bonefairy Castle, and it didn't look like Sir Hunter was going to make it.

The festival was going strong into the night. As the night came, so did the drunks. When there was a festival in town, there was always extra work for the fairies. One of the things the queen wanted for her powers was what the fairies would collect from the men who were drunk. Pieces of clothing or pieces of hair were always needed for the queen. The men whom the queen used were usually drunk or dead. Sir Hunter had brought back a wagon that was full of pieces of men and clothing for the queen. That was why the black smoke was coming from Bonefairy Castle. As time went on, the smoke would stop, and many men would come up missing, never to be seen again. No one could ever explain this but knew that when there was smoke coming from Bonefairy Castle, the queen was not available to talk to. Sir Hunter was in charge when this happened.

Three days had passed, the festival was winding down, and everything started to get back to normal. The townspeople had celebrated the victory of winning the battle and the return of all the soldiers. It was time for Sir Hunter to leave the queen and Bonefairy Castle and get back to Isabella. Isabella had put in her time at Bonefairy House and was now returning home. One of the drunks she had had trouble with the day before decided to follow her down the street. Isabella made it down the street and turned the corner when Sir Hunter ran into her. Isabella immediately told Sir Hunter about who was following her and stood behind Sir Hunter as the drunk came around the corner. Sir Hunter had just come from Bonefairy Castle and was still in his uniform when the drunk ran right into him.

Sir Hunter looked at the drunk and said, "Are you following my lady?"

The drunk said, "I just wanted to get to know her a little bit better."

Sir Hunter pushed him back a little and said, "You need to turn around and go back where you came from. I will forget that you were following Isabella."

The drunk agreed, turned around, and went in the other direction.

Isabella held on to Sir Hunter as the drunk left and said, "I am so glad you showed up when you did. That guy was at Bonefairy House all day, and I really didn't need him around bothering me anymore."

"I don't think he will be a problem anymore, so let's go home," Sir Hunter said encouragingly.

Isabella smiled as she looked up at Sir Hunter. "It's nice to have you around."

Sir Hunter put his arm around her as they walked for home. "Looks like it's going to be a nice night, my lady."

"I certainly need a nice night. A festival is always good to have, but it's all the drunks and clean up that I don't like," declared Isabella.

"Let's not think about that anymore tonight. Is there any food at home?"

"I think we can find something."

"Well, that's going to be worth a kiss, my lady. Come here!" Sir Hunter grabbed her and kissed her.

Isabella blushed. "Maybe I need to cook a little more often, if that's what it takes for you to give me a kiss,"

Sir Hunter said, "You know I like your cooking."

"I know, but I also know you just don't want to have to do it," Isabella teased.

As they arrived home and was walking to the front door, they could see a note that someone had left. Isabella took the note, read it, and handed it to Sir Hunter. She sighed. "Well, so much for something to eat."

Sir Hunter read the note. It said that he was wanted back at Bonefairy Castle right away. Sir Hunter looked at Isabella and said that he had to go. He gave her a quick hug. "I'll be back when I can."

He turned and went to get Wheels from the barn. Sir Hunter knew it had to be something serious whenever he was sent for. It wasn't very far to Bonefairy Castle, and he rode away.

Some of the queen's Royalmen were waiting for Sir Hunter as he arrived. Sir Hunter asked the captain what the problem was.

"Sir Hunter, the dragon has been seen, and we are afraid that it is going to make trouble for us. Some of the animals out in the fields have gone missing, and the dragon has been seen. We think that we are going to have to go after it, or we will keep losing animals," the captain explained.

"All right, Captain. Get the men together. I'll be back after I talk to the queen," instructed Sir Hunter.

He went looking for the queen and found her talking to some of her other men about what was going on.

"Sir Hunter, I'm glad that you are here. I'm sure the captain has told you what has happened. I'll leave it up to you to decide what we can do about it," the queen said.

"Yes, Your Highness. I saw the captain and told him to get the men together. We will be going after the dragon immediately," Sir Hunter assured her.

"Sir Hunter, do you know what you are going to do?" the queen asked.

"Your Highness, I believe that we're going to have to go to where the dragon's cave is, in the mountains, and fight it there. We'll have to get it to go into the cave, where we can trap it. We can build a big fire inside the cave. It will see smoke and light coming from the cave, which should bring it in. Once we have it inside the cave, we will have some of the animals there that it likes to eat. When it comes toward the animals, that is when we will attack. If we have time to build a fire, we can make a large amount of poison, which is made from dragon berries. We can then put the poison all over an animal's back. The dragon will go after the animal and eat the poison, which will make it sleep. Once we have the dragon asleep, we can go out, close the entrance to the cave, and seal it forever."

"Sir Hunter, I think that is a great plan—if you think we will be able to do it."

"Well, Your Highness, that is what we're going to try to do. If that doesn't work, we'll have to think of something else." Sir Hunter admitted. "Captain, are the men ready to go?"

"Yes, Sir Hunter, their ready!" the captain affirmed.

"Okay, then, let's move out!"

"Yes, sir!"

"You take the men, and I'll catch up to you in a little while. I have a few other things I have to take care of," commanded Sir Hunter.

As the captain moved out, Sir Hunter went back to the queen. The queen was just coming out from her private quarters and asked, "Hunter, did you have the men move toward the dragon's cave?"

"Yes, Your Highness. They should be there by tomorrow," Sir Hunter responded.

He then decided to head back home before following his men. Isabella was home and didn't have any idea that Sir Hunter was going to have to leave.

"Isabella, the queen has asked me to go with some of my men to kill the dragon, so I will be leaving after I get a few things together," Sir Hunter informed her.

"How long do you think you'll be gone?" asked Isabella.

"I'm not sure, but I don't think it will be long. It really depends on the dragon and how much trouble it gives us. We are not sure exactly where it is or if we can find it. I will have to figure that out when I get there," Sir Hunter clarified.

Sir Hunter put a few things together along with some food for Wheels, and he said goodbye to Isabella. The men were about three hours ahead of Sir Hunter. He knew that he had time before he would have to face the dragon. As he climbed up on Wheels and turned to ride off, he looked back at Isabella and waved. Isabella stayed on the porch and watched as Sir Hunter rode out of sight.

It wasn't very long before Sir Hunter reached the main bridge out of town and crossed it. Sir Hunter hoped to catch up to his men before they reached the cave. There was a place that Sir Hunter told the captain to stay for the night with the men, and it was about a half a day's ride before reaching the cave. Sir Hunter figured he would catch up to them by then.

As Sir Hunter arrived at the camp where the men were, he could see the cave in the distance. It was high, about halfway up on the mountain. The fog had set in and it wasn't going to be long before they would be able to see the cave. They knew the dragon wasn't going to be an easy fight, so it was time to relax and do some drinking around the fire. Sir Hunter told the captain to not let the men drink too much, because tomorrow was going to be hard enough without the men still being drunk. The captain agreed and said that he would keep an eye on them.

As the next morning came, most of the fire had burned out, and there was just a little smoke. One of the men came to the captain and told him that he had just seen the dragon come out of the cave and fly off. The captain told Sir Hunter what was happening and said that this would be a good time to move toward the cave, before the dragon returned. Sir Hunter agreed and told the captain to get the men ready to head out. He also told the captain to send some of the men to look for some dragon berries, so they wouldn't have to look later.

While the men reached the bottom of the mountain, there were several other occasions that they sighted the dragon in the distance, and they knew that it could return at any time. The men started up the mountain. The trail was very rough, narrow, and dangerous. There were a few places where the horses had a hard time, and the men had to get off their horses and walk them. When they finally reached the cave, the sun was bright, and most of the fog had lifted.

Sir Hunter said to the captain, "Have some of the men stay outside the cave to watch for the dragon to return. The rest of the men should go inside to build a fire. They need to be ready for when the dragon comes back."

Inside the cave, there were different tunnels to many different parts of the cave. They were dangerous, but there was just one place that looked like where the dragon stayed, because they could see bones of animals.

Sir Hunter said to the captain, "Put a couple of the animals over there and tie them up. Put the dragon berry juice over their backs."

It wasn't long after the men moved the animals to the other side of the cave that some of the Royalmen ran in and said they saw the dragon coming back. There was a small pond of water in the middle of the cave, and Sir Hunter told the men to put as much of the dragon berry juice as they could into the water so when the dragon drank it, it would make the dragon helpless. All they could do then was wait. The fire was built and burning very bright, and the animals were tied up on the other side of the fire and the water.

"Men, you need to get back into some of the other parts of the cave and wait until we hear the dragon," Sir Hunter commanded.

The men had to keep putting more wood on the fire to keep it big and smoking, and others threw dragon berry juice in the fire for more smoke. About two hours went by, and the cave was very smoky. Some of the men came and told Sir Hunter that the dragon had returned; it noticed the bright fire and smoke and was coming back. The dragon was big and had been around for many years. It had caused many deaths and destroyed too many things. No one ever thought of doing anything about the dragon because it was so big and dangerous to fight. The queen said it was time that something be done about the dragon, and it was up to Sir Hunter to see that it got done.

All of the men hid in the cave, waiting. The dragon landed outside the cave. The smoke was coming out of the cave, and the dragon wasn't sure why but decided to investigate. The dragon slowly went in the cave and immediately saw the animals behind the fire. It started to move toward the animals, using slow predator movements to sneak up on them. Some of the men came out from behind rocks and shot their arrows at it. The dragon swung its large tail and blocked a lot of their shots. It then lunged after one of animals. The men tried to keep the dragon from getting too many of the animals to keep the collateral damage at a minimum. The dragon did get hold of an animal with its sharp claws and teeth. The animal tried to escape, but it couldn't get away from the dragon's grip. The dragon ripped the animal to shreds, eating flesh and bone. The men kept firing their weapons, but it didn't seem to faze the dragon one bit.

Sir Hunter asked one of the men to pour more of the dragon berry juice in the fire, which caught the dragon's attention as the smoke billowed up into its face. The men continued shooting their arrows, which forced the dragon into a different part of the cave. This allowed the men to get the remaining animals out of the cave so they could seal it up. The fire was still large enough to continue burning the dragon berries for smoke. The dragon stayed back in the deepest part of the cave as the men used their horses to pull rocks across the entrance of the cave. The smoke built up more and more, and more rocks were put in place to cover the entrance of the cave. The poison was working. The dragon was getting weak and defenseless. It still tried to move around, but it didn't get far. The men continued to place rocks in front of the cave entrance. It was hard work for the men and horses.

The men were tired, but finally the cave was sealed. All the animals were back out of the cave, and the men were all safe. They cheered with relief and started to drink. Sir Hunter and the captain were glad that everything had worked out.

Sir Hunter said, "Now, I just hope that this dragon can't get back out of the cave."

Word got out that the fight with the dragon was successful, and the townspeople planned for another celebration. Sir Hunter told the captain to order the men head back to town but have a few stay behind for a couple of days, to make sure that the cave stayed sealed. The captain also had many of the men plant dragon berry bushes all around the cave's entrance. The aroma from the berries would constantly be in the air, which helped keep the dragon asleep. Sir Hunter and the rest of the men headed back to town to tell the queen what had happened with the dragon. No one knew just how old the dragon was or how long it would live. Sir Hunter decided to place guards at the cave entrance every day and night until they were sure that the dragon could not get out.

Sir Hunter knew that Bonefairy House would be the place to go when he got back to town. Isabella and Agenda would be there making plans for the celebration, and with all the townspeople, that would mean wild drinking. The whole town was still cleaning up from the festival from a few days ago. As Sir Hunter and his men arrived back in town, Sir Hunter told the captain to have the men go to their cabins before coming back into town to celebrate. The men went in different directions. The captain and Sir Hunter then went to Bonefairy House to get some spirits. That would give Sir Hunter a chance to see Isabella again. He needed to let her know that he was back, and the celebration could begin.

As Sir Hunter and the Captain entered the Bonefairy House, Agenda saw them, stood up and with a mug in his hand, he cheered, "Welcome the safe return of Sir Hunter and the Captain."

Isabella was out back behind Bonefairy House, taking out some trash to burn, when she heard the cheering going on inside. As she started back inside, Sir Hunter met her at that back door and said, "I was looking for you."

Isabella smiled, gave him a hug, and said, "I had to take some trash out to burn when I heard the cheering. I had a feeling it was you, and I'm glad you're back." She pulled him inside the door. "I bet you're hungry."

Sir Hunter knew that the food was good and said that was exactly why he was there. Isabella looked at Hunter and said, "Really? I thought it might be to come and see me."

Sir Hunter smiled and sat down at the table where the captain was.

"Agenda, can you bring Sir Hunter and me some spirits?" asked the captain.

"Yes, sir. I'll see what Isabella has made up for you to eat. I'll be right back!" Agenda responded.

It wasn't long before some of the men who had come back with Sir Hunter came into Bonefairy House, where the celebrating had started.

Sir Hunter raised his mug to his men and said, "You all did a great job the last few days, and you deserve to relax now. Enjoy Bonefairy House and all that it has to offer."

The men cheered and held their hands in the air. Agenda returned to where Sir Hunter was with some spirits, raised his mug, and said, "Thank you, Sir Hunter."

"Agenda, you need to make sure my men get what they want. They did a great job, and everyone in here should raise their mugs to them," Sir Hunter praised.

"Yes, sir. I will see to it," Agenda agreed.

"Good! Captain, I will celebrate here with you and the men for the rest of the day. I will then go to Bonefairy Castle to give my report to the queen," Sir Hunter said.

"I know that is what you need to do. The queen needs to know, but for now let's have some more spirits," replied the captain.

"I like the way you think. Agenda, more spirits! Captain, I'll be back in a few minutes," Sir Hunter said.

He got up from the table and went to find Isabella. She was clearing off some tables when Sir Hunter took her arm and said, "Come with me. The tables can wait."

Isabella smiled and held on tight to Sir Hunter's arm as they moved upstairs. Bonefairy House had several rooms upstairs that were available to people when they came into town; it was for those who needed a place to stay for the night. Sir Hunter didn't plan on staying for the night, but he did want to be alone with Isabella for a while. As Sir Hunter and Isabella moved upstairs, he looked down at the captain and raised his mug. The captain looked up, and he knew that Sir Hunter and Isabella were going to be busy for the rest of the afternoon. Isabella was beautiful with long black hair and blue eyes. Sir Hunter had strong feelings for her. He was very lucky that she wanted to be only with him. Sir Hunter was always gone doing things for the queen, and they never had time for each other, but today wasn't going to go by without Sir Hunter and Isabella spending some time together alone.

Just after they closed the door to their room, it opened again, and Isabella called down to a girl who was working there and told her she wanted water brought up for a bath. The girl waved and said, "All right, in a minute."

Sir Hunter was at one of the windows looking out, as the girl brought in water for the bath. Sir Hunter told the girl to bring back some spirits, and Isabella looked for some towels. The bath was ready, and the door was closed again. Isabella poured some spirits in two mugs as Hunter got undressed and climbed into the hot bath. Isabella then gave Sir Hunter some spirits and started to wash his back.

Sir Hunter smiled. "I really needed this bath."

Isabella laughed. "Yes, you sure do!"

Sir Hunter put his mug down on the floor next to the bath and pulled Isabella into the bath with him. He smiled. "Well, you can use a bath too! After all, you've been busy at work."

It was quiet for the rest of the afternoon as they had their time together. Downstairs was just the opposite. There was loud laughing, and everyone had spirits in their mugs. A few of the men were starting to get drunk and falling down.

Sir Hunter came out of his room and yelled down to the captain, "Captain, do I need to come down there and take charge?"

"No, Sir Hunter. I will quiet the men!" the captain assured him.

"Okay, Captain. I'll be back down in a few minutes," Sir Hunter commented. "Isabella, I'm going to have to go downstairs. The men are starting to get a little wild, and you don't need the place busted up."

Isabella replied, "Okay, I'll be back down in a few minutes. We made a mess, and I want to clean up this place a little. It's nice to have you back."

"Thanks, my lady. It's nice to be back," Sir Hunter agreed. "Agenda, bring me some more spirits over here, and bring the captain some too."

"You clean up pretty well," complimented the captain.

"Well, I know how to get that done," Sir Hunter said.

"Yes, I can see that," the captain said as Isabella came back downstairs. She had changed her clothes because the other ones were wet.

Sir Hunter said, "Maybe you'll find a lady too someday."

The captain smiled. "Do you think there will be any left for me?"

"You never know. Captain, let's you and I go walk around the town a little and see what else is happening." Sir Hunter looked back, waved to Isabella, and said he'd be back later. He and the captain went out the door and walked through the town.

There were a lot of different things happening all over town as people celebrated. There were different tents set up on the street, and food was being cooked. They could hear music playing as children ran through the streets. Many people waved at Sir Hunter and thanked him for what he and his men had done about the dragon. As the captain and Sir Hunter walked, they could see Bonefairy Castle in the distance. The smoke was coming out, which meant the queen was busy.

"Captain, it looks like I'm going to have to leave you here and go on to Bonefairy Castle. I know when the queen needs me there," Sir Hunter explained.

"Sir Hunter, I think you'd better let Isabella know before you go," the captain said.

"She'll be all right, but I'll stop back in and tell her what I'm doing."

Sir Hunter went back to Bonefairy House, but Isabella was too busy to stop and talk. Sir Hunter asked the captain to inform her that he was heading back to Bonefairy Castle and would return when he could. Sir Hunter went on to Bonefairy Castle and left the celebrating for later.

When he arrived at the Bonefairy Castle, the queen was showing one of the fairies a scroll that was never seen by anyone. In the scroll were words that the queen had written down and explained how she used the things that were brought back from battles, as well as how she made DNA. The queen knew that the words in the scroll would be helpful to someone in the future. Several hundred years had to pass, and the world would become very different.

CHAPTER 8

"You know, Grandpa, they were lucky that thirty-eight of the Royalmen survived the battle," I pointed out.

"You're right. Many men did get killed, but they weren't the Royalmen. The Royalmen are highly skilled and are heavily guarded by other men to protect them because they serve the queen. They are like the Secret Service agents who protect the president of the United States," Grandpa said.

"That's cool. I'd love to be a Secret Service agent. They are loyal to the president like the Royalmen were loyal to the queen."

"That's right," Grandpa replied.

"What are spirits? I thought those were ghosts or something, but you said Sir Hunter was looking forward to having spirits with his men," I mentioned.

"Spirits are what we call alcohol today, like beer and whiskey," Grandpa explained.

"That's a shame Sir Hunter had to go see the queen the next day. So soon after getting home? I'm sure he was tired," I noted.

"The queen needed all the stuff that Sir Hunter brought back with him, remember? She needed the items as soon as possible. At least she gave him the night to rest. I'm sure he would have rather spent the night celebrating, but he was too tired to even do that. The celebrations usually lasted several days, so when he was done with the queen, she would send him back—as long as he wasn't needed for something else."

"Agenda is an unusual name. I wonder where that came from?" I inquired.

"Well, it certainly is an unusual name. He got his name because his father was a planner. He was a builder and wanted a big family. Agenda, as you know, is a list of activities in the order they are to be completed. So he got his name because having a son was on his father's life agenda," explained Grandpa.

"Oh, I would never have guessed that, but it makes sense. Sir Hunter sure loved Wheels. I think it was really cool how he named his horse that. Wheels pulled a wagon with wheels." I giggled.

"Yes, Wheels was Sir Hunter's most loyal friend. They had been through a lot together," Grandpa agreed.

Grandpa and I worked hard on the chair. It made me feel good to be able to help Grandpa. I could tell Grandpa was enjoying me helping him too. I could also see why he needed help. There was no way he'd be able to fix this chair without someone holding it. As we got closer to completing it, I had to ask Grandpa to tell me more. As he hammered the final nails, he picked up where he had left off.

Although I asked Grandpa a lot of questions, I still had more. Grandpa and I completed the chair. It was a very old chair, but it was made well, with really good wood.

"Great job, my son. I couldn't have fixed this chair without you," Grandpa praised.

"It is a really nice chair. Is it Grandma's chair?" I asked.

"No, Hunter. You know your grandma doesn't come out much on the porch. When she does, she likes to sit on the bench swing over there, but that is broken too, so I'll have to fix it sometime. This chair was once your father's. Before him, it was mine. My father made it for me, and it has been around ever since," Grandpa explained.

"Wow, really? So this is for me, Grandpa?" I said excitedly.

"It sure is," Grandpa said with a big grin.

Grandpa asked me to help it carry it up to the porch. We carried the chair to the porch and placed it right next to Grandpa's chair.

"Give it a try," Grandpa stated.

I sat down on the chair. It was perfect. I rocked back and forth with glee.

"Well, now we can rock together as I tell you more," Grandpa proclaimed.

We both sat in silence for a while rocking back and forth, listening to the birds sing, and watching the cats chase the birds. This was heaven. There was always something to watch or listen to here.

"Grandpa, why doesn't our family still live in Europe? Whatever happened to the queen?" I asked.

Grandpa smiled. "Well, that's a good question, but I don't have any answer to give you. I just know what my parents have told me, which is what their parents told them. It goes all the way back to hundreds of years ago. Your ancestors left Europe to come to America."

"I don't know if I'll be able to remember everything that you have told me," I said.

"It was a long time ago, but that is where we came from. You'll be able to tell your teacher and the rest of the class what you know now. I'm sure that you'll get a lot of questions. Now, let's go inside and get a little something to drink. All that work has made me thirsty and hungry. I think your grandma has made something for us," Grandpa announced.

As we walked into the house, we could smell something cooking.

"Wow! Something smells good. What are you making, Grandma?" I asked.

"Oh, I just made some cookies. I thought you may want to take some home with you for your mom and dad," Grandma decided.

"Oh, yes Thanks, Grandma!" I said as I sat down at the table to eat a cookie with some milk.

Grandma put some of the cookies in a bag for me to take home. All the while, Grandma asked me how school was going and how the rest of the family was doing.

I said, "Everything's good. I had to find out about my ancestors from Grandpa for a class assignment. That's why I came out to see you guys."

"Any time we can help with your school assignment, you know you can always ask. Now, don't eat too many of those cookies. I made a nice, big pot roast with potatoes and carrots, so I don't want you to spoil your dinner," Grandma preached.

We all sat down for dinner. It was amazing how much Grandma did for her age. All the laundry, cooking, and cleaning—and the best part of all was the baking. She made an apple pie for dessert. I was sure going to miss all the treats from Grandma. Mom gave me treats, but they were store-bought. I once asked Mom why she didn't make homemade cookies like Grandma, and that was a mistake. She went into how many hours she worked, saying that she didn't have time and that I should be thankful for getting any cookies at all. I never asked Mom a question like that ever again. I felt really bad.

After dinner, Grandpa got another cup of coffee. Working on that chair wore him out, and he looked really tired. I thought I had a lot to share at school when I got back, but I knew I had more questions. Maybe I'd take tonight and write some of it down, so I could remember. I knew I was leaving tomorrow and was going to miss sitting with Grandpa, especially on my new rocking chair. He was so wise, and I couldn't believe how much he remembered. I bet he had more stories, but I didn't want to push him. Maybe I could come back out again soon to hear more. I'd try to be prepared with more questions.

Sunday came around, and I knew my parents were coming to get me. I couldn't wait to tell Dad all the stories that Grandpa had told me, although according to Grandpa, he had already told Dad. But maybe Grandpa had told me more, or maybe Dad didn't remember some of it. I bet he didn't write anything down. If he did, I believed he would have shared with me. I was able to write a lot last night, and I couldn't sleep because I wanted to get it all down. I kept thinking of Sir Hunter and how he had to deal with that dragon. I'd like to see a dragon, but I knew they were dangerous, and it would probably try to eat me.

Mom and Dad soon pulled up in the drive way. I had my stuff ready, especially the papers on which I had written down everything.

"Hi, Mom and Dad," I yelled.

"Hey, Hunter. Did you have fun?" my dad asked.

"I sure did. Look what Grandpa gave me," I said, pointing at the chair.

"Wow, Dad. I didn't know you still had that. I certainly remember sitting on that next to your grandpa," Dad proclaimed.

"I helped Grandpa fix it," I boasted.

"That's great, son. I'm proud of you. I bet your grandpa sure appreciated you helping him," Dad replied.

I hugged Grandma and thanked her for everything. I went up to Grandpa, and he put out his hand.

"I reckon you're too old for a hug, young man," Grandpa pointed out.

I put my arms around him. "Never, Grandpa. I really appreciate you telling me all the stories of our ancestors."

"Well, it was my pleasure. Come back again soon, and we'll continue where I left off. Maybe we'll even tackle fixing the old bench swing on the porch for your grandma," Grandpa said while messing up my hair.

I smiled. "I'll be back again with more questions."

I stepped off the porch. As I walked toward the car, I turned back and hollered, "Oh, by the way, someday I'll have my own Wheels, just like Sir Hunter, but I'll literally have wheels. Then I'll be able to visit more often."

As they drove away, I could see my grandparents standing on the porch waving. I waved back until I couldn't see them anymore, and tears filled my eyes.

When I was back home, I put the bag of cookies on the table.

"Grandpa sure knows a lot about where we came from. Did you know that our ancestors lived back when there was a queen and a Bonefairy Castle, and even a dragon?" I said to Mom.

"Oh, really? I hope that you wrote everything down," she said.

"I did. I told Grandma and Grandpa that I'll be back to see them again soon. I want to hear more of Grandpa's stories."

"Well, I'm sure they'd like that. Now, go get washed up for lunch."

The next day at school, I told my teacher that I had spent some time with my grandparents over the weekend, and my grandpa had told me all about my ancestors—where they had lived and come from.

The teacher said, "Well, why don't you take a little time and write everything down, and this way you will have something to remember and pass on to the rest of your family so they will know?"

I said, "I already started, but I have more to do. I know it will be something that I can save, if I can remember everything that my grandpa told me."

"I can't wait to hear what you have. Maybe you can share with the class sometime this week," the teacher said.

"I really want to get more information. Can I have more time?" I asked.

"Sure, that's fine. We have more from the other kids yet," the teacher said.

I asked my mom to buy me a journal. She went to the store and bought a leather journal. She knew how important this was to me, so she got a nice one.

The week seemed to drag on forever, but by the time the weekend arrived, I was already making plans to go back to see Grandpa and Grandpa. I want to write down what Grandpa told me in my new journal. I also wanted to go back to see Grandpa several more times to keep adding to my journal, until it was finally finished.

Mom and Dad took me out to the farm again. Of course, Grandpa was sitting on his rocking chair waiting for us. As we came up the long driveway, Grandma came out, and they both stood there waiting for us. We pulled up to the house. I ran out of the car and went up on the porch.

"Well, look here. Have you grown some more since I saw you last weekend?" Grandpa said.

"Oh, Grandpa, that can't be possible," I said.

"I swear you look a couple inches taller. Did you have a good week?" Grandpa asked.

"Oh, it was okay. You know how it is. Same ol', same ol'," I said.

"Come on in. I've made some rice crispy treats," Grandma said.

"Oh. yummy, I love those!" I said.

We all went in the house. Grandma got out the treats and some milk. I sure did love coming out to the farm. I didn't dare mention that I loved Grandma's baking in front of Mom. I didn't want to hurt her feelings.

"So how is everything going, Dad?" my dad asked Grandpa.

"Everything is fine here. I don't have anything to complain about. Of course, it wouldn't do any good anyway," Grandpa responded.

Everyone sat at the table and talked for a while. It seemed like a lot of small talk to me. I wanted to dig right in to asking Grandpa more questions and him continuing where we had left off. I made sure I had brought my journey. The night went on, and everyone was winding down for the evening.

"Hunter, you and I have a project to work on tomorrow," Grandpa said.

"Oh, that's right. You need me to help you fix the bench swing on the porch," I commented.

"That's right. It shouldn't take as long to fix as it did your rocking chair. While we're doing that, I can pick up from where I left off from last weekend, but only if you remember where I left off at," Grandpa said, winking.

"I remember! I wrote a lot of stuff down in my journal," I said as I pulled it out of my bag to show Grandpa.

"Well, look at that. Don't you look all important with that nice journal," Grandpa said.

"I know. Mom bought it for me so I can keep my notes in something nice."

"Dad, you know we can't stay the whole weekend. We both have so much to work to catch up on, but Hunter can stay till Sunday again, if that's okay," my dad said.

"I would really like that. Hunter and I have a lot to catch up on ourselves," Grandpa said, ruffling my hair.

The next day, Mom and Dad left to go back home for work. Grandma was in the kitchen cooking up some breakfast.

"Now, you boys need to eat a good breakfast before you begin on that bench. I got some country-fried steak, eggs, and hash browns," Grandma said.

"Wow, Grandma. If Grandpa eats all that, he'll have to go lie back down," I said, giggling.

"Oh, don't you know it, but it is some good stuff," Grandpa said.

The three of us sat at the table and had our breakfast. Boy, was that good. I wanted to have seconds, but I was afraid I'd be the one who would want to go back to bed. After breakfast was done, Grandpa got up and sat out on the porch with his coffee. I got up and helped clear the table.

"Thank you, sweetheart. I appreciate your help," Grandma said.

"Grandma, it's the least I could do. You made such a wonderful breakfast. I can't tell you when was the last time I had such a good breakfast. Oh, yeah, it was here. Don't tell Mom I said that," I said nervously.

"Oh, well, I'm sure your mom cooks just fine, but mum's the word," Grandma said while crossing her heart with her finger.

"Can I help you with anything else?" I asked.

"No, sweetheart. You go on out with your grandpa. He's waiting for you"

I went out to the porch. It looked like Grandpa was dozing off, so I sat next to him in my rocking chair. I loved this chair. I thought it was really cool that it was mine now. We sat there in silence. I watched all the animals around the barn. There were so many critters.

Finally, Grandpa began to move. "How long was I asleep?" he asked.

"Oh, not long. Maybe thirty minutes," I said.

"Well, are you ready to tackle that bench over there?"

"Sure, let's do it!"

Grandpa got up and went out to the barn. He said he needed to go get some tools. As I sat there waiting for Grandpa, I tried to come up with some questions I had, wondering how I could get him to start telling his stories again. Grandpa came back with some tools, and it looked like he was having trouble carrying everything, so I got up to help him.

"Let me help you, Grandpa."

"Thanks, my son. I didn't realize how much I needed, and I tried to bring it all at once," Grandpa said.

We got all the tools up on the porch. Grandpa laid them out so he could see what he had. We started to work on the bench.

"Now, we will need to replace the bolts and hangers on the ceiling up there. We're going to have to take down the swing. You think you can hold the one end up as I do this side, and then we'll do the other side?" Grandpa asked.

"Sure, I can. Should I get a latter to hold it up?"

"That won't work, son. I need the bench part to be held level to not damage the springs. So I think I remember where I left off from last weekend. Are you ready?" Grandpa asked.

"I sure am. Never been readier," I said excitedly.

"Well, you remember Sir Hunter had to go back to Bonefairy Castle …"

CHAPTER 9

S moke and vapors really flowed out from the top of Bonefairy Castle. It could be seen all the way into town because the wind was blowing and swirling the gray smoke all around. The fairies had to stay inside the castle when this happened. The queen always kept the fairies busy cleaning Bonefairy Castle.

Sir Hunter was with some of the Royalmen in another part of the castle, talking about the queen and wondering whether they would ever be able to learn how the queen changed her appearance. Sir Hunter informed the men that he had seen the queen and one of the fairies with a scroll. He believed the queen shared some of the information that was written in the scroll with the fairies about what she did when the smoke came out of Bonefairy Castle. No one knew where the queen kept the scroll. They knew only that it was hidden inside the walls of Bonefairy Castle somewhere.

The captain came back from town and walked into the room where Sir Hunter was. "Sir, I can see the smoke from town and thought that I had better get back here," stated the captain.

"It's okay, Captain. Just a lot of the same of whatever the queen is doing with any materials brought to her. But because you are back, I'm going to leave you and head back to see Isabella for a little. Then I will go on to my cabin in the woods. I've got a few things that I need to take care of. Send one of the men if something comes up."

"Yes, Sir Hunter."

Sir Hunter headed back into town to see Isabella. The celebration was still going on, and Sir Hunter was tired. He wanted to get something to eat and see Isabella before going back home to his cabin. Isabella was just coming out of Bonefairy House, when she saw Sir Hunter, and she said, "Hey, I was just heading home."

"Good. I was stopping by to let you know that I was going to go back to my cabin, because I need to do a few repairs on some things that I couldn't get to before I left for the battle. I'll be gone for about a week, or until I get everything fixed. Then I'll be back," Sir Hunter said.

The cabin was where Sir Hunter really liked to be. It was where he could relax. The barn was in need of some repairs, along with a few other things, and now that he was back, he could start before something else came up. Sir Hunter put Wheels in the barn, grabbed some wood for a fire, and went into the cabin. A fire always had to be made for one thing or another, but this time it was simply to have a fire. The evening was very quiet, and it was time for Sir Hunter to relax and think about the day. He could think only about the scroll that the queen had, and he wondered whether he would ever know what was in it. If he could only get the queen to trust him enough to tell him where she kept the scroll. There were many hidden walls and passages in Bonefairy Castle, and only the queen and the fairies knew how to find them. The scroll had to be in one of those walls somewhere. Bonefairy Castle was very old and had been there for hundreds of years. The queen kept the scroll in an old box and never brought it out until she needed to write something in it. Sir Hunter knew that the best time to see the scroll, or where she kept the scroll, was to be at Bonefairy Castle when the queen was adding information to it.

The next day, Sir Hunter went out to the barn and put Wheels outside. He wanted to build a water trough for Wheels so he wouldn't have to take him to the river all the time. Suddenly, one of the Royalmen rode up and said the captain wanted him to know that some of the men back at Bonefairy Castle were planning to confiscate the scroll from the queen. Sir Hunter told the rider to go back and tell the captain that he would be back tomorrow and would meet him at Bonefairy House at noon.

It was noon the next day when Hunter arrived back in town, and he went straight to the Bonefairy House. Isabella was there working when Hunter came in. Hunter waved at her, asked for some spirits, and sat down.

Isabella came over with the spirits and asked, "What are you doing back in town?"

"Well, my lady, it seems that some of the Royalmen at Bonefairy Castle are planning to try to look for the queen's scroll that she keeps hidden from everyone so they can learn her powers. I would also like to know what is in the scroll, but I can't let anyone else know. The powers of the queen are only known by the fairies."

Isabella asked Sir Hunter, "What are you going to do?"

"I'm supposed to meet the captain here at noon, and we're going to decide then what we're going to do. So until the captain gets here, you can keep bringing me some more spirits."

Isabella smiled. "If you keep drinking spirits, I can only imagine what kind of scheme you and the captain will think of."

The captain walked through the door, and Isabella waved and said that she would bring another mug of spirits over.

"Sit down, Captain. I need to know what's going on with the men," Sir Hunter said seriously.

"Well, after you left the other day, some of the men went off and had a meeting. They were talking about going to find the queen's scroll. She has lived for hundreds of years, and the men said that what is written in the scroll explains how she is able do that," said the captain.

Sir Hunter said, "How does anyone know that? No one knows what's in the scroll."

"Sir Hunter, that has to be what's in the scroll, don't you think?" the captain countered.

"I have a strong opinion that it may be, but it is going to be very hard to prove what is in the scroll without actually retrieving the scroll and looking inside."

"Yes, that is what the men are thinking."

"I cannot allow the men to take control of the queen or find the scroll. The queen has to be protected from any takeover. If the queen thinks that her Royalmen are not loyal to her, she will have them removed. She will disappear to her private quarters and will not be seen until some time has passed. She is the only reason we live here and have the things that she allows us to have," Sir Hunter emphasized.

"Okay, so what do you want to do?" asked the captain.

"Right now, let's finish our spirits. Then we can head to Bonefairy Castle and talk to the men. How does that sound, Captain?"

"I knew you would have a good plan. I like it so far."

Sir Hunter and the captain finished their spirits, told Isabella that they would see her later, and left for Bonefairy Castle.

The queen was always demanding. She had a way of knowing when something was going on or was going to happen, and this day was no different. Sir Hunter and the captain arrived at Bonefairy Castle. They wanted to find the men who were plotting to take the scroll. The queen knew something was about to happen because Sir Hunter and the captain were looking for the men, but she didn't know why. The queen commanded the fairies to bring Sir Hunter to her when she got word that the men were congregating. Sir Hunter stood before the queen, and she didn't look happy. He could feel the tension in the air and the heat coming from her. It was very intense.

"Sir Hunter, why are the men congregating here? I have not asked for them for any work. I demand to know," the queen stated.

"Your Highness, I'm not totally sure, but I will find out and let you know," Sir Hunter assured her.

Sir Hunter obviously did know what the men were up to, but he didn't want to say anything to the queen until he had talked to his men. Sir Hunter told the captain to get the men to leave Bonefairy Castle immediately. They should go into the woods, and he would meet them when he could get away. The captain did what he was told and ordered the men to go into the woods and wait. The queen saw the men leaving and knew that something was going on.

"Sir Hunter, I want to know what's happening right now. Why are the men leaving Bonefairy Castle?" the queen demanded.

"Your Highness, the men are asking for a meeting. They are asking questions. I believe that there is a problem with the men, and I didn't want anything to start here, so I ordered the captain to have the men go into the woods. I will go meet with them," Sir Hunter said.

"Okay, Sir Hunter, but I want to know what the problem is," the queen commanded.

"Yes, Your Highness," Sir Hunter responded.

Sir Hunter left the queen to meet the men in the woods. The group of men who were there wasn't as big as many as he thought it would be, but he did want to know why the men were starting to cause trouble. The men told Sir Hunter that they heard about the scroll in the queen's possession, and they wanted to know what was in it.

Sir Hunter replied, "Well, I can understand why you all want to know that, because I would like to know myself, but we can't ask the queen to reveal what she has in her scroll without causing turmoil. This would make her very mad. Then there's no telling what she might do. As you all know, the queen controls all of the fairies. She can make them do whatever she wants. They are going to always protect her. The powers that they have are so much more overpowering to us men, and you know that."

"Yes, but then how are we going to find out what is in the scroll?" one of the men asked.

"All I know is that if you challenge the queen, you'll lose. She has been around for a long time and will be here long after we're all gone," Sir Hunter reminded the men.

"Well, Sir Hunter, what can we do then? We want to live as long as she does, and we know that what she has written in the scroll is the answer," declared one of the men.

"You don't really know what she wrote on the scroll. You are just guessing and assuming that's what is in the scroll," Sir Hunter insisted.

"Yes, sir, but where else could we get that information, if not from the scroll?" one of the men asked.

"I'm not sure, but I'm telling you that if we challenge the queen for the scroll, and she finds out what we're up to, we'll lose her trust. The queen trusts us now because we have always kept Bonefairy Castle safe. I will ask the queen if she will tell me what is in the scroll, but I know that will start trouble, and she will know this is why we're all here in the woods having a meeting. So for now, Captain, let's wait and see what I can find out without causing suspicion," Sir Hunter said.

"Yes, Sir Hunter, I think that is the best solution for now," the captain agreed.

"Okay, then. You men to go back, and let's not have any more of this talk about the scroll. I'll see what I can find out."

Sir Hunter returned back from the woods to meet with the queen again. The queen told the fairies to watch for when the men left the woods and to let her know when Sir Hunter came back. The queen asked Hunter when he came back what the problem was with the men.

Sir Hunter said, "Your Highness, the men have heard that there is a scroll with writings, and that explains how you get your powers to live forever. They believe there's important information in it that will help with the future of the region."

"Sir Hunter, you have been a loyal servant of mine, and I know that the men want to know about the scroll. I knew the time would come when these questions would be asked, so I have a very important task for you to do. I will have you and some of my fairies go to the cave that was sealed. You will take some things that must never be found, and you will bury them deep in the cave. I will have the fairies put together everything that you will be taking and let you know when the time is right for you to go. You must not tell anyone of this," the queen explained.

Sir Hunter didn't know what to say and stood there contemplating a response. All he could come up with was, "Thank you, Your Highness. I will do anything you ask of me, and I will not tell anyone."

Sir Hunter left Bonefairy Castle and headed to Bonefairy House to see Isabella and tell her that he would be gone again for a while. He didn't know what could be so important that the queen wanted him to protect it in the cave, but he would soon find out. He knew this was going to be a very important mission.

"Hello, my lady. I have bad news. The queen has given me another mission that is very important to her."

Isabella asked, "What is it now that she asks of you? Everything is always so important."

"I don't know yet. The queen told me that I would be sent for, and that's when I will be told what I must do. In other words, she doesn't want anyone to know about the task. I can't even tell you how long I'll be gone."

"I wish you safe travels, and please come back to me in one piece. I don't want anything bad to happen to you," she replied.

"I don't think it is a dangerous mission, but I will be safe, and I promise I will come back to you as soon as I can."

The next day, the captain was sent to gather Sir Hunter and bring him to Bonefairy Castle to talk to the queen.

Sir Hunter and the captain returned to Bonefairy Castle, and he looked at the captain and said, "I will be gone for a while. I need you to be in control of the men until I return."

"Yes, Sir Hunter, I understand. Have you any idea how long you are going to be gone?"

"No, I don't, because I haven't talked to the queen yet. Once I know what the queen wants me to do, I will try to let you know some answers to your questions."

The captain left Bonefairy Castle to tell the men about Sir Hunter leaving on a mission. Sir Hunter was brought to the queen's private quarters by the fairies. As he stood there waiting for the queen, another fairy suddenly appeared before him. She looked slightly different than the rest of the fairies. Her wings were bigger and brighter, glowing with gold hues. She had long flowing brown hair, but what caught Sir Hunter's eye more than anything was the pulsating blue lines through her face, as if it her blood vessels were on the surface.

"Sir Hunter, my name is Galaxy. I am the leader of the queen's fairies. You were brought here to stand before the queen to receive your mission," Galaxy said.

"Nice to meet you, Galaxy," Sir Hunter responded.

The queen suddenly appeared and said, "Sir Hunter, I want you to return to the same cave where we sealed up the dragon. With the help of the fairies, I want you to take most of the gold that we have, along with a map, and bury it there. As I've already said, no one must ever know about any of this. The fairies will know where to bury everything. The right time will come when this gold and the map will be used. If the townspeople ever found out about any of this, then the gold will be gone. This is why no one can know about it."

Sir Hunter said, "I understand and will do as you ask."

Galaxy said, "I will take you back out of the queen's private quarters. You will not remember how to get back to her quarters. You are to return here tomorrow to begin your mission."

"Yes, I understand," Sir Hunter replied.

Sir Hunter left Bonefairy Castle, went to see the captain, and told him that he could not tell anyone about what the queen has asked of him. He did say that he was going to be gone for about a week. Sir Hunter then went to Bonefairy House and told Isabella the same information and was leaving tomorrow morning.

The next morning, Sir Hunter returned to Bonefairy Castle. The fairies had everything ready for the trip. There were three wagons full of gold along with two men whom Sir Hunter had never seen before. Galaxy appeared to take Sir Hunter to the queen's private quarters again.

"Sir Hunter, the queen would like to see you before you leave," Galaxy said.

When he arrived, the queen said, "Sir Hunter, I wanted you to know that I have taken two of my fairies and changed them into men, so no one will be suspicious."

After getting some last instructions from the queen, Sir Hunter started out for the cave. After a few days, they arrived at the cave. Sir Hunter thought that it was going to be hard to reopen the cave. Little did he know what powers the fairies had. When they reached the entrance to the cave, the cave looked as though it had never been sealed at all and was wide open for the wagons to go right in. Sir Hunter remembered the dragon was captive in the cave and was worried they'd disturb it.

"What about the dragon?" Sir Hunter asked.

One of the "men" explained the dragon berries still surrounded the dragon. It was still asleep and would not be disturbed.

The wagons moved into the cave and out of site. Once inside the cave, some of the fairies appeared, including Galaxy, and told Sir Hunter that the gold was to be placed at the bottom of the small lake in the middle of the cave. This was the only place where it could not be seen. He didn't think he was going to be able to do that himself.

"How am I going to do that?" Sir Hunter asked.

"Just leave that up to the fairies," Galaxy said.

It took several hours for the gold to be placed at the bottom of the lake. Sir Hunter watched as the fairies did their work.

After finally finishing with the gold, Galaxy told Sir Hunter that there was one more thing that needed to be done. The fairies showed him a box that was sealed back at Bonefairy Castle and told him that they would place the box at the bottom of the lake with the gold. Sir Hunter didn't ask what was in the box and watched once again as the fairies took the box under the water. Once that was done, it was time for the wagons to be taken back out of the cave. Once out of the cave, the fairies resealed it like no one had been there. They then headed back to Bonefairy Castle to report back to the queen.

Days later, they arrived back at Bonefairy Castle. Galaxy took Sir Hunter to the queen's private quarters.

The queen said, "Sir Hunter, thank you for completing your mission. Remember that you must tell no one. You don't want to know the consequences will be if you do. The time will come when all of this will be known," the queen said.

"I thank you for the honor and trusting me. I don't understand why it had to be me that took those things to the cave. Why couldn't your fairies do that?" Sir Hunter asked.

"There is a reason that it had to be you. Your ancestors will hold the secret for eternity. I chose you for your utmost loyalty to me—more than any other servant I've ever had. The time will come all will be revealed and will make sense, but unfortunately that time is not right now," the queen explained.

"I'm not sure what that means, but I'll have to take your word for it."

The queen then disappeared on the spot.

"I will take you out of the queen's quarters," Galaxy said.

Sir Hunter left the castle to find the captain and let him know that he was back. Then he would find Isabella, who was probably at Bonefairy House. Sir Hunter was ready for a few drinks, and that was the place to get them. As Sir Hunter rode into town, he could see that Agenda's horse was in front of Bonefairy House.

When he walked in, Agenda yelled out, "Sir Hunter, it's about time you get back here. I'm tired of drinking alone."

Hunter smiled. "Agenda, what if I don't have any money for drinking?"

Agenda said, "Well, then, I guess I'll just have to keep buying. Isabella, look who is back in town. We need a couple more drinks here."

Isabella said, "Why, yes, I see that. When did you that back in town, Sir Hunter?"

"I just got here, my lady. Did you miss me?" Sir Hunter teased.

She smiled. "Well, I can't lie. Maybe a little bit. We're hoping that you will stay a while now that you are back."

"You know I will, or at least until the queen calls on me again," Sir Hunter replied.

"She needs to give you some time to yourself so you can rest a little," Isabella said.

"I know, but that is why she always calls on me: because she trusts me to do what she asks," Sir Hunter pointed out.

"Well, she's not here now, so let's drink," Agenda said.

CHAPTER 10

Several years went by, and I graduated from high school. My parents bought me a car for my graduation present. I was so excited when I saw it. My dad handed me the key and said, "Well, son, now you have your own wheels, so you won't need to use our car."

I thought about what I had said to Grandpa: that one day I'd have my own wheels, like Sir Hunter had his horse, Wheels. That put a smile on my face and tears in my eyes. My grandparents had both passed on. Grandpa died first, and then Grandma passed from loneliness. I cried for days after Grandpa died. I wished the good ones could live forever, like the queen.

With the memories of what Grandpa told me about my ancestors and what I wrote in the journal I kept, I decided to go to a library to do some research. I didn't quite know how to start, but while there, I ran into one of my old classmates, Samantha.

"How are you, Hunter?" Samantha asked.

"Hey, Samantha. I'm doing good. How have you been?" I asked.

"I'm good too. Getting ready to go to college. Did you ever decide where you were going?"

"Yes, I got accepted at Marshall University. I'm starting my major with computer science," I said.

"Oh, wow, that's sounds great. You always were interested in computers. I hear it is the future. I'm heading to Keiser University in West Palm Beach, Florida, to study law. You know me: I've always wanted to live in Florida."

"Lucky you. That should be an adventure for you. Law, huh? That certainly suits you."

"So what are you doing here? Didn't you get enough books in high school?" Samantha joked.

"I want to do a little research on something."

"What are you researching? Oh, whatever happened to that journal you kept?" she asked.

I said, "Well, I'm not sure how to explain what I'm researching, and I've really just started. I still have the journal."

Samantha asked, "Hunter, is what you wrote in your journal really true?"

I said, "My grandpa said it was true."

"Is that what you're researching? You should go there and find the castle," she suggested.

"Yes, that is what I am trying to research, but I don't know how to begin. That is a good idea. That would be a real adventure, wouldn't it?" I exclaimed.

"It sure would. Well, I wish you good luck. It doesn't sound like it's going to be easy."

"I think you're right, but I've got to know, and I want to at least try. By the way, what are you here for?"

"I wanted to research what kind of law I want to study. I am leaning toward doctor of judicial science. That's the highest you can go," Samantha said.

"Wow, you don't mess around. Going all the way to the top, huh?"

"That's me. I want to learn it all. Well, I'll let you get back to what you were doing. I need to head over to the law section. It was great seeing you, Hunter. I wish the best for you. Whatever you do, stay safe in your travels. It is crazy out there."

"It was great seeing you too, Samantha. I really hope you do well. I sure wouldn't want to in any dispute with you. I bet you'll knock them dead!" I responded.

Samantha and I hugged, and she went in another direction. I sat down at one of the tables and began to ponder. I couldn't stop thinking about what Samantha had said about going to see the castle, and I decided to go back home to find my journal and remember what I had written down so many years ago. I knew that it was going to take a lot of research, but I really wanted to discover whether what Grandpa had said was true or not. It wasn't like I didn't believe him. I simply want to see it for myself.

I got back home and started digging through my closet. I looked through box after box and began to panic because it wasn't there. I knew it had to be here. I took everything out, even from the top shelf. Nothing. Maybe I had moved it to my desk? I went to my desk and started digging through all the drawers. Still nothing. I sat down at my desk and thought. When did I have it last? Then I remembered. I had it back on the farm when I was talking with Grandpa, but I knew my parents have already packed up the farmhouse. *Think, think, where could it be?* Instead of wasting more time, I went looking for Mom to ask her.

"Mom, where is all the stuff you packed up from Grandpa and Grandma's house?" I asked.

"We put everything up in the attic. Why do you ask?" Mom asked.

"I think I left my journal there. Did you see my journal in any of the stuff?"

"I don't remember seeing it. There is a box of photo albums. Maybe it got put in there."

"Are the boxes marked?"

"Some of them are, and some of them aren't," Mom said.

"Oh, great. Okay, I need to see if my journal is in any of those boxes," I said.

"Okay, well, they're all in the one corner on the left side of the attic. You can't miss them."

I went up in the attic and started going through boxes. There were so many. I tried looking for a box labeled "photo albums" but didn't see one. I went through several boxes. It was kind of nice looking at all my grandparents' stuff and remembering certain knickknacks that Grandma had. Finally, I came to a box that had all the photo albums. I pulled some of them out and looked inside, reminiscing through all the pictures. A lot of them were of when I was young, and some were of Dad when he was young. It was amazing how much we looked alike when we were young. I was near the bottom of the box and was getting discouraged when, finally, there it was on the bottom. Relief came over me. I had been worried it was gone. I put all the other boxes back because I knew Mom would not be happy with the mess I had created. I took my journal and climbed down out of the attic.

"Did you find it?" Mom asked.

"Yes, thank goodness. I was so worried I'd lost it," I said.

"Oh, sweetheart, I'm so sorry. I'm sure your grandparents got confused and put it with their photo albums. And I'm sorry I didn't notice it."

"I'm just glad I found it. I'm going to my room to read it. I want to remember what I wrote."

"Okay, honey. Dinner will be ready around six o'clock."

I went to my room and started reading. Some of my handwriting was hard to read, not to mention really funny with the words I used. What did one expect from a ten-year-old? The more I read, the more I remembered. It was such an amazing story.

The next day, I went back to the library to start my research. Again, I didn't know where to begin, but I took a stab at the actual castle. I asked the librarian several questions, and she looked at me funny. I thought I should probably see if I could do the research myself.

I kept going to the library every day with no luck, so I finally decided that I would do my research by going to where Bonefairy Castle was. That was going to be a challenge because I had no idea how to find it. It took a few days to build up the courage, but the day finally came when I decided to go on an adventure. I told my parents not to worry. I wasn't sure what was going to happen or where I was going to wind up, but I knew that I had to go. I saved enough money from the many small jobs I had so I could buy a plane ticket. I said goodbye to my parents and said that I'd be in touch when I found something out.

I was about to go to another part of the world that I didn't know anything about, so I would have to ask questions to see if anyone could help me. My plane landed in Europe. Once there, I left the airport in a cab and asked the cab driver, "Have you ever heard of Bonefairy Castle?"

The driver said, "I know there's a Bonefairy Castle that has been left abandoned on the other side of the country that the government owns."

"Do you know exactly where it's at?"

"It is a few hundred miles away. It is near a town called Harbor."

"Okay, well, can you take me to a hotel here close by for now?" I asked.

"Sure can. There's one a mile down the road that is very popular," said the driver.

"That will be good enough for now. Just drop me off there," I requested.

As the cab driver drove up to the hotel, I could see why it was so popular. The parking lot was full of cars with very few parking places left. I paid the driver, thanked him for what I had learned from him, and went into the hotel.

I walked up to the front desk and asked, "Do you have a room available?"

"Yes, we have a room available. How many occupants, and how many days do you need?" asked the desk clerk.

"It is just me, and I need it for one night," I responded.

The desk clerk looked in the computer. "I can have you in room 1205 with a king bed."

"That's perfect. Do you have room service so I can get something to eat?" I asked.

"Just call on the phone once you get into your room, and they will take your order," the clerk said as she handed me the room key.

The next day, I looked at my journal. I wanted to start looking right away for Bonefairy Castle. After breakfast, I asked the hotel clerk, "Can you please give me the number to a car rental place so I can rent a car?"

The town of Harbor was a few hundred miles away, and I did not know anything about where I was going, so it was going to be an adventure all in itself. But that was what made this so wild and challenging. I called the rental car company, and they said they'd bring the car to me, so I sat and waited in the lobby.

The rental car finally showed up, and I filled out all the necessary papers and started for the town called Harbor. I got a map to help me navigate. I knew it was going to take me about four or five hours to get there, but it was a nice little trip. It was a beautiful country with vast lands of farms. The map made it easy, and I was able to find the town Harbor. I wanted to find out where Bonefairy Castle was. Harbor was a nice little town, and the people were very friendly as I drove through what looked like downtown. I needed to get some gas and find a place to eat. I saw a little diner and decided to stop there. There was only one person in the diner other than the cook, and that was the waitress. I sat down and waited for her to come over.

"Hello, can I get you some coffee?" the waitress offered.

I smiled. "No, thank you. I really don't drink much coffee."

"All right, then, do you need a few minutes?"

"Well, I guess. What are your specials, if you have any?" I inquired.

"We have everything that is on the menu over the counter," replied the waitress.

"Okay, thank you. Oh, by the way, what do I call you? What is your name, if you don't mind me asking?" I asked.

"No not at all. My name is Isabella, but my friends call me Izzy," she stated.

I smiled and laughed a little.

"What? Why are you laughing?" Izzy asked.

"Oh, nothing, I just thought about something that my grandpa told me," I said

"Really? Can you let me in on it, or is it something that you don't want me to know?"

"Well, Izzy, it's a long story. If I knew you better, or if I was going to be in town longer, I would tell you all about it."

"Okay, well, I understand. Just how long are you going to be in town? By the way, what is your name, now that you know mine?"

"Oh, I'm sorry. My name is Hunter," I answered.

"Well, Hunter, nice to meet you. What are you doing here in town, if you don't mind me asking?" Izzy asked.

"I live in the United States, and I came here to see where my ancestors came from. My grandpa told me stories about them when I was little, and I decided to come over here to see if it was all true, so I could learn more about my ancestors."

"That sounds like you could be here for a while," Izzy stated.

"Yes, maybe I will, but it all depends on whether I can find this castle called Bonefairy," I proclaimed.

"Really? Bonefairy Castle is just down the road a few miles."

"Oh, wow, really? I can't believe it. Well, I guess I just need to get a little something to eat, and then maybe you can point me in the right direction to where it is," I requested.

"Sure, I can do that. I used to go there back when it was open to the public, but it has been closed for a while," Izzy explained.

"Izzy, can I ask you what time you get off work today? I would pay you if you would show me what you know about Bonefairy Castle."

"My shift is over by the time you finish eating, and I'd love to go with you to show you Bonefairy Castle, but I don't know you. I simply don't go off with some stranger in his car when I have met him only fifteen minutes ago," Izzy warned.

"Oh, I'm sorry. I didn't mean anything by asking. It's just that you seem to know what I don't. That is why I was asking," I explained.

She paused. "Because you are new in town, and I really don't have much else planned, I guess I can show you."

"Izzy, that would be spectacular!"

"If I'm going to do this with you, I'd like to know a little bit more about what your grandpa said and what you wrote in your journal. If that's all right," Izzy said.

"Well, it's not a secret. I'll let you read it, if you'd like," I responded.

"It's just that I have always been a history nut, and I love this kind of stuff," Izzy confessed.

"I think we are going to get along just fine. By the way, tell the cook the food is great."

I waited until Izzy's shift was over, and we left together. Izzy and I were about the same age, and she seemed like she like me.

Izzy asked, "Would you mind if we stopped by my house so I can change my clothes? My work uniform isn't really what I want to wear we go to Bonefairy Castle."

"I don't have any problem stopping. I can wait in the car while you change," I responded.

Izzy told me where she lived. It was a little tavern, and I was a little confused. She laughed and said, "I live over the tavern. I'll be back in a few minutes."

I grabbed my journal and started looking through it again as I waited for Izzy to return. In a few minutes, she came down, jumped into the car, and pointed me in the direction of where to go.

"Bonefairy Castle is just a few miles out of town," Izzy said.

It was really something for me to get to actually see the castle that Grandpa had talked about. We drove a few miles and came up to a gated area, and I saw the Bonefairy name. There was a large wall all the way around it. It was a little overwhelming—something that looked like it came out of a fairy tale. I stopped the car and got out.

I wanted to take a few pictures of Bonefairy Castle so I could prove that I was really here. I took some pictures and got back in the car. Then I drove through the entrance of Bonefairy Castle and could see there was a security guard.

"How can I help you?" the security guard asked.

I rolled down my window and said, "I'm from the United States. I just want to look at the castle, if I can," I responded.

The security guard said, "There isn't anything here to see anymore, only some empty rooms. All the furniture, pictures, and everything that used to be here have been moved out a long time ago."

I said, "Okay, but I really just want to look around."

The security guard said, "I really don't care or have a problem with it, just as long as you don't destroy anything."

I thanked the guard and parked the car. We got out of the car and moved into Bonefairy Castle through the front doors.

"Wow! The guard was right when he said that there wasn't anything left here," I said.

There were a lot of big, empty rooms and hallways. It was still very beautiful and overwhelming, and my curiosity made me think that what I was seeing for the first time may make sense of what I had written in my journal. I knew that I had written the queen had private quarters behind the walls, high up in the castle, that no other person knew about. I also knew that it was going to be dark up there, and it was going to take some time to look closely at all the rooms and walls. There were probably secret passages to other rooms.

Izzy and I moved to the upper part of Bonefairy Castle. There were many hallways and a lot of smaller rooms. This was where I needed to look around. In my journal, it said that there were secret doors and walls here, but I didn't know where to look. I had to start touching or pushing on the walls to see what happens.

"Izzy, why don't you take that wall over there, and I'll try over here? We'll see if anything happens," I suggested.

Izzy agreed and moved to the other side of the room. Over where Izzy was looking, there seemed to be a wooden box on the wall with a little door. When she opened it up, there was a window, and we could see outside and down to where the car was parked. The sunlight came in through the window. A bright reflection from the window formed on the other wall across the room that wasn't there before, when the door was closed.

Izzy yelled, "Hunter, look at the wall with the reflection and all the wild colors."

I said, "Maybe that is what we're looking for. Let's touch that wall and see what happens."

Izzy moved her hand over the wall where the reflections were. Nothing happened. She stood back from the wall and took a different look at it. That was when the sun shined on Izzy's back and not on the wall. Part of the reflection was on Izzy's back, and that made the reflection on the wall different. We could see the reflection on the wall now pointed to a piece of stone that had a different color to it when the sun was shining.

Izzy said, "Touch the stone over there."

"Where?" I asked.

"Look at the reflection, Hunter. Right there—touch it."

I touched the colored stone. It looked like it started to move. I then pushed in, and the wall on the other side of the room moved.

"It's opening up!" yelled Izzy.

"Do you think I should go in? Just make sure that the box on the wall over there doesn't close. I think the sunlight has something to do with the door staying open, and we don't know what we are going to see or find on the other side of that wall. We sure don't want to get stuck behind something that we don't know about and be unable to get back out," I said.

"You're right, but isn't this exciting? I bet no one even knows about this other room."

"Well, we do now, so let's go in through the opening and see what's in there."

"Okay, you first," she proclaimed.

"Look! There are all kinds of stuff in here, and it looks very old. I'm going to take some pictures so we have it all on film."

"What is all this stuff, Hunter?" Izzy asked.

"I'm not sure, but in my journal, it says that there was a queen who lived here at Bonefairy Castle, and she had powers that she never told anyone about. That the queen would disappear behind doors that no one knew about or could ever find, and that was when you could see smoke come out from Bonefairy Castle," I explained.

"Hunter, look over here. It looks like some kind of treasure chest. Maybe there's something in it," Izzy said. She opened the chess. "Wow! It's a scroll of some kind."

"Izzy, I don't believe it. In my journal, it says that hundreds of years ago, that queen kept a scroll that she wrote things down on and kept it hidden from everyone. I'm going to take pictures of what is in it."

"What is in it?" she asked.

"I don't know, but someone will. I want to have a record of it. This scroll is very old, and I know that if this gets in the wrong hands, it will disappear. I know that it talks about DNA. My grandpa told me that back when he was young and just a boy, he was told about our ancestors. There were things that went on here in Bonefairy Castle. The queen and her fairies always did things when they were here in this room. That was when you could see smoke coming from the castle. Let's look around and see what else we can find. There is what appears to be a round pot over there next to a ire place. Let's take a look at that. I'll bet whatever was put in this big pot was put in this fireplace and caused the smoke," I said.

"What do you think it was?" asked Lizzy.

"I'm not sure, but I can only speculate," I pondered.

"All of this all happened so long ago. How are we ever going to find that answer?" she asked.

"Let's look around at everything here and see if we can take a few things with us now, including the scroll. We'll come back again later. What's over there behind that wall?" I asked.

I walked over and looked, and it seemed the floor opened up when I stood on it.

"This is amazing. There are stairs that go down. That's got to be another way out of here. Let's go down the stairs, because we may never see the sun reflection on that wall again to get back in here. There has to be another way," I said.

"Okay, but you first!"

"Izzy, I wouldn't ask you to do something if I didn't know where these steps were going, and I don't, so maybe you should wait a minute while I see where the stairs go."

"I like the way that sounds, Hunter!" Izzy agreed.

"Okay, here I go. Give me that flashlight we brought. It's pretty dark down there. It looks like there is another door at the bottom of the stairs. Just a second; I'll look and see what's there." I walked down the stairs. "All right, there is another door to get out, so come on down. We can get out from down here, through this door."

Izzy went down the stairs. We were at the bottom when the door from the floor closed back up behind us.

"That is why no one ever knew these stairs existed," I commented.

"I wonder how the floor closes back up once we leave?"

"Well, if you think about it, it must have to do with our weight. Once we leave and our weight is no longer on the stairs, the stairs close up the floor. This castle is pretty cool. I'm surprised that some of these things still work. All right, we are back on the lower level now, and we can come back tomorrow. Let's get out of here. "What was that?"

"Where?" Izzy said.

"You didn't see that?" I said, pointing in the corner.

"What is it?"

"There was a shadow on that wall, and now it's gone," I said, confused

"No, I didn't see anything. Are you sure you saw a shadow?"

"Yes, I'm positive. Look over there. There it is again!" I pointed.

"Hunter, I don't like this right now, so let's get the heck out of here," Izzy said nervously.

"Okay, but did you see it? I'm not sure what I saw. It looked like it floated in the air and had wings. Do you think that maybe it could have been a fairy, or maybe even the queen who lived here long ago?" I said.

"How the heck do I know? I didn't know about any of this until now. Can we go now?" begged Izzy.

CHAPTER 11

Izzy and I went back to town and were curious about what we could learn from the scroll. There were some pictures and drawings that were not easy to understand. Some of the writings were in a different language, and it would take time to learn what they meant. I wanted to talk again with my grandpa. It made me sad again just thinking of him. I decided I would take a few pictures of some of the things that were in the scroll and mail them back home.

"I want to go back to Bonefairy Castle tomorrow to continue looking around and see if I can see or find those shadows flying around again," I said.

"I won't be able to go because I have to work," Izzy said.

"Oh, okay. Well, I'll just go by myself," I replied.

"Good luck. I hope those flying shadows don't spook you too much," Izzy teased.

I dropped Izzy off at the tavern and headed back to the hotel. It had been a full day. I wanted to get a good night's rest so I can go out there early.

The next day, I woke up early, had some breakfast, and headed out to the castle. When I got there, the security guard was there again.

"Back again so soon?" he asked.

"Yeah, well, this place is so big I know I didn't get through all of it yesterday," I replied.

"The same rule applies. I will only let you go in if you don't do any damage or disturb anything," he reiterated.

"I won't. I just want to look around some more. Like I said, the castle is so big, and there is so much to look at," I said.

The security guard let me go in. I parked the car and walked into the castle. It wasn't long after walking in that I saw some of the shadows again. I tried to follow them. It was next to impossible because they appeared and then were gone again. I decided to sit down in one of the large rooms and wait to see what would happen. I could see the shadows come and go as I sat there. An hour later, suddenly one of the shadows appeared and moved toward me. The shadow looked like it wasn't real, but I could see it. Unless it was a figment of my imagination? I didn't move and didn't know what was going to happen until the shadow appeared as real, with a face and wings. It looked like a fairy and was so beautiful. The fairy floated in the air right in front of me. The fairy floated down to the floor and stood there.

The fairy asked, "Why are you here at Bonefairy Castle?"

"My ancestors lived in the area hundreds of years ago. I'm trying to learn what I can about them," I answered.

"Do you want me to show you around the castle and some of the passages?" the fairy asked.

I could hardly believe what I was hearing, but I wasn't going to refuse the opportunity to see and learn. I brought the scroll back with me and had it in my hand. "Can you help explain what it says in the scroll?" I asked the fairy.

The fairy took the scroll and opened it. "What is written in the scroll was put there so the people of the new world would be able to understand what was written. There are still many fairies who live in Bonefairy Castle. Shadows are often seen, but the fairies haven't been seen until now."

"Do you have a name?" I asked.

"My name is Galaxy," the fairy said.

"Why do you appear now?" I asked.

"It is time for the rest of the world to be aware of what was written in the scroll. Everything that was written in the scroll will help people all around the world," Galaxy replied. She took the scroll from me, opened it up, and told me to look at the pages that had some formulas on it. I looked at the pages.

"The formulas are for what they call DNA. The queen knows that every living person has his or her own deoxyribonucleic acid, and in the future, it would become known for its uses. When the queen was in her own private quarters, she would take many things that were brought to her by one of your ancestors, Sir Hunter. He was the leader of the Royalmen for many armies that the queen had, and he would bring the queen pieces of fallen men who were killed in battle for the queen—things like hair, clothes, and body parts. The queen needed them to get their DNA. She knew that someday this information would be very helpful to the rest of the world so they could recognize people," Galaxy explained.

"I do know a little about all of this. My grandpa told me about it. I wrote a lot of what he told me in my journal," I said has I showed Galaxy my journal.

"Yes, that is what was expected. So now you will continue where Sir Hunter left off," Galaxy said.

"I want to continue writing down everything that you tell me in my journal, because there is so much, and I know I won't be able to remember everything. Am I allowed to stay here at Bonefairy Castle for the night?" I asked.

People have stayed overnight from time to time. The fairies will look after you," Galaxy responded. Then just as quickly as she appeared, she disappeared. Poof!

I decided to stay instead of going back to town. There wasn't much of anything left at Bonefairy Castle, and there was nothing to sleep on, so I slept in my car.

The next morning, I went back into the castle before going back to see Izzy in town. I waited for Galaxy to return because I had a few questions. Eventually, Galaxy appeared and asked, "What questions do you have for me?"

"Is the queen still around? Where is she?" I asked.

"The queen doesn't come out to be seen anymore. The only reason you're able to see me is because all of the fairies and the queen decided that it was time to let the rest of the world in on what is in the scroll for the DNA."

"Will I ever see the queen?" I asked.

"There may be a time that you will, but I will let you know when that time is. Are those all the questions you have?"

"That is all I have for now. I am going to leave. Thank you for everything. I will return again when I can," I replied.

"Goodbye, Hunter," Galaxy said, and she was gone again.

I left the castle, got in my car, and drove back to town. I went straight to the diner where Izzy worked. I wanted to talk with Izzy and get something to eat.

Izzy said, "Hi, Hunter. Did you go back out to Bonefairy Castle again yesterday?"

"Yes, I did. I met a fairy called Galaxy," I said.

"You're kidding, right? You actually saw and talked to a fairy?"

"Yes, and I stayed out there last night. I stopped here to get something to eat and tell you all about it, because I know you'll never believe me. I was there, and I don't even believe what I saw. There are many fairies who still live there, but I talked to only the one. Galaxy told me about my ancestor, who was the leader of all the Royalmen. He was in charge of the armies. His name was Sir Hunter, and that was where I got my name from. There was a dragon that lived up in the mountains in a cave back then, and Sir Hunter and some of his men had to find it and destroy it, because it was killing all the animals."

"Wow, really?" Izzy asked.

"Yes, and Galaxy also told me all about the scroll that we found, as well as what was written in it and what to do with it when I go back home. Izzy, I can't believe everything that I've learned about Bonefairy Castle and my ancestors. It's so exciting. I want to go back out there. I'm sure that there is more to learn."

"Well, why don't you go back out there, then?"

"I may, but I need to start thinking about what I have and plan my trip back home to America."

"Oh, I see," said Izzy.

"Well, right now I'm starving. What have you got to eat?"

"I just boiled some chicken. How's that sound?"

"That sounds great. I'll have some of that," I said.

"Okay, I'll be right back."

Izzy and I spent the rest of the day together and talked about everything.

"Izzy, why don't you come back with me to America for a while?" I inquired.

"I've never been to another country before, and I don't know anyone there," she answered.

"You know me, and I can show you where I live. You can meet my parents," I offered.

"I don't know, Hunter. That all sounds great. I'd love to, but I hardly even know you."

"I know, but we get along pretty good, so why not?"

"I do have some vacation time coming. I could ask and see if I could get the time off," Izzy conceded.

"That's great! Let's do it. I'll see what another plane ticket will cost, and you can ask your boss. Then we can get together later, okay?"

"All right, I'll ask," she confirmed.

Izzy went to see if she could get the time off, but she couldn't get it until next week. I really wanted Izzy to go, so I said, "Everything is going to be all right. That will give me more time to go back to Bonefairy Castle and talk to Galaxy," I said.

The next day, I did just that. I wanted to add more to my journal and record as much information as possible. After I reached the castle, I immediately looked for Galaxy, but Galaxy wasn't around, so I did some exploring. Bonefairy Castle was very big inside, and after finding the secret rooms in the upper part of the castle, I thought there could be more. I just had to find them.

It wasn't long before Galaxy showed up. "Hunter, why are you back at the castle?"

"I have a little more time before returning to America, and I wanted to see what else I can find or add to my journal. Because the queen has been here for so long and was the ruler of the region, is it true she is very rich?" I asked. I was very curious and wanted to know what had happened to all the wealth.

Galaxy said, "The wealth is still here, but it isn't where anyone knows about it."

That got me thinking, and I asked Galaxy all the questions I could think of.

Galaxy said, "The queen told the fairies to move everything of value and hide it so the townspeople could never find it."

"I remember my grandpa told me that the queen had Sir Hunter hide some gold. Do you know where all the gold was hidden?" I asked.

"I do. Why do you want to know?" Galaxy asked.

I tried to explain that if there was a significant amount of gold available, it would help many, many people. I knew that I had to try to make Galaxy understand why it was so important, but I didn't know if I would be able to do so.

I asked, "Is there any way that you could tell me where the gold is?"

Galaxy said, "There is a way to find it, but first you have to look in the scroll that belonged to the queen."

"I have the scroll. Izzy and I found the scroll the other day when we were looking around in the upper part of the castle. But I don't know how to read it," I stated.

"Yes, Hunter, I know you found the scroll. The writings in the scroll will tell you where the gold is, but you have to look at it very closely to read the clues."

"Why can't you just tell me? That would save time? I don't understand why I have to figure it out when you know where it is," I said.

"The queen wrote the clues in the scroll specifically for you to discover. That is the only way you will learn what it says. If it is told to you, then you will not have learned it by yourself. It must come from the thoughts in your mind," Galaxy explained.

I was very confused and didn't understand what thoughts from my mind had to do with getting my hands on that gold. If it was meant for me to have, why couldn't I be told where it was?

"How am I to learn what the queen wrote in the scroll, when it seems to be in a language that I'm not familiar with?" I asked.

"You may not understand now, but you will. Walk through the castle. Take pictures and study them. Write down everything you see," Galaxy said, and then suddenly she was gone.

This was very upsetting. I wanted to find that gold. How was walking around the castle going to help me find it? I punched the wall. The wall was so solid that it didn't even leave a mark, except for on my hand. That was stupid because now my hand really hurt. I sat down in a big chair that was comfortable. I wondered to myself how such a chair was built back in the days of when Sir Hunter was here. I hunched over with my elbows on my knees and my face in my hands, and I sat there thinking. After a while, I got up and stood in the middle of the huge foyer.

"Okay, I'm ready. What do I need to do?" I asked aloud.

Suddenly, Galaxy appeared. "I know you'd come to your senses. Come along with me."

I spent the rest of the day walking around Bonefairy Castle with Galaxy, writing down as much as I could in my journal, and taking pictures.

"You are wasting your time taking pictures of me, because fairies can't be seen on film. I can be seen only by you, and that is because I want you to see me," Galaxy said.

"How did you know I took a picture of you? Oh, never mind," I said.

CHAPTER 12

A fter a grueling day of walking around the castle, I decided to head back to where Izzy worked. I was hungry and wanted to see if Izzy could make me a couple of sandwiches to go.

Izzy asked, "What have you been up to?"

I smiled. "I went back out to Bonefairy Castle and saw the fairy again. Galaxy told me that there are many clues in the scroll and to make sure that I didn't lose it."

"What kind of clues, and for what?"

"Galaxy wouldn't say, but she did say that if I could figure out what the writings in the scroll meant, I'd be able to find a fortune in gold. We just have to figure out the clues, which will tell us where to look," I explained.

"Do you think you can figure out what the clues are?" Izzy asked.

"Well, maybe if you help me, we can figure them out together."

"I don't know how much use I'll be. Do you have the scroll on you now?" she asked.

"No, I'll have to go back to the hotel to get it," I said.

"Why don't you go get the rest of your things, and check out of the hotel? You can stay here so we can figure out the clues together," Izzy offered.

"Are you sure? I mean, I think it is a great idea, but I don't want to impose."

"Yes, I'm sure. As long as you don't mind sleeping on the couch," Izzy said with a wink.

"No, I don't mind at all. Your place is a lot more comfortable than the hotel room," I confessed.

I left to get my stuff and check out of the hotel. I told Izzy I would meet her at her place in a little while. I got to the hotel and went to my room. I didn't have much with me, so it didn't take long to pack my stuff. Checking out was a different story. When I came down to the lobby, there were a few people checking in, so I went to the small café to get something to eat; I hadn't gotten a chance to ask Izzy to make me some sandwiches. It didn't look like there was much food already made, except for some pastries and muffins, so I grabbed a blueberry muffin and a small carton of milk. I sat at one of the small tables and ate while I waited for the lobby to clear.

About twenty minutes later, the lobby cleared a little, and I was done eating, so I got up to check out. I checked out and headed to Izzy's.

The hotel was far from the diner where Izzy worked. I knew she was still working, but I thought she would be getting off soon. I arrived at the diner and walked in. It wasn't very busy. I went over to one of the tables that I knew Izzy covered and sat down. She walked over when she saw me sit down.

"You know, I feel like I'm living in a dream and don't want it to ever end," I said.

Izzy smiled. "If someone would have told me a week ago that a man was going to come into town, and I was going to meet him, and then a week later I asked him to move into my home; I would have said they're crazy. But here you are. So, where is the scroll? Let's take a look and see what we can figure out."

"I know what you mean. It is happening very fast. You know, I appreciate your hospitality. I don't know what I would have done if I hadn't run into you," I said.

I took the scroll out of my backpack. As Izzy and I began looking at it, we saw something in the writings of some kind of formula talking about DNA.

"What does that writing right there mean?" Izzy asked.

"I'm not sure about anything right now, but I do know Galaxy said that the clues are in the scroll and tell us where to find the gold, so we just have to figure it out," I proclaimed.

"Well, the writings are talking all about this DNA stuff and nothing about any gold," Izzy pointed out.

"I know, but there has to be some other clues here somewhere.

Maybe the clues aren't in the writings. Maybe there's something in the scroll itself."

"Let's look a little closer at the scroll," she suggested.

"I'm looking. I don't see a thing. Hey! Remember when we found the scroll in that secret room at the castle?" I said.

"Yes, I do. Why?" Izzy inquired.

"Well, we wouldn't have found the room without the sun coming through the window, remember?"

"Yes, I remember. What are you saying?"

"Maybe we need to take the scroll back to that room."

"Hey, I'll try anything. Let's go find out!" Izzy offered.

"We'll have to go tomorrow during the day for the sun to shine, and hopefully it won't be an overcast day," I said.

Izzy finished with her shift at work, so we headed to her house over the tavern. Of course, we had to go in the tavern for some drinks. As we sat there, we both seemed to be in a daze, thinking about what an unusual adventure we were about to be involved with. Izzy got tired and said she wanted to go home, so we went up to her place. Izzy got a blanket and a pillow for me to sleep on the couch, and we both got ready for bed. I made my bed. As I lay there drifting off to sleep, I couldn't help but think about that gold.

Izzy and I woke up the next day and had some breakfast. We then drove back to the castle. We were excited to go to see that the sun was shining. As we pulled up to the gate, the guard was there again.

"Boy, you sure like this place," he said.

"Well, it is so big. There are so many rooms, and the rooms are huge. I just want to make sure I see it all," I explained.

"The same rules still apply. Come on through, and have a nice day," the guard said.

We pull up to the castle, got out, and walked in.

"We need to go back to where saw the sun shine on the wall, so we can get back into the room," I said.

"Yes, I remember. It's this way," Izzy said.

We got to the room and opened the box over the window to allow the sun to shine in.

"Okay, Izzy, let's put the scroll over where the sun is shining to see if anything happens," I said.

Izzy walked over and unrolled the scroll and spread it on the wall directly in the sunlight. "I don't see anything happening."

"I know, but let's wait a little. Look! The sun is shining on the scroll and is making a reflection off of it onto the wall," I shouted.

"What does it say, Hunter?"

"I'm not sure. It must be a clue of some kind."

"All right, so maybe it's a clue, but what does it mean?"

"There are letters on the wall. Look, there are fifteen letters. HOMEOFTHEDRAGON. Do you see it?" I asked.

"Yes, I do see it, but I wonder what it means?" she asked.

I took my journal out and wrote out the letters.

"I wrote out all the letters, and it makes out the words 'Home of the Dragon,'" I said, scratching my head.

"Well, what the heck does home of the dragon mean? I know, I know—you're going to say it's a clue, but the clue doesn't make sense," Izzy said.

"Yeah, I know it has to be something important. I think I need to find Galaxy again and see if 'home of the dragon' means anything."

"Well, Hunter, do you think Galaxy will tell you? Didn't she say you had to figure out the clues on your own?" Izzy asked.

"I don't know, but I'll try anything right now. Let's see if we can find Galaxy," I suggested.

"Do you know where to look for Galaxy?" asked Izzy.

"Not really. Galaxy says she knows when we are here, and she knows what we are doing, so it shouldn't take very long. Maybe you should wait in the car, because I don't know if Galaxy will come out if you are here. I'm the only person who has seen Galaxy."

"All right, but I don't want to be there all day," Izzy said as she left, pouting.

"I know. If Galaxy doesn't show in thirty minutes, I'll let you know, and we can decide then what we are going to do," I assured her.

Izzy stayed in the car while I walked around a little, calling out for Galaxy. It wasn't long before Galaxy showed up.

"Yes, Hunter, I am here," Galaxy said.

"Galaxy, I think I may have found a clue from the scroll, but I have no idea what it means. I thought I would ask you and see if you can help me," I pleaded.

"Hunter, I know what you have found, Remember I'm a fairy, and I know everything," Galaxy reminded me.

"Okay, well then, can you help me with the meaning of home of the dragon that I found on the wall?" I asked.

"I cannot tell you what the clue means."

"Well, it has to mean something! This isn't fair!"

"Hunter, I know you are angry, but if you really stop to think about this, you will figure it out," Galaxy said, and then she was gone.

I couldn't believe it. She keeps appearing and reappearing. That is so aggravating and quite rude, if you ask me. What am I saying? I'm getting angry at a fairy. I sat there looking at the words I had written in my journal. *Home of the Dragon.* I remember something I wrote in my journal about a dragon that Grandpa told me about. I can't quite remember it all. I opened the journal and started looking through it. I got so engrossed with reading my journal that I forgot about Izzy being out in the car. I went out to the car and said that she could come back in.

"Well, Izzy I did see Galaxy. She wouldn't tell me what the words mean, but I think I figured it out," I said.

"What does it mean?" Izzy asked.

"Galaxy told me to stop and think about what the words could mean, so that's what I did. I thought there might be something that I wrote in my journal, so I looked through it. Sure enough, there notes about a dragon that my ancestor Sir Hunter had to deal with. The queen had him and his men capture it in a cave up high on a mountain."

Izzy smiled. "Well, it doesn't look like I need to figure on going to America anytime soon."

"Izzy, I'm sorry, but we have to find where this dragon lived," I apologized.

"Do you have any idea what you sound like? You want to run around the woods and the mountains to find a dragon that hasn't been seen for hundreds of years? You could look for the rest of your life and not find anything," Izzy said, raising her hands.

"Take it easy. I know it sounds outrageous, and you're right, but I do have to try."

"Well, I think we need to go back in town and get drunk. We can think about all of this tomorrow. I don't think that dragon is going anywhere. What do you think?"

I laughed. "I think that is a good idea. I sure could use a drink about now."

Izzy and I drove back into town and went straight to the tavern. "Come on, Hunter. I'll buy the first one," she offered.

"Okay, but I'm serious about looking for where that dragon lived," I announced.

"I know, but please, not now. Tomorrow you can go and get all the equipment and tools you want, and we can spend as much time as it takes to find where the dragon lived. I have one question, though. What are you going to do once we find where this dragon lived?"

"Izzy, that is a very good question, but I can't answer that until I get there and see what is there. Okay, where's that drink you were going to buy?" I teased.

CHAPTER 13

The next day couldn't come soon enough. I got up early and wanted to get everything in motion.

Izzy laughed and said, "Hunter, do you have your mosquito repellent to take with you? You may not find a dragon, but I bet you'll find a few thousand mosquitos."

"Hey, I know this is a crazy and wild adventure, but what the heck. You coming?" I asked.

"I wouldn't miss it for the world. I love adventure, and besides, you may get lucky and find that place where the dragon lived. Maybe even find a few dragon bones. I wonder what dragon meat tasted like back then?"

"I know you are making fun of me, but I don't care. I'm going!" I declared.

"I know, and so am I! Let's get going before I change my mind. You have everything?" she asked.

"I think so. We can only take the car so far, and then we'll be on foot. There is a bridge just up ahead of us, and we can park the car there. Then we'll take a boat down the river. That should get us a good start."

"Okay, but what then?"

"Well, I don't know. I'm just as new to this as you are. You can see what looks like a cave about halfway up this mountain, and we might as well try to go toward that and see if it is anything. If we can get there, we can stay there for the night in the cave. We brought our sleeping bags, and we can build a fire," I offered.

"Oh, really? Now, how do you know if there is anything in that cave?" Izzy asked.

"I don't, and I won't until I we get there. Once we get there, I'll let you check it out first before me," I teased.

"Hunter, you know what you can do with that idea," Izzy said while doing a hand gesture that was not too friendly.

I looked at Izzy with astonishment while laughing. "Well, I never. We'll be all right. Look, there's a trail that looks like it is going to lead us right to the cave."

"All I know is that by the time we get to the cave, I'm going to be so hungry that I could probably eat a dragon," Izzy declared.

"Well, we'll build a fire and cook up something," I assured her.

About three hours later, Izzy and I reached the entrance to the cave.

"I think this is it. It looks like it's all grown over with trees and bushes. No wonder no one knew this cave was here," I said.

"Yes, I see that. How are we going to get into the cave with all those bushes in front of it?" inquired Izzy.

"I'm sure we'll have to dig through some of it. It looks like there are some rocks too. This may be harder than we thought," I confessed.

I had no idea it was going to be this difficult, but I remembered now what Grandpa had told me. They had to block the entrance to the cave to keep the dragon captured. I had to think a minute on how we could do this. I looked through some of the tools we brought. We had a hammer and a small axe.

"I think we'll have to pull away some of these bushes and maybe even chop some of the down. I can give you this axe. I will use the claw side of the hammer and yank away at the bushes. What do you think?" I asked.

"That looks like the only way we'll be able to get in," Izzy agreed.

"Are you sure you want to do this? We don't know what's on the other side once we get through, even though it doesn't look like anything or anybody has been up here in a long time."

"I have to agree with you. Only us crazy people would even want to come here."

"Well, we're here, and so far we're good, right?" I asked.

"Yeah. Home of the Dragon—that's just where I've always wanted to be," she commented.

"Hey, you didn't have to come," I blurted.

"Take it easy. I was only kidding. I told you I wanted to see for myself too. Let's get to plowing down some of these bushes, so we can get in the cave, build a fire, and look around a little bit before it starts to get dark and we won't be able to see anything."

Izzy and I started pulling, yanking, and hacking away at the bushes, and we moved some of the rocks. It was hard work, but we made a pretty good clearing so we could get inside the cave. We both couldn't fit through the clearing, so I went in first. Izzy handed me some of the tools, our backpacks, and the sleeping bags, and then I helped her climb through.

"Okay, it looks like there's a spot right over there where we can set up camp," Izzy noted.

"I'll go back out and get some wood for a fire," I said.

I climbed back out through the clearance and gathered some wood. I got what I could find that I thought would catch fire easily. I brought it all back through the cave, and Izzy set up our sleeping bags.

She said, "Wow, this cave is pretty big. I was looking around, and there are a lot of different tunnels going in all different direction. How are we going to know which one to take?"

"One at a time, I guess. Look, there's a lake over there, and there are some bones that I said we might see in here."

"You mean dragon bones?" Izzy asked.

"I don't know, Izzy. All I know is that there are bones. They look pretty big too. Maybe they are dragon bones."

"Well, at least it's only bones. I'd hate to run into a real dragon."

"If there were dragons still around, I sure wouldn't be here. I think I want to build that fire a bit bigger," I suggested.

"I'm not sure I like this cave thing," Izzy confessed.

"We're here, and I don't think we are going to have to worry about anything," I said comfortingly.

"Hunter, I just want you to know that I'm a fast runner, and if there is anything in here, I'll be gone so fast that it will be only you standing here with whatever it is."

"All right, there's no need to talk like that. Let's stop with the worrying. The only things that we may see are a few bats. We are in a cave, you know," I reminded her.

"You just make sure that wherever you sleep tonight, I'm close by."

"All right Izzy, I promise."

The morning came after a long night of worrying. We crawled back outside and looked down the mountain from the cave. The fog was heavy, and we couldn't see the bottom of the mountain.

"Hunter, I think it's time to build another fire. This cave is kind of cold," Izzy suggested.

"I know, Izzy. Most caves are."

"Now, just how many caves have you been in?"

"Well, counting this one, just one. But I read that caves are always damp and cold inside."

"This is some kind of a place. I wonder what we're going to find in here?" she said.

"It may take a while with all the different tunnels. All right, we need to have some kind of a plan so we can find our way back each time from the different directions we go. Let's put a mark on the walls of the cave so we can follow it back," I suggested.

"I think we should use a rope. If we put a mark on the walls, then we are going to be looking for marks all the time. It is pretty dark in here, not to mention when it gets dark outside later, then we're really going to have a hard time finding all any marks."

"Ah, right. I think you are right. Yes, that does make sense, but I don't know if we have enough rope."

"Then let's do both. We can put a mark on the wall so we can always find it, and then we can use the rope to go where we make our next mark. How's that sound?" Izzy inquired.

"It works for me. Okay, let's go."

"I wonder why no one has ever been in this cave?" Izzy said puzzled.

"The front of the cave was sealed off with big rocks, remember? They did that to keep the dragon captured," I explained.

"What do you mean?" Izzy asked.

"Think about it. If this is the home of the dragon, wouldn't you want it to be sealed off, because this is where the dragon lived?"

"Well, yes, I guess you are right. That does make sense. So maybe those are dragon bones over by the lake."

"I bet the queen hid all her gold here because she knew that no one would ever go into the cave where the dragon lived."

"It makes sense. The dragon couldn't get back out once the cave was sealed to eat, and it died in here. Those bones have to be the dragon's bones," she said excitedly.

"All she would have to do is wait for time to pass, and then the dragon would die from not being able to get back out of the cave and find anything to eat. The queen would then send her men back here, open the cave back up, and find the dead dragon. Then they could come back with all of her gold, put it in the cave somewhere, and seal the cave up again," I said.

"Yes, but if that was true, then someone would know that there was gold in here. Someone had to bring the gold, right?" Izzy said, confused.

"I remember I wrote in my journal about what my grandpa said, where the queen changed two of her fairies into men, and they and Sir Hunter brought all of the queen's valuables to this cave. I never understood that because the people couldn't see the fairies anyway, but I guess it would look kind of weird with carts being pulled by horses with no driver. No one would ask questions with Sir Hunter leading the way."

"Yes, that would look kind of funny. So maybe the gold is in here somewhere, but how are we going to find it? Let's take a look at the scroll again and see if there are any more clues, or maybe in the writings," Izzy offered.

"Okay, bring the scroll over here by the fire so we can see what it says."

"I really don't understand this language written in the scroll, Hunter. After we look down all these tunnels, what if we don't find anything?"

"Well, there is a possibility there isn't anything down these tunnels, but we have to look. Izzy, why don't you just stay here by the fire, and I'll go down each tunnel? I'll yell back if I don't find anything, and then I'll come back," I suggested.

"Well, now, that's the first bit of sense that I will agree with," she said, grinning.

"Okay, you sit right here, and I'll be right back—I hope. I don't think these tunnels go very far, so it shouldn't take long."

I started down the first tunnel and yelled back, "I'm at a dead-end, so I'm going to go on to the next one."

Izzy yelled back, "Okay, just be careful."

After about two hours of looking, I came back and said, "There isn't anything down any of the tunnels."

"Well, it looks like we've had all the fun we are going to have, so can we get out of here?" she begged.

"Izzy, I know you want to go, but I can't believe we have come this far and nothing is here."

"Maybe someone has been here, found the gold already, and took it out of here. There's got to be another clue in the scroll, so let's look again. What about these drawings on the back?" Izzy asked.

"I don't know. Let's see. This looks like a small waterfall that runs down some rocks and into what looks like a lake." I pointed.

"I bet it is this lake, and there is water running down that rock over there into it. Maybe that is the clue. Hunter, maybe the gold is in the bottom of the lake," she said.

"Oh, wait! I remember now. I have an entry in my journal where the fairies put the gold at the bottom of a lake. Sir Hunter couldn't do it; the fairies had to. The water is so dirty that we can't see the bottom. Hand me that flashlight. I'll try to go down in the water to see how deep it is," I offered.

"Too bad you don't have any scuba equipment," she said.

"All right, give me some of that rope we brought. I'll tie it around my waist," I suggested.

"Wait a minute. Let's tie something heavy on the rope first and lower it down to see how far it is to the bottom," she suggested.

"That's a great idea. Give me that rock over there," I said.

"How are you going to tie a rock on the rope?"

"Good point. That won't work. So give me one of those bags that we have food in. I'll use one of them. I'll put a couple of rocks in a bag and tie the bag and the rope together."

"Yeah, I think that should work," she said.

I got the bag of rocks ready and lowered it into the lake. I slowly fed the rope as it went farther down in the water. Finally, the rope was no longer taut, which meant the bag of rocks had found the bottom of the lake.

"Well, that's not so bad. It can't be but about fifteen feet to the bottom. Give me the shovel that we brought. I'm going to dig a little trench that leads down this little hill and let out some of the water," I said.

"Hunter, we are doing all this, and we don't even know there is anything down there."

"I know, but we have to try. Where else can that gold be? I looked down all the tunnels."

"Okay, but after we get the water out of the lake, if there isn't anything there, like gold or anything, we can go home, right?" Izzy begged.

"I guess so, but what if there is?" I hinted.

"Well, mister explorer, start digging, and we'll find out."

I grabbed the shovel and started digging as Izzy kept looking at the scroll for more clues. I finished digging the trench from the side of the lake. Some of the water ran out and down the hill. This made the water become clearer, and we could better see the bottom of the lake.

"Hunter, I think there is something down there. Look!" she hollered.

"Shine the flashlight down there."

Izzy turned on the flashlight and pointed it in the water. We could see several bags tied with rope.

"Oh, my goodness, Hunter, is it the gold? It has to be it. We found it! We found it!" Izzy bounced around.

"What in the heck are we going to do now?" she asked.

"Well, we need to get it all out of this lake. Are you going to help me or just stand there jumping up and down?" I demanded.

"All right, but wow!"

"I knew it had to be here."

"I know, but you do have to admit that it was a pretty wild idea and was kind of hard to believe," Izzy countered.

"Well, I bet you will start to believe me now," I proclaimed.

"Okay, smarty pants. How are we going to get the gold out of the lake?" Izzy asked.

"I think we should wait for more of the water to clear out of the lake. I'm going to dig the trench deeper so more water comes out. Then I should be able to go down in the lake using the rope," I explained.

I dug out the trench some more, and more water flowed out.

"There something else down there, Hunter," Izzy said, shining the flashlight in the water.

"I see it too. I'll have to get a closer look when I get down there," I said.

The water continued to drain out. I tied the rope around a big rock nearby. I figured I could lower myself into the water, grab the bags individually, and throw them up to Izzy. I hoped the rope held me. I tied the rope tight around me and lowered myself in the water.

"Oh, wow, this water is so cold," I said.

"I bet it is. This whole cave is freezing."

"This is going to be easier than I thought. I can feel the bags."

I grabbed the first bag. It was heavier than I thought it was going to be, but I was able to throw it up over the edge. Izzy grabbed it and moved it out of the way. This process continued until all the bags were out of the lake.

"Okay, that's all the bags. I'm going to have to go down there to see what else is there," I said.

"It looks pretty big from here," Izzy noted.

"Keep an eye on the rope. Make sure it is still tied tight. I'm going down there," I said.

I fully submerged myself and took the flashlight with me. When I got down there, I could see it was a big wooden box. I shined the flashlight on the top of it. It read, "Property of Bonefairy Castle." I took off the top of the box and couldn't believe what I saw. I shined the flashlight inside the box. The brilliant and luminous light was overwhelming. I backed away and took the box top with me as I swam back up.

"Izzy, you're not going to believe this," I said.

"What was the bright light I saw?"

"There's a big wooden box, and it is full of precious stones!"

"Are you kidding me?" Izzy hollered back.

"Bring some of those empty bags over here. I'm not going to be able to bring that box up, so I'll fill the bags up with the stones."

Izzy stood there frozen. She had a stunned look on her face.

"Izzy, please! This water is freezing. I'm beginning to feel numb," I shouted.

"I'm sorry! Here," she said.

Izzy handed me the bags. I took one at a time. This wasn't going to be easy doing this all underwater. I went back in the water and put the flashlight in my mouth. I scooped the stones, put them in a bag, and took the first bag up to Izzy.

"Make sure the bags I bring up are tied tightly. I don't want any of the stones to fall out," I said.

I dropped the bag near the edge. Izzy looked inside and then at me. Her eyes were huge, and her mouth dropped open. I know what she was thinking, but I needed to go get the rest, so I went in again. This process continued until all the stones were out. I came up with the last bag.

"That's all there is. I need to get out of this water," I said.

I pulled myself out of the water as Izzy helped me. Izzy handed me a blanket, and I wrapped around me as I shivered.

"You might want to take off your jacket and then wrap up in the blanket," she suggested.

"Good idea," I said.

I took off my jacket. Of course, it was soaking wet. The blanket was cold as well, but it was dry. Izzy went out of the cave to get more wood for the fire. I sat there in front of the fire, staring at all the bags sitting there in front of me. I couldn't believe this was all real.

"Izzy, let me see the top of the box I brought up," I said.

Izzy handed me the top. I was astonished how the writing, "Property of Bonefairy Castle," was still so visible. Someone must have burned the letters into the wood. I flipped the box top over to see the other side. I could barely see it, so I turned on the flashlight. My jaw dropped open this time.

"We are going to have to figure out what we are going to do with all this gold and stones," Izzy said.

"I know, but look—there's a map engraved on the bottom of this lid to the box," I said.

"Really? What does it say?" Izzy asked.

"I don't know. Right now, I don't care. I just want to get everything out of this cave."

"Hunter, how are we going to get all of this out of this cave without anyone knowing what is going on? We can't do it by ourselves."

"You're right, but first I want to look at the map more closely. It looks like just a map, but wasn't there something in the scroll that said something about a map."

"Yes, I think so, but it didn't make much sense," Izzy acknowledged.

"Maybe now it will because we have the map. Okay, here's what I think we should do right now. Let's take the map along with a few of the stones and some of the gold, and then we can hide the rest of it," I suggested.

"Right, and how are we going to do that?"

"Well, let's just pile some of the wood and some of the bones over there to cover everything up, so people can't see anything."

"Where are we going to take the gold and stones?"

I said, "I'm not sure yet. I don't know if we can make a claim to your government. It's not going to be easy without telling them where all of this gold is."

"We can come back and get the stones. We don't have to tell anyone about that until we have to," Izzy said.

"Okay, let's cover up the gold and hope that nobody comes here until we have everything figured out. Let's move everything from one our backpacks to the other. We can use the other pack to take out what we want," I suggested.

"Hunter, did you ever think that we were going to find this kind of wealth?"

"Well, no, but I never thought that I was going to be talking to a fairy in a castle either. Let's get out of here and head back to your place to get a little rest before we do anything else. We should then go back to the castle so I can talk some more with Galaxy. Galaxy must know about this other map, and she can help us understand what it says. Maybe there is more to this wealth than what we have found. Maybe there's more somewhere else."

CHAPTER 14

Izzy and I climbed back down the mountain with what we could carry in our backpacks. We tried not to look conspicuous—just two people hiking in the woods. It seemed like forever going back, but we finally reached the car and put our backpacks in the trunk. We headed back to town to Izzy's place.

Izzy asked, "What are you going to do first now that we're back?"

"Really? You have to ask that? I'm going to celebrate in that tavern right there and have the biggest drink they have," I gloated.

"Yes, I think that we should celebrate a little too. Tomorrow we can go back to the castle and talk to Galaxy about the other map we found. Have you looked at it at all?"

"No, not really. I'm so excited about what we have already found. I think I'm going to make a few phone calls tomorrow to people back in America to get some advice. I didn't really figure on all of this when I decided to come here. I was coming just to learn a little bit about my ancestors, not all this other stuff. Izzy, when I go back to America, I want you to go with me. I think that with what we have found here, you won't need to worry about working anymore."

"I would like to see America and travel a little," Izzy admitted.

"Well, I think that you'll be able to travel anywhere you want now."

"It's something to think about, so let's get something to eat and have another drink."

"Okay, but after that, I think we should stop with the drinking and figure out what our next move is."

"We are going to have to figure out how we are going to get all that gold out of the cave," Izzy stated.

"I think we need to contact the National Treasury Agency. Let's make some phone calls tomorrow and see what we can find out. We can't keep all that gold, so if the National Treasury Agency can take it off our hands, I think that would be the smartest thing to do."

"What about all the precious stones?" Izzy asked.

"We can keep some of them and sell some. We are going to have to make some kind of deal with the National Treasury Agency to have them come out with a helicopter and get all that gold out of the cave. I think we should do that before we start anything else."

"What do you mean, start anything else?" Izzy asked.

"You know, like that other map we found."

"That map isn't going anywhere. We have it with us, and no one knows about it. Are you going to write all that has happened in your journal?"

"Don't you think that I should?" I replied.

"Yes, I do. I was just asking."

"Izzy, I've had enough to eat and drink. I think we should go get some rest."

"Okay, that's cool. Let's go," she agreed.

The next day started, and I definitely got a good night's sleep. I got up and made a few phone calls, with one of them being the National Treasury Agency.

"Izzy, the National Treasury Agency said that they will meet with us in a couple of days to talk. What do you want to do in the meantime?" I asked.

"Well, we can go into town and see what some of the stones we have are worth. We do need some money to continue doing all this crazy stuff," Izzy recommended.

"Okay, and then maybe we can get a big safe-deposit box or two, to keep the rest of the stones in until we need them."

Izzy and I went to a jeweler in town. Izzy said it was the better store, and she trusted the guy who owned it. We walked in and asked for the owner. An older gentleman came out of an office.

"How can I help you?" he said.

"I found some stones that look like they might be valuable, and I was hoping you could take a look at them," I said.

"Sure, let me see them," the owner said.

I pulled out the stones and slid them across the counter. The owner looked at them and had an unusual look on his face.

"What's wrong?" I asked.

"Well, these look pretty old. I'd like to put them in some solution to clean them up a little, if you don't mind?" he asked.

"No, not at all."

As the jeweler put the stones in a cleaning solution, the stones came to life. They were so beautiful with illuminous colors. My eyes grew wide.

"They're something, huh?" the jeweler said.

"Yeah, they sure are," I commented.

"Where did you get these?"

"Oh, they've been around with my family for quite some time," I said.

The jeweler looked up at me with a suspicious look, as if he knew I was lying.

"So, what do you think they're worth?" I asked.

"Well, they are quite valuable, but I'd like to take a little more time and examine the more thoroughly with my partner. Would you mind if I keep them for a while?" the jeweler asked.

"Well, I'm only in town for a little bit. I was just hoping to get a quick quote on them. I can come back another time," I said nervously.

The jewelry took them out of the solution, dried them off, and laid them on a soft cleaning cloth. "That's a shame. I'd like to look at them more closely. They are quite magnificent."

"Thank you for your time. I'll come back another day when I have more time," I said as I removed the stones and placed them back in my pouch.

"That would be great. I'll be here," the jeweler said with a funny grin.

Izzy and I left the jeweler and got in the car.

"He had a funny way about him, didn't he?" I said.

"What do you mean?" Izzy asked.

"Well, it was like he's seen the stones before and knows where they came from."

"Oh, Hunter, you're paranoid," Izzy said.

"Maybe. Let's get out of here. I want to get a safe-deposit box," I said.

"Okay, well, they have them at the bank on the corner, down the road," Izzy suggested.

Izzy and I went to the bank, and she got a safe-deposit box because she lived here. We put the stones and the small amount of gold in it and locked it up. I then dropped off Izzy at the diner for work and went back to her place. I sat down at the table and began studying the map on the bottom of the box lid. I then brought out the scroll to examine the map on that too. My eyes were going buggy. I needed to get something to eat, so I headed to the diner for something to eat.

"I'm going nuts just sitting around," I said to Izzy.

"You want something to eat?" she offered.

"Yes, I could use a big sandwich. We didn't eat very much while we were ..." I was about to say what we were doing yesterday, but I stopped when Izzy put her figure to her lips in the gesture of, *Shh*.

"It will be coming right up. Our Reuben sandwich is the special today," Izzy offered.

"Perfect, I'd love a Reuben."

I sat there waiting for my sandwich. When Izzy brought over my sandwich, she sat down. "I have a few minutes for a break. I'm glad we tucked away our stuff. It will be safe there. So now what do we do?"

"We wait," I said.

A couple days later, the National Treasury Agency called us and said that they were ready to meet with us. We agreed to meet and drove to where the meeting was supposed to take place. The National Treasury Agency office was just outside of town. As I drove into the parking garage and parked the car, a van with three men drove up next to us, stopped, and told us to get in the van. We did as they said, and the van drove back out of the parking garage and out of town.

"What is going on? Who are you, and why are we being taken in a van out of town?" I asked.

One of the men in the van said, "We don't know why. We are just doing what we are told."

I looked at Izzy, and she looked worried, like something was not right.

After about thirty minutes, the van pulled up to a house in the country.

"I don't understand. We have a meeting scheduled with the National Treasury Agency right now," I explained.

One of the men said, "Not anymore. Just get in the house, sit down, and keep your mouth shut."

One of the men grabbed Izzy and took her into another room. Izzy hollered, "Hunter, what's happening? Why are we here, and why are they doing this?"

The door closed behind Izzy. One of the men told me to sit there and be quiet. A few minutes later, another car drove up, and some more men came into the house.

One guy was dressed in a suit and did all the talking. He asked me, "Do you know why you are here?"

"No, I don't have any idea. Who are you?" I asked.

"Well, Hunter, who we are is not as important as why you are here. Let me fill you in on why. You see, we know that you have been going out to Bonefairy Castle for the last couple of weeks, and so has your girlfriend in the other room. Any time anyone goes into Bonefairy Castle, we are contacted. We have a close relationship with the National Treasury Agency. There was a queen who lived in Bonefairy Castle and was very wealthy. As the years went by, the town people wondered where all the wealth had gone. After the castle was no longer occupied by the queen and the government took it over, we have been watching it. Now, you and your girlfriend show up, and for the first time in many years, someone is going into the castle again. We would like to know why, what you were doing there with your friend, and why you keep coming back," explained the agent.

"How do you know my name?" I asked.

"We know everything," the agent said.

"Are you from the government?" I asked.

"Like I said, who we are is not important. Tell me what you are doing at Bonefairy Castle."

"I am from America, and I'm in town for a few weeks to try to find out about my ancestors, who lived here hundreds of years ago," I stated.

"Hunter, who is that girl in the other room?" the agent asked.

115

"I met her when I came into town. I stopped at a diner to eat, and she works there. I asked her if she had ever heard of a place called Bonefairy Castle. She told me that she did and that it was a few miles outside of town. I had just gotten into town and didn't know where to go, and I didn't know anyone. Izzy told me that she would show me where the castle was if I had a few minutes to wait until she got off of work. She lives out by Bonefairy Castle and said she didn't mind showing me where it was. We just became friends, and she wanted to go with me when I went to the castle. We didn't know what there was to find or what was there. We asked if we could go in, and the security guard said it was all right," I explained.

The agent then asked, "So what did you find?"

"We didn't find anything," I said.

"Why do we think you're lying, Hunter?" the agent accused.

"I don't know why."

"Well, like I said, we have been watching you and your girlfriend since you started going to the castle. We got a phone call from a jeweler today, and he said a guy and girl who matched your description was in his store and had a few precious stones. They were trying to find out what they were worth. Now, is any of this starting to ring a bell? You know that we can take you to the jeweler and see if he recognizes you," the agent declared.

"Okay, so I found a couple of stones while we were at the castle and wanted to know if they were worth anything. We went to the jeweler and asked. What's the big deal?" I confessed.

"Well, anything that you find at Bonefairy Castle belongs to us," he declared.

"So you *are* the government. I didn't know," I muttered.

"I didn't say that. Hunter, do you have the stones on you?" he asked.

"No, I don't."

"Well, we're going to need to get those from you. What is your girlfriend going to say? Is it going to be the same story?" the agent asked.

"She isn't going to say anything, because she wasn't with me when I found the stones. I showed her what I found later," I informed him.

"So you are saying that is why you and your girlfriend kept going back to the castle."

"Yes, but we also liked Bonefairy Castle and wanted to explore it."

"I have just a few more questions, Hunter. Are you guys going back to the castle anymore?" the agent asked.

"Well, yes, we want to. We haven't been able to see everything yet."

"All right. I'm going to have these nice men take you and your girlfriend back to your car. Just remember that if you do go back to Bonefairy Castle, we will be watching. Oh, and if you do find anything, make sure that you don't take it off the premises because it doesn't belong to you," the agent threatened.

"Why did you have to bring us all the way out here, to this house, to tell us this? Why couldn't you just say all of this back in town?" I huffed.

"Hunter, let's just say that we have our reasons, and that's all you and your friend need to know. Go get in the van, and we'll bring your girlfriend out in a minute," the agent commanded.

The men took me back out to the van. I waited for Izzy to be brought out. It was about ten minutes before the men brought Izzy out to the van.

"What took so long?" I asked.

"Hunter, you need to stop with the questions before you get into more trouble," the agent threatened.

Izzy sat there next to me in the van and didn't say anything. I looked at Izzy and could see that something wasn't right, so I did what I was told and stopped talking. The men drove us back into town and to our car. Izzy and I got out.

I looked at Izzy and said, "Let's get out of here."

They got in their car and left the parking garage. I thought it was best to drive in silence for a while. We both needed to catch our breath.

I finally asked, "Did that man question you while you were in the other room?"

"Yes. He wanted to know why we were at Bonefairy Castle and if we found anything," Izzy said.

"What did you say?" I asked.

"I told him that we didn't find anything and were just looking around. Then he asked me about the stones that you had. I told him that I didn't know anything about that. I didn't want to say anything more about it until I talked to you again, because I figured we were in enough trouble already."

"Good. That was a very smart move. I think something isn't right with those men who grabbed us. They may be with the National Treasury Agency, but I think they are crooked. We had a meeting scheduled with the National Treasury Agency, so why were we questioned all the way out there in that house? They are crooks, and I think they are simply trying to get whatever they can for themselves."

"Hunter, if you're right, what are we going to do? They're watching Bonefairy Castle and will know when we go back out there."

"I know. I told them that we were going to go back out there a few more times, but I didn't say why. We are just going to have to remember that we are going to be watched and make sure that whatever we do, they can't know what we found out about the castle or about any of the things we discovered. Tomorrow, after we have some breakfast, let's drive back out there as if nothing has changed or happened. We can pretend that we are doing what we said we would be doing: exploring. We know that they're going to be watching us, but what they don't know is how to get into the secret room in Bonefairy Castle. If they came in there, they wouldn't be able to find us. I will ask Galaxy if it is all right for you to be with me when we talk again. Galaxy already knows what is happening and will see that you are a friend of mine. If I ask, I think you'll be accepted. It's a funny thing about fairies: they already know everything that has happened and is going to happen, but they can't say anything. They are forbidden to tell the future, but they can talk about the past."

"Hunter, what are we going to do about all that gold?"

"No one knows about that. It has been there for hundreds of years. I don't think we are going to have to worry about it for a little while longer. Let's try to keep thinking about Bonefairy Castle and the other map. We've put the stones in a safe-deposit box. No one knows about that, so they're safe."

"All right, so what's for breakfast?" she asked.

"You're kidding, right? Let's just get going, and we can eat later."

"But I'm hungry," Izzy said, sulking.

CHAPTER 15

The next day arrived, and Izzy and I were on our way to the castle. As we pulled up to the gate, I could see the security guard on the phone.

"Look, Izzy, the guard is making a phone call right now. He probably called those men when he saw us coming, so they know we're back out here again," I said.

"Well, let's just wave and smile like we have been, and move on. Wait—the guard is waving at us and wants to say something."

The guard said, "I'm sorry, but I've been told that I can't allow any more visitors into Bonefairy Castle."

"Really? Why is that?" I asked.

"No one is allowed inside Bonefairy Castle anymore. Sorry," the guard reiterated.

I acted confused. "Well, okay, but we don't understand. We were allowed in before."

"Yes, I know, and I don't make the rules, so I'm sorry."

Izzy and I got back in our car. I was very upset and just sat there.

"Hunter, let's go," she said.

"No, Izzy. We are just going to find another way into the castle. There has to be another way in somewhere. We have that other map, and only Galaxy is going to be able to help us figure it out. Let's drive around the back of the wall that surrounds Bonefairy Castle. We'll find a place somewhere that we can climb over and get in. If we can do that and get into the secret room, then the guard won't even know we are there."

"That's pretty risky," Izzy said, concerned.

I backed up, left the gate entrance, and drove down the road. As we drove a little farther, I could see a side road on the other side of the wall that surrounded the castle.

"Look, I think there's a place over there where we can climb in. We can park the car under those trees and climb that tree to get over the wall," I explained.

"Hunter, are you sure you want to do this? We could get in a lot of trouble," she said nervously.

"Izzy, I'm not going to think about that. We've got to get in there."

"Wait! There's another guard coming down the road with a dog. Oh, great. Let's get out of here. We'll come back later," Izzy pleaded.

"All right, but I'm coming back, Izzy."

"I know. I'm coming too."

"Those guards aren't going to keep me out of there. There's something funny going on. They let us go in the other day, and now we can't get in."

"It's probably those guys we talked to yesterday. We told them that we were going to come back out here a couple more times. It has to be them," Izzy suggested.

"Well, I don't trust them. I bet they think we know something, and that's why we wanted to come back."

"Hunter, we do know something, just not everything yet. Let's go back out front."

"Look! There's that same van out by the guard shack, with those men who grabbed us yesterday. I knew they're crooked. I think we should come back later because we know they're here now."

"Yeah, Hunter I think that's a good idea."

"I'm going to go back to your place to relax and think a while."

"Okay, that's cool," she said invitingly.

"Oh, by the way, how long have you had that place you're at?" I asked.

"Well, I haven't had it very long, but it's been in my family forever."

"Really? What do you mean, forever?"

"Well, it has been handed down from my ancestors for a couple of hundred years."

"How long have you been living there?" I asked.

"Up above the tavern, there are a bunch of rooms that they used to rent out a long time ago. Then when I got it, I made a few changes so I could live there. I took the name down when I started living there. That's why it just says tavern out front," she explained.

"So what was this place called before?" I asked.

"The sign was old and falling down anyway, but it was called Bonefairy House."

"Oh, wow, really? My grandpa told me about this place, but I didn't realize it was here," I informed her.

"Your grandfather told you about this place? It has been here for a long time."

"I can't believe it! I'll have to let you read my journal sometime. My grandpa told me that Sir Hunter use to come in here all the time with some of his men. Maybe my ancestors knew your ancestors. Wouldn't that be wild? I've been here in your country for a short time, and I would've never believed that I could find out all this. The longer I'm here, the more that is happening. I need to add more to my journal before I forget what has taken place so far."

"You know, I was thinking we don't need to tell anyone about the stones we found, so we don't have to worry about that for a while," she said.

"Yes, but what if the map that we have has more history to it?" I asked.

"I don't know, but how are we going to find out?"

"All I know is that we are going to have to get back inside Bonefairy Castle."

"So when do you want to try that again?"

"Let's wait until tomorrow and try then," I suggested.

"All right, so what do you want to do now?" she asked.

"I don't know, Izzy. I'm new around here, remember? What do you want to do?"

"Well, we still have all that gold that we have to figure out what we are going to do with."

"I have an idea. Let's go find out about the land where the cave is and see if there may be a way to buy that piece of land. Nobody knows that there's gold in the cave, and we're not going to tell anybody. So let's ask to see who owns the land. Someone has to know. All land belongs to someone, right? We can ask around, and we sure have enough gold to buy it. We simply have to find out whom to ask."

"Hunter, before you came to town, my life was quiet with not much to worry about. Harbor was a small town and never exciting, but now that you're here, things have changed a lot. I've been back out to Bonefairy Castle, and now I'm finding secret rooms and doors no one knows about. Then we find all that gold and the precious stones in a cave, and another map. I can't believe everything that's been happening since you've been here."

"Well, I think that we are just getting started. There's definitely more that's going to happen—I can feel it. I can hardly wait to get back inside Bonefairy Castle and talk to Galaxy," I said.

"Okay, but for now, let's slow down a little and see whom we can talk to about buying the land. Let's go back in town and see what we can find out. Maybe the town clerk can give us a little direction. Someone must pay taxes on that land or something. If we can find who owns it, maybe they will be willing to sell it."

"Izzy, I know we need to find out all this stuff, but what if the map that we have leads us in another direction?"

"So what do you want to do first?" she asked.

"The gold isn't going anywhere, and I think we have some time before we have to worry about it. This map is going to lead us somewhere. So maybe we can put the gold wherever the map leads us to and not even buy the cave," I stated.

"Okay, that makes sense So I guess we are going back out to Bonefairy Castle, then?" Izzy asked.

"Yes. Come on. Let's go see what Galaxy knows about it."

Izzy and I went back out to Bonefairy Castle. We drove down the back road behind the castle wall and parked the car under the tree. I helped Izzy climb up the tree and over the wall, and then we dropped down. We hurried inside the back door of the castle.

"Hunter, how are we going to find Galaxy?" she asked.

"Galaxy is a fairy and knows every time we're here, or anybody else. Let's get to the secret room and wait. Galaxy will show up. I think Galaxy will see that you are a friend of mine, and then you will be welcome."

"So where's this Galaxy?" Izzy teased.

Galaxy suddenly appeared and said, "I'm right behind you."

Izzy shrieked. "Wow, you scared the heck out of me!"

"Izzy, this is Galaxy. There's nothing to be afraid of," I assured her.

"Ask her about the map!" Izzy said.

Galaxy said, "Young lady, I know why you're here, and I know that you have found the map that was with the gold and stones in the cave. I am not allowed to tell the future about anything, but I can give clues so you can figure it out for yourselves. The gold you found in the cave will be safe, and no one will find it, so you don't have to worry about it. You already have put the stones in a safe place, and no one will find them either. Now you have a map that you need to follow. Hunter, if you and Izzy look at the map, you will see there's a place that the cave is at, so you'll know where to start from. I cannot tell you how or where to travel—I'm not allowed to. As you both know, the queen had Sir Hunter and his men capture a dragon that threatened the town's livestock, and they sealed it in the cave before the gold and stones were put in there. After time passed, the dragon died, so those are the bones you and Izzy found inside the cave. Now, with the map that you have found, you can start following the trail that will lead you," Galaxy explained.

"To what?" I asked.

"Like I told you before, I cannot tell the future to anyone."

"So, Galaxy, what you are saying is we need to go back to the cave with the map?" I asked.

"Yes. The queen had the map put there hundreds of years ago knowing that it would be found and that the secrets to the map would be known. I can tell you this, because you already know that. If you remember when you and Izzy were in the cave, there were several different tunnels there, and they didn't look like they went anywhere. Take the map and look again at the tunnels, and maybe you'll find what the map is trying to show you."

"Okay, Galaxy, we'll go back to the cave, but I looked when we were there before."

"Hunter, you looked, but did you *really* look?" she asked.

"Well, it was dark down those tunnels. I didn't look very good, but when I looked and didn't see anything, I moved on," I admitted.

"Go look again, and look closer. Take a better light," Galaxy suggested.

"Okay, Izzy, let's go back to the cave. Galaxy, we'll be back to see you again if we don't find anything," I stated.

"Hunter, remember that I can see the future, and I already know whether you'll find anything. I simply can't tell you, or tell you where to look," Galaxy reiterated, and then poof—she was gone.

Izzy and I left the castle through the back door. We hadn't thought about how we were going to get back over the wall to the car. I noticed a big tree on the inside of the wall farther down.

"We can climb that tree to get over the wall," I suggested.

"Well, you're going to have to go first and help me up," Izzy said.

I climbed the tree and helped Izzy climb up. We got over the wall and ran back to the car.

"I don't know how much more we'll be able to do this. I'm sure eventually the guards will notice us," I said.

"I bet you're right."

We drove back to the main road, where the entrance to the castle was. There was a guard in the shack, and he saw us driving away. He immediately got on the phone when he saw us.

"Izzy, I bet that guard is calling those men we don't like," I said.

"Well, let's not stick around long enough to find out. Let's go!"

Izzy and I drove back to town and went to Izzy's place.

"Izzy, look. That van is at the tavern again," I pointed out.

"Yeah, I see it. You were right about the guard calling them. Now they're here waiting for us, wanting to know why we went to Bonefairy Castle again."

"Izzy, that's okay. We simply went back to the Bonefairy Castle and were looking around. We don't have to tell them anything. Let's go in and see what they want."

"Hunter, you know why they're here."

"I know, but we don't know anything. Izzy, just be cool. I'll see what they want and ask why they are following us around."

Izzy and I walked in and saw the men waiting at one of the tables. I walked over and said, "Well, you guys really get around, don't you?"

One of the agents said, "Sit down. We have a few questions to ask you. Why did you go back out to Bonefairy Castle yesterday and then leave when you saw our van there?"

"Izzy and I don't want any trouble with you guys, so we left and went back out today," I answered.

"You know the guard called us when they saw you there again today. That's why we are here," the agent said.

"Look, as you can see, we don't have anything. We went back out there because we're just as interested as you guys are to see if we can find anything."

"Hunter, we told you that if you find anything, it belongs to us, remember?" the agent reiterated.

"Yes, I remember, and we haven't found anything, so why don't you guys back off a little bit?"

"Why don't you go back where you came from? Then you won't have to worry about us following you and your girlfriend anymore."

I smirked. "Hey, I'm going to be here for maybe another week or so, and then I'll be gone. You'll never have to see me again."

"Hunter, I have a suggestion. Why don't you leave right now?"

"I don't want to leave right now because I haven't done anything wrong!" I shouted.

"Okay, play it your way, but we are going to be around until you leave town."

The men got up, walked out of the tavern, and drove away.

CHAPTER 16

Izzy and I went upstairs to her room. "Why in the heck won't they leave us alone?" she said.

"Izzy, it doesn't matter. Tomorrow, we'll go back out to the cave. They can sit at Bonefairy Castle and wait for us to show up all they want. They won't have any idea where we are at, and we can look all over that cave and maybe find what Galaxy said was there. In the meantime, let's get something to drink," I decided.

"Okay, Hunter, I think that's a great idea. I'll meet you downstairs."

I went back downstairs and waited for Izzy. It wasn't long before she came back down and sat at the table with me. I looked at her face, and she didn't look happy.

"Izzy, let's take it easy tonight. We can get a good night's sleep and start early tomorrow, before anybody misses us," I suggested.

"Those men are making me very nervous," Izzy said.

"I know, but we will be fine."

"Is there anything we need to get before we leave?"

"No, I think we have everything that we'll need," I stated.

The next morning, Izzy was up early and made breakfast while I loaded the car with the equipment.

"Hunter, come and eat before it gets cold," Izzy hollered out the window.

"I'm ready, and it smells good," I said, my mouth watering.

"Well, I figure we'd better have a good breakfast before we leave. It may be a while before we eat again."

"I know. I've also packed some food in the car for us to have later."

"You did pack the map, didn't you?"

"Yes, Izzy, that was the first thing I put in the car. Nothing like getting all the way back to the cave and not have the map, right?" I asked.

We ate our breakfast and finished with last-minute things we might need.

"Breakfast was good and the car is loaded, so let's get going before those agents come around again," I suggested.

I drove back out to where we had parked before at the bridge and left the car in the parking lot. We went down the river and headed to the trail that led to the cave. It didn't seem to take as long this time because we knew where we were going. We finally made it back to the cave again. I built another fire so I wouldn't have to do it later. Izzy was trying to set up some kind of a campsite so it wouldn't be so difficult for us to do later, because she didn't know how long we were going to be here.

After the fire was built, I said, "Let's take a look at that map again and see if we can figure out what we are supposed to find. I'm hoping it will tell us which tunnel we are supposed to look down."

I looked over on the other side of the cave at all those dragon bones.

"It looks like there may be something there, where all those big rocks are. Izzy, there's another tunnel behind these rocks. I didn't see that the last time we were here."

"I bet we'll find something down that one because there wasn't anything down the other ones," Izzy stated.

"Okay, well, are you going to stay here, or are you coming this time?"

"Hunter, as long as you stay close to me, I'll go."

I laughed. "Don't worry; there's nothing to be afraid of. At least, I don't think there is."

Izzy smiled. "Just remember what I said before. I'm a fast runner."

"I remember! Come on. Let's check it out"

"You have the map, Hunter?" Izzy asked.

"Yes. You have the light?"

Izzy gave a thumbs-up. As Izzy and I started down the tunnel, I could see that it was getting narrower, and we came to a stone wall that we had to go around. We went around the wall, and then I could see a doorway. We went through the doorway, and as we did, the chamber opened up into a room that looked exactly like the secret room that was in the castle.

"Hunter, it looks exactly like the room in the castle," Izzy said.

"Yes, it does," I agreed.

"How can this be?"

"I have no idea, Izzy."

Izzy and I walked into the room and looked around, and Galaxy suddenly appeared.

"Galaxy, how are you here?" I asked.

"Hunter, I can go many places anytime, and now that you and Izzy are here, I can help you. I couldn't help you before because I am not allowed to tell you what is going to happen in the future. I want you to hold Izzy's hand and follow me," Galaxy instructed.

We did what we were told and followed Galaxy across the room. Just like the secret room in the castle, there was a stairway that went down. Galaxy led Izzy and me down the stairway. Just like the stairway in the castle, once our body weight was on the stairs, it opened up another door.

Galaxy told us, "Go through the door, and you'll understand why we have been waiting for you to show up."

"Galaxy, I don't understand," I said.

"You will. Now, go through the door."

Izzy and I walked through the door way with Galaxy, and the door closed behind us. We now were in a much larger room. We had to close our eyes because it was so bright. We turned to look at Galaxy with a questionable look on our face, and all of a sudden, the queen appeared.

Galaxy said, "Hunter, you and Izzy need to bow down to the queen. The queen has been waiting for you to arrive for a long time. The queen also can see the future and knows that you were the person who was going to show up."

We did as we were told and bowed down to the queen.

"Hunter, you and Izzy can rise up now and listen to what the queen has to tell you," Galaxy said.

"Hunter, I am the queen of Bonefairy, and I was here when your ancestors were here. Yes, I did know your ancestor, Sir Hunter. He was the leader of my Royalmen and was with me at Bonefairy Castle. He also was the only one whom I really trusted. He led all of the knights and other Royalmen into battle. Hunter, you know about Galaxy, but you don't know about all the other fairies I have. There are many, and they have been around for hundreds of years. They will still be here after you are gone. Hunter, when you and your friend found the scroll in Bonefairy Castle, it told me that you had arrived. As you know, the scroll that you found really doesn't tell you very much because you can't understand what is written in it. I have another scroll that I'm going to give to you. You will then be able to understand it, but not until you go back to America. Your ancestor, Sir Hunter, used to bring me many different things after there was a war or battle, from the men who died there. I took these things up into my private chambers in Bonefairy Castle—things like hair, bones, skin, and clothes. Many of these things were needed for what I was doing. I have mentioned all these things in this new scroll, so you'll be able to understand once you get back to America.

"I want you to take everything that is written and keep it so no one else will ever know what it says or means. If by chance someone else finds the scroll, they will not be able to understand it, because I will know that someone else has it. What is written in the scroll will not be understandable to them or anybody else. When you get back to America, I will also move the gold that you found here in this cave. My fairies will move it when the time comes. You will know where it is by looking in the scroll you now have. This gold will help you in the future, along with what is written in the scroll. Now, Hunter, do you have any questions for me?"

"I certainly do. I'm so confused about what has happened. There have been some men who have been following us and trying to get information out of us for the last few days."

"Yes, I can understand that, but what you need to know is that I have been waiting for a very long time for you to show up. Now that we have you, we can move on with what I just told you. You won't be having any more problems from those men. You are going to go back to America and follow what is in the scroll. No one will be able to understand how you know all this. Galaxy will always be with you if you have any trouble. Galaxy is going to be to you, as Sir Hunter was to me a long time ago, but Sir Hunter wasn't a fairy. Do you understand?"

"Yes! I understand," I claimed.

"Then you and your friend can leave now and never return here. I will be moving everything that has been found in here, so you won't need to come back," the queen said.

We bowed once again to the queen and thanked her for the new scroll and telling us everything.

"Before we leave this cave, I want to get one of the bones of the dragon. Just a small one, and then we can leave the cave," I said.

"Hunter, why do you want one of those old bones?" Izzy asked.

"I'm not sure myself, but why did the queen take bones from all the men who died?" I wondered.

"Heck, how do I know? I'm more confused than you are," Izzy admitted.

"Well, think about it. The bones have something to do with it all, and this dragon bone is going with me, if nothing else as a souvenir. Besides, if the queen knows the future like she says, then she knows that I was going to take it, and she didn't say I couldn't."

"Okay, can we get out of here now?" Izzy asked.

We left the way we came in and went back to the cave. We gathered our stuff, and I took one of the smaller dragon bones, although it was still pretty big. We went back down the mountain and drove back into town. We didn't look back. I had a new scroll that didn't make any sense to me, but I knew that once I was back in America, it would.

"What has just happened here is unbelievable. I had no idea that I was going to find out about my ancestors and where they lived. Izzy, you mean an awful lot to me now, and you know as much about what has happened as I do. Do you want to go back to America with me?" I asked.

"You can always come back here to visit, but what will I do there, Hunter?" Izzy asked.

"We will take the scroll and do what it says. We'll figure it out as we go," I concluded.

"Well, it is all pretty unbelievable, isn't it? That castle has been there all this time, and no one ever would have known about any of this if you hadn't shown up."

"No one knows anything but us. When we get back to America, we can get a place together and ask Galaxy where the gold is. Then we can start a company," I suggested.

"What about my place here? This old tavern has been in my family for centuries."

"We can use some of the gold to fix it up. We can get someone else to run it, and we'll always have it to come back to when we want. What do you say?"

"Well, it does all sound good, Hunter. I guess I'll give it a try," Izzy proclaimed.

"All right, then. Let's start packing up a few things that you want and see if we can find someone to run the place until we come back. We shouldn't have too much trouble finding someone that would stay here, at least for just the room and board. Give them free rent just to take care of it until we get back," I suggested.

"Well, I can ask a few of my friends in town if they would mind staying here to take care of the place for me," Izzy replied.

CHAPTER 17

Izzy and I made some quick plans. We were also able to make arrangements with a friend of Izzy's to stay at the tavern. They put a sign in the window saying that the tavern was closed for now to do some renovation. In the meantime, Izzy would stay in touch with her friend and touch base once a week to see how everything was going.

With all the arrangement made, Izzy and I headed to the airport by cab. The flight seemed to last forever, but we finally made it to America. We wanted to see my parents and tell them everything we could about the trip. I had been gone for over a month and could hardly wait to see them. We went to my apartment in town. I didn't know how to tell everyone that I was bringing back a friend to live with me, but I knew as soon as my parents met Izzy, they would see why I liked her. Izzy was just what I needed, and we had been inseparable. We went everywhere together.

My parents lived in Huntington, West Virginia. I called my parents to make sure they would be home. They were a little older now and didn't go out much. They were home and said to come over, so I drove to my parents' house. My mom met us at the door. We got out of the car and walked to the house, leaving our stuff in the car for now. We walked in, and I hugged my mom and shook my dad's hand.

"Come on in. It is so good to see you. I've missed you. Who's your friend, Hunter?" my mom asked while gesturing us to move into the living room.

I said, "Mom, I'd like you to meet my friend Isabella, but she likes to be called Izzy."

"Well, Izzy, it's nice to meet you. We don't ever get a chance to meet any of Hunter's friends. How'd you and Hunter meet?" my mom asked.

Izzy explained, "It was by chance. Hunter came into the town where I lived and stopped at the diner where I worked. He stopped for a sandwich and a drink, and that was when I met him. We started talking a little bit, and he told me that he was from America and was in town to see if he could find anything out about his ancestors. I asked him if he knew who they were, and he said not really. All he had was a journal that he was writing in and what his grandpa told him. Hunter then asked me if I had ever heard of Bonefairy Castle. I sat down at Hunter's table and said yes. The castle was just down the road, and that's how we met. You have no idea what Hunter and I have gone through in the last thirty days."

"You're right, we don't, but we would love to hear all about it and your trip," my mom said.

"We wanted to talk to you and Dad to tell you everything that has happened. So much has happened to us, and some of the things that have happened you're not going to believe, but you can't tell anyone," I explained.

"You know you don't have to worry about us saying anything," Dad said.

"I know, but we made a promise not to tell anybody," I informed them.

"It sounds like it was a pretty wild trip," Dad chimed in.

"Mom, Dad, you have no idea."

"So can you tell us where you were at and what you saw?" Dad asked.

"Yes, it was a little town called Harbor, and Bonefairy Castle was just down the road. Izzy showed me the castle, and it had a guard outside it. There was a big, high wall that went all the way around it. The castle was huge and high. You can tell it has been around for many years, but they've kept it up somehow. The first time that we were there, we asked the guard if we could go in, and he let us. But soon after that, we weren't allowed back in anymore. There wasn't anything in the castle; the government had taken everything out of it. Well, at least that's what we thought. Izzy and I took some pictures of Bonefairy Castle and some of the rooms, so we had proof that we were there."

"Hunter, when you were walking around, did you find anything?" Mom asked.

"It was just by accident that we found a secret room," I testified.

"What do you mean, a secret room?" Mom inquired.

"Well, we saw a box on the wall upstairs in Bonefairy Castle and decided to open it. It was a window where you could look down and see the guard shack, but what happened next was when everything started to change," I described.

"What do you mean?" asked Mom.

"When we opened the box and looked down at the guard, we didn't pay any attention to what was happening. The sunshine came through the window and made a beautiful reflection on the wall. That was when we found it," I stated.

"What, Hunter? What'd you find?" Dad asked.

"We found a secret room in Bonefairy Castle. The reflection on the wall was so beautiful that when we touched it, the wall moved and opened up to the secret room. After the sun moved a little bit—or maybe it was a cloud—the reflection disappeared, and the wall closed back up," I described.

"You and Izzy were inside the secret room?" Mom asked.

"Yes, and there were a lot of things still in that room. I guess because no one ever knew about the room to get into it, they couldn't move any of the things out," I realized.

"So what did you find in the room?" Mom asked.

"Well, there were some pictures on the walls, a few stone statues, and chairs with a table. Then we saw a box on the floor. We took the box, put it on the table, and opened it. That was when we saw a scroll of some kind. We looked at it, but it had different writings on it, and we didn't know what it meant. We kept it because we thought nobody knew about it. If they did, it wouldn't be there. We then started moving around some more in the room, and that was when the floor opened up to a stairway leading down some stairs. When we looked down the stairway, we couldn't see the bottom. The same stairway that appeared for us to get into the room had closed up on us. We decided to go down the stairs. When Izzy and I started down the stairs, our body weight made the stairs move, and that is when a door at the bottom opened up for us to get out."

"Wow, Hunter, I guess you and Izzy did have an unusual trip," said Mom.

"I'm just getting started, Mom. Do you remember what Grandpa said? That a few hundred years ago, there was a queen who lived at Bonefairy Castle?" I asked.

"Yes, I remember, but they still have a queen, if I'm not mistaken. Isn't that right, Izzy?" I asked.

Izzy responded, "Yes, but she doesn't live at Bonefairy Castle anymore, and it's not the same queen who lived back then. Well, if it was, she would be several hundred years old by now."

"So what else happened while you were there?" Dad asked.

"We had some trouble with some men in a van. We wanted to set up a meeting with the National Treasury Agency in town, because we found some things that were very valuable. That was when these men in a van grabbed us and took us out to a house outside of town," I stated.

"Oh, wow. Did they do anything to you? Did they hurt you? Why did they do that, Hunter?" Dad asked.

"No, no, they didn't hurt us. The guard who was at Bonefairy Castle called them to let them know if anyone ever went inside the castle," I explained.

"Hunter, I thought you said that they let you go in," Dad said confused.

"Yes, they did the first time. But soon we weren't allowed to go in anymore. The men who were from the National Treasury Agency questioned us for a couple of hours. They thought we had found something or knew something. After the questioning, they finally took us back to our car and let us go. Mom, that was when Izzy and I figured there had to be a reason for those men doing that, so we decided to go back out to the castle. The only problem was we weren't allowed back in, so we waited a day, and then we went back out and climbed over the wall around back and snuck in. Then we met someone, and I can't tell you who it is, because they made us promise that we wouldn't tell anyone about them if they helped us," I divulged.

"Hunter, sounds a little far-fetched. Are you really expecting us to believe all this?" Dad said.

"How would they know if you said anything to us here?" Mom asked.

"I don't know how, but they said they would know," I confirmed.

"Okay, so now that you and Izzy are back home, what's your plan?" Dad asked.

"Izzy and I want to look into starting a small company," I announced.

"What kind of a company, Hunter?" asked Dad.

"We're not sure yet, but it will have to do with some of the things that happened to us when we were at Bonefairy Castle. You still own Grandpa and Grandma's farmland. Is there any chance that you would be willing to sell some of it to us?" I asked.

"Hunter, that land has increased in value and isn't cheap," Dad declared.

"I know but, I wanted to ask anyway," I stated.

"How much of the land do you want?" Dad asked.

"I know there's five hundred acres, so maybe five or ten acres to start. Then it will depend on how the company goes. Izzy and I have some silent investors who have money, and this is how we are able to do this," I shared.

"Well, Hunter, your mom and I will have to talk about it first before we can give you any kind of an answer. We don't do much with the land anymore but lease it out to people, so they can put some crops on it. That can always change. Hunter, do you want to build something on the land?" Dad asked.

"It is possible, but not right away. We have to get the company going first," I explained.

"Hunter, your mother and I will work with you and Izzy and see what we can do. The day may come when you own this land anyway. For now, how about us all go to the dinner table for something to eat? Your mother made a pot roast. That sounds pretty good, don't you think?" Dad suggested.

"I didn't know you were going to make dinner, Mom. Izzy and I were going to stop and get something to eat after we started back home, but I definitely prefer your home cooking," I admitted.

We sat down at the dinner table as Mom brought out the food. After we finished dinner, Izzy and I said that we had better head back.

"Hunter, you and Izzy keep us posted on what's going on," Dad said.

We said our goodbyes and waved as we left.

"So, Izzy, what do you think of my parents?" I asked.

"They're wonderful. I wish I had some," Izzy said.

"I think you do now." I winked.

We drove back to town and arrived just as the sun was going down. We went into my apartment and weren't there but a few minutes when Galaxy appeared.

"Oh, wow, Galaxy. What are you doing here? How'd you know where to find us?" I asked.

"Remember that I'm a fairy—or have you forgotten already? I know everything. I know that you were out to see your parents today and were talking about the things you and Izzy did on your trip to Bonefairy Castle," Galaxy stated.

"Yes, but we didn't say anything about you or the queen," I disclosed.

"Yes, I know. That is why I think that I needed to appear here, and now," Galaxy explained.

"Did we do something wrong or say something that we shouldn't have?" I asked.

"No, Hunter, you didn't. That is why I'm here. The queen wants you to be able to start your company without having any problems, so I will be around for you. Your company will be very successful, and we'll make sure of that. When you told your parents that you had some silent investors, that was very smart. No one needs to know who we are. Now, tomorrow you'll need to start getting your company moving, so we have moved the gold over here and put it where no one can get it."

"What do you mean, Galaxy? How can I get any of it?" I asked.

"We want you to open a bank business account and put in a small amount of money to keep it open. As you need things for your company, your account will grow just as if you were putting money into your account. You found the gold, and there is a lot of it, but it is still our gold, and it will always be our gold. We knew that you were going to find it. We even allowed it to happen, but it is still our gold. Next, you'll need to take the two scrolls that you have, and you'll base your company on what is in them. That is where I will be able to help. But for now, you just got back home, so I'll let you and Izzy relax for a few days before I appear again."

After Galaxy disappeared, I said to Izzy, "Wow, are we ready for all of this?"

"Hunter, I don't have any idea. I'm just as confused as you are, and besides, the queen and Galaxy already know what we are thinking and going to do anyway," Izzy stated.

"I guess I'll open a bank account tomorrow, and we'll go from there."

"Don't we have to know what we're going to call the company before we can open a business account?" Izzy asked.

"Yes, I think you're right," I said.

"So what do you want to call the company?"

"I don't think that's going to matter. We can call it anything and then change the name of the company to something better when we think of something. How about H and I, for Hunter and Izzy?" I suggested.

"Really, Hunter? I like I and H better," she teased.

"The *H* does come before *I*, remember?" I said, laughing.

"Well, not anymore! We'll think of something," Izzy affirmed.

"I've got it. Let's call it Bonefairy Company!" I shouted.

"Oh, Hunter, I love it! That's really what this is all about anyway, right?" Izzy smiled.

CHAPTER 18

Izzy and I decided to call the company Bonefairy Company, and the next day we went to open a bank account. Later that day, after we got back home, Izzy got a phone call from her friend staying in her home. Her friend's name was Victoria, and she was very upset. Victoria told Izzy that someone had broken into the tavern when she was gone. Izzy's place was ransacked. Someone was obviously looking for something. The door that was locked wasn't locked anymore.

Izzy asked Victoria, "Can you tell if anything is missing?"

"No, not that I can see. It seems they were looking for something," Victoria explained.

"Okay, Victoria. Are you okay?" Izzy asked, concerned.

"Yes, I'm okay. I locked the tavern back up and straightened up things as much as I could."

"Thanks, Victoria. I'm glad you are my friend, and I appreciate that you called me to let me know what happened. I'll tell Hunter what happened. We will be coming back sooner than we wanted to now."

After Izzy told me about the break-in, I said, "Maybe we should go back now before we start up the company, to check everything out. I think once the company gets up and running, we'll be busy, and we can't stop and leave for Harbor anytime that we want."

"Okay, let's go back now and see what's happening," Izzy agreed.

We arrived back and were relieved that there was very little damage done. It looked like some kids had broken in, couldn't really find anything, and then left. Now that we were back, we told Victoria that we were going to stay for a while and that she could still stay with us because we were going to be coming and going all the time.

The next day, Izzy and I wanted to do more exploring in Bonefairy

Castle. We had the scrolls with us and headed back to the castle. This time we drove right past the guard's shack and went to the back, where we climbed over the wall. It was a nice day, and we didn't have any problems this time.

After we were back inside Bonefairy Castle and inside the secret room, Galaxy appeared again. "Hunter, I see that you and Izzy came back to the castle again."

"Yes, Galaxy, we had to come back to Izzy's place in town because there was a problem, but it's okay now," I explained.

"I know. The queen wanted you and Izzy to come back, so we made it look like a break-in, knowing that you would come back. We know that you and Izzy want to start your company back in America, but there are a few things here that you need to do and see first. You brought the scrolls back with you, and we are going to make the scrolls open up so you and Izzy will be able to understand what is inside. You need to take the first scroll and open it up now. I'll show you," Galaxy instructed.

I did what Galaxy said and opened up the scroll. All the writings that were written inside before, which didn't make any sense, now changed. I could understand what was written.

"Hunter, do you see the part that says you need to go find Sir Hunter's cabin in the woods?" Galaxy asked.

"Yes, I see it."

"Well, that is the first thing that needs to be done. You and Izzy will know where Sir Hunter's cabin is by using the scroll. You see, there is a map that will lead you to the cabin."

"Wow, this is great. Izzy, do you want to see if we can find it?" I asked.

"Hunter, if Galaxy says that's what we need to do first, then I think we'd better get going. We don't know how long this is going to take, so let's go," Izzy said.

"This is true. The sooner you start, the sooner you'll find the cabin," Galaxy said.

"Well, okay, then. I guess we'd better get going," I replied. Then Galaxy was gone.

We left the castle with the scroll and started to follow the map, which led us toward the forest outside the town of Harbor. As we reached the forest, we could see that there were many different trails going in all different directions. The scroll said to follow the trail that was lined with wildflowers growing down the middle.

"Look, Izzy: there's the trail with wildflowers," I pointed out.

We got out of the car because we had to walk the trail; it wasn't big enough to drive down it. After about an hour of walking, we could see an old cabin that was overgrown with weeds and bushes, and there was also a barn.

"Izzy, I bet that's where Sir Hunter lived."

"Well, it looks pretty bad, if you ask me."

"I know, but back when Sir Hunter was around, I bet it was kind of cool to live out here. Let's see if we can push open this door and get inside," I suggested.

"Why? It's just an old cabin that hasn't been lived in."

"Izzy, remember what Galaxy said about us needing to find the cabin. Well, there must be a reason, so let's go inside and find the reason."

I pushed the door open, and the inside almost looked as bad as the outside, with a lot of weeds growing up through the floor.

"Hunter, I don't want to say anything, but there's nothing here, just an old cabin," Izzy announced.

"Let's look around a little. Galaxy said that we needed to do this. Look what's that over there in the corner."

"It's just a big cedar chest," Izzy said.

"Well, I want to look inside, and then we can go." I tried to open it, but it wouldn't budge. "Izzy, I think we may have to break it open somehow. Look, there's an old iron rod in the fireplace. That should work."

"Okay, I'll get it," Izzy offered.

"It shouldn't take much to bust it open," I said.

Izzy handed me the iron rod, and I hit the latch on the chest.

"Look, Izzy: I bet this stuff inside here is what Galaxy wanted us to find."

"Looks like some old tools and clothes to me," Izzy said.

"Well, see if the scroll says anything about it," I asked.

"The scroll says to take a piece of clothing," Izzy said while reading from the scroll.

I frowned. "I don't understand. We came all the way out here for a piece of clothing?"

"Well, just grab something, and let's get out of here, Hunter. I'm getting hungry," Izzy pleaded.

"All right, I've got something, so let's go." I looked around once more as we left the cabin. "Can you imagine living here?"

"No, not really, Hunter. I'll take my place over this anytime," Izzy confessed.

"Okay, well, let's go to your place," I suggested.

We started back down the trail toward town when Galaxy appeared.

"Galaxy, what are you doing here?" I asked.

"Hunter, the scroll wanted you and Izzy to go to the cabin to look around, and you did, but not enough. You looked in the cabin but not in the barn," Galaxy stated.

"No, Galaxy, we didn't. We didn't think that there was anything in the barn to find," I replied.

"Well, please go back to the barn and then look at the map you found in the cave. There is something that you need to find in the barn," Galaxy instructed.

Izzy and I glanced at each other with puzzled looks. We agreed to return to the barn, and Galaxy was gone. When we got back to the barn, it looked like it was in worse shape than the cabin.

"Hunter, what can be in the barn? It looks like it is about to fall down."

"I know, but Galaxy knows more about it and wants us to go inside," I reiterated.

"All right, but we need to be careful."

"Let's go over there, where the light is better. Maybe when we look at the map, it will tell us something." I read the map. "Okay, there is the barn, and the map's saying to go to the middle horse stall and dig."

"What for, Hunter?" Izzy asked.

"I don't know. Let's do a little digging and see what we find."

I looked around for a shovel or something to dig with. I found an old rusted spade that was covered with dirt. I kicked some of the dirt off and then thought to myself, *What does it matter? I'll be digging in dirt anyway.* I started to dig, and after getting down about five feet, I hit some wood.

"Look, Izzy," I exclaimed.

"What is it, Hunter?"

"I'm not sure. I need to dig a little bit more. It looks like there are some hinges on a door," I explained.

"A door?" she asked.

"Yes. Wait just a second. Let me get some of the dirt out of the way. Yes, it's a door with a chain on it," I described.

"How are we going to get the chain off?" Izzy asked.

"I'm not sure. Maybe we can bust the door open," I suggested.

"There is a chain, but there's no lock or anything on it," Izzy stated.

"Okay, let me take off the chain. There, now let's see if I can open it. The door was very heavy, so we both had to pull it open.

"Wow, I can't believe it. There's a stairway going into the ground," I said, surprised.

"Hunter, I don't like this. We don't have any idea where it goes," Izzy said with concern.

"I know, but remember Galaxy told us about this, knows what's here, and wants us to find it. Give me the flashlight in my backpack, and I will go down a little way and look," I offered.

Izzy got the flashlight and gave it to me. The stairway went down about twenty steps, and then there was another door.

"Izzy, there's another door down here," I yelled back up.

"Can you open it?" Izzy asked.

"I think so. There's nothing but a door. I'll try. Yes, I got it to open," I explained.

"What do you see?"

"There's a cave down here. Come on down and bring another flashlight with you," I instructed.

Izzy got her flashlight and walked down the stairs.

"Hunter, I can't believe it. I bet nobody even knows about this cave," she stated.

"Yeah, nobody but Galaxy."

"Yeah, but what's down here?"

"Galaxy wanted us to find this, so let's look around and see what we find," I suggested.

"What then?"

"I don't know, but what I do know is that my ancestors lived here, and I bet that he was told to build this barn over this cave so nobody would know about it. Sir Hunter came here when he could get the time away from the queen, and he built his cabin and barn. There has to be a reason for doing this, don't you think?"

"Well, yes, I guess so," Izzy stated.

"Let's look around and see what we find," I suggested.

"Hunter, I'm not sure about all this."

"It looks like there's a river over here. I wonder where that will take us?"

"We can't go down that river. We have no way of doing that," Izzy said, confused.

"I know, but if we did have something, we could, right? It has to go somewhere. Let's look at the map and see what the map says," I suggested.

"I'm not going down this river unless we go back in town and get a blow-up raft," Izzy decided.

"I think you're right. Let's stop and go back in town to get something to eat. Then we can buy a raft and come back out here tomorrow. I know we will need some things before we take on this river."

"All right, cool. I'm starving, so let's go," Izzy pleaded.

We left the barn and went back into town to the tavern. Victoria was making a pot of soup and asked if we wanted some.

"Victoria, the soup smells great. Yes, we would both love to have a bowl," Izzy said.

Victoria asked, "What have you guys been doing all day?"

"Izzy and I have been trying to learn a little more about my ancestors, and we have been reading a couple of scrolls and a map that we found at Bonefairy Castle. The scroll said for us to go back into the woods outside of town. That's why we look the way we do," I commented.

"What are you talking about? You're not making any sense. May I make a suggestion, Hunter? You both need to go get cleaned up and at least wash before I give you some soup," Victoria teased.

"Okay, Victoria," I said.

Victoria smiled. "Go on, get going. I'll get the soup."

We went upstairs to wash up. A few minutes later, we came back down.

"Okay, sit down, and be careful—it's a little hot," Victoria warned.

"The soup tastes great, and we really needed this," Izzy said.

"Well, you guys look like you've been crawling around under some rocks with all that dirt on you," Victoria noted.

"You really have no idea," I replied.

"So what's this all about a scroll you found?" Victoria asked.

"Well, we really can't tell you a whole lot. First, we were told not to, and second, you wouldn't believe us or understand anyway," I replied.

"That probably is best," Victoria said.

We finished eating our soup and turned in early. We had a full day planned for tomorrow. The following day couldn't come soon enough. We got up early and went straight to a sporting goods store to buy a blow-up raft and a pump. As we were leaving the store, we ran into one of the men who had held us at the house for questioning. We didn't say anything, but we did recognize them. We bought what we needed at the store, got into our car, and left. I watched in my rearview mirror as I drove away to make sure that we weren't going to be followed, and then I drove out of town to where the trails started. I remembered the trail wasn't big enough to drive on, so we would have to carry the raft to the barn, down the stairs, and through the cave to the river.

Once back at the barn, we made sure that we weren't followed and went straight to the stairs in the ground. We walked down to the cave with the raft, and I used the pump to blow up the raft. The raft was big enough for about four people and some equipment. The current in the river wasn't bad, so we were able to get everything in the raft and move out without any problems. We started down the river and followed the map. The river kept going, and after what about a mile, it opened up into a large lake.

"Hunter, where are we?" Izzy asked.

"The map says that there will be a lake, and here it is. The map is saying to cross the lake and adds that there is another cave on the other side somewhere."

"I wonder if anyone even knows about this lake?"

"Well, I bet Sir Hunter did," I claimed.

We paddled on the raft to the other side of the lake, and as we got closer, I could see what looked like the opening to another cave.

"Hunter, I had no idea that there were so many caves around here," Izzy said.

"Well, I love it. This is great, and who knows what we will find?"

"I think we have been a little lucky that we haven't had any problems."

"I don't think that is going to happen because nobody even knows about this place," I concluded.

Izzy turned around and looked at me because I was sitting behind her in the raft. Then she saw a couple of men on the other side of the lake.

"Hunter, look! We've been followed. Those are the men who were at the sporting goods store. They must have followed us," Izzy said.

"Come on. We have to move faster. We're almost there. Paddle, Izzy, hurry! We've got a little time before they'll get here, so let's hide our stuff so they can't find it. Then we will watch and see what they do. You were saying that we didn't have any problems, but I think we just got some."

"Sorry, I didn't mean to jinx us," Izzy said.

"There's no way those men can know what we know. They are waiting to see what we find and then will take it away from us," I stated.

"Well, we have Galaxy on our side, and that should make a big difference. When we get to shore and hide our stuff, I think that Galaxy will keep us safe. At least, I hope so," Izzy prayed.

"Okay, we're just about there. Be ready to hop out," I said. We were coming up the edge of the river. "All right, Izzy, hurry! We have to move."

"Hunter, what if those men find us?" Izzy asked.

"I don't know. Let's just get out of here. Let's put our equipment and the map over here, behind those trees, and cover them up. They'll never look over there," I suggested.

"All right, and what do we do then?" Izzy inquired.

"I think that we shouldn't go into the cave right now, because we don't know where it goes or what we will run into."

"That works for me. We don't need any more surprises," Izzy concurred.

"They'll be here in a little bit. We can hide and watch to see what they're going to do. Izzy, you know that those men may know everything we know and simply may be doing something that they were going to do all along. We just happened to stumble across them by accident," I said.

"Well, I'm not going to stay around and ask them, so let's get out of here and watch," Izzy replied.

The men were just now getting to shore and really didn't look like they knew we were even here. They did know about the cave, because they went right in without any hesitation.

"Look, Izzy. I bet they think we went into the cave, and that is why they went right in. Let's give them a minute to get in there, and then we can get closer and check it out. If they find us, we can say that we are exploring the cave and didn't know they were here. They don't know that we have a map," I said.

"What if they get mad and mean? We may be running into something that they don't want anyone to know about," Izzy said.

"That's possible. We'll have to wait and see."

"Look over there. There they are."

"Yes, I see them. Get down," I urged.

"What are they doing?" Izzy asked.

"It looks like they are looking for something."

"Yeah, I think you're right."

"They have to have been here before. This cave is a perfect place to keep something, or hide something so no one would ever find it. Here they come. Get down," I ordered.

The men left the cave and looked like they were leaving.

"Hunter, I can't believe that they didn't see us," Izzy said.

"Well, they didn't know that we were here, so that may have helped. Let's give them some time to leave and make sure that they are gone before we do anything," I suggested.

"We don't even have any weapons of any kind."

"Let's make sure they are gone. We'll be all right," I stated. Some time passed. "I'm going to check to see if they are back out of the cave yet. Yeah, there they go."

"I wonder what they were doing in there?" Izzy asked.

"I don't know, but let's get our stuff, and then we can check it out. It's not likely that they'll be back anytime soon," I suggested.

CHAPTER 19

W e had the map and the scrolls, and we knew that the cave was
going to tell us something. Now that the men had left, it was
time to get back to thinking about why we were there.

"Izzy, we really need to look closer at the map. I know that it tells
us about this cave, but there has to be a reason for us to be here," I
commented.

"I know, but how are we going to be able to figure the map out
without some help?"

"We'll figure it out somehow, so let's take the map inside the cave
and try that way. There are pictures on the map, and maybe we can
recognize some of them in the cave."

We went in the cave and started looking around.

"Look, Izzy, over here. There's a panel box with a lever on it," I
pointed out.

"Pull it down and let's see what happens," Izzy suggested.

I pulled the lever down. "Okay, wow. There are lights in here. Izzy,
those men have been here and must have done all this. There's also a
generator, so that's how they get the lights," I said.

"Well, now we can see the map better, and also the cave," Izzy
stated.

"Yeah, a lot better. Look how big it is in here. Okay, let's look at
the map. You see, it looks just like the inside of the cave, and it says that
there's a secret tunnel over behind all those big rocks," I said.

"How are we going to move all those rocks to find the tunnel?"
Izzy asked.

"I don't know. I bet those men doesn't know about the tunnel either, or they would have equipment in here already. There's got to be some way to do it. Where's Galaxy when we need her?"

"The next time Galaxy shows up, we need to ask her what we have to do for her to show up when we need her," she said.

"Izzy, Galaxy usually knows when we want her," I said.

"Well, why isn't she here? I think now would be a great time, don't you?"

"Yes, it would. Okay, Galaxy, where are you at? We need to talk to you," I requested.

Galaxy appeared. "Yes, Hunter, I know what you want to ask. I cannot tell you. I am not allowed to, but I am allowed to give you clues. The clues are in the scrolls that you have brought with you, and you need to look there for the answers." Then she disappeared.

I said, "Ugh! I can't believe she keeps doing that. It looks like we're going to have to figure out the clues ourselves. Galaxy knows what's happening and can help us only when we really it, I guess. Where are the scrolls? Bring them over here where the light is better."

"We don't even know what we are looking for," Izzy stated.

"I know, but it must have something to do with this cave, right? The map says that there is a tunnel behind those big rocks, so let's see what the scrolls say about it. Galaxy said the clues are in the scrolls. I think we need to look at both of them together."

"Okay, so let's take the scrolls over by those big rocks, because that's where the map says there is a tunnel. We can spread the scrolls out on the rocks," Izzy suggested.

"That sounds like a good idea. I'm willing to try anything at this point. Okay, spread the scrolls, and let's see what happens. Hold the end of the two scrolls together. I'll pull out the scrolls."

"Look! When you put the two scrolls together here on these rocks, and the lights hit them, it shows that there's a reflection just like back at Bonefairy Castle. Remember the reflection at the castle, when we found the reflection on the wall and pushed on it? It opened up that secret wall with the other room in it," Izzy said.

"Yes, I remember, so let's look at the reflection here and start pushing on the rocks," I suggested.

"Right, I'll start over here. Those men didn't even know what was here when they were here."

"Well, we don't either until we can get these rocks moved out of the way. Look at the reflection: it looks like there's a head of a dragon right now on the rocks," I noticed.

"You're right, Hunter. I see it. The eye on the dragon is red and looks different," Izzy agreed.

"Well let's push on the eye and see if anything happens," I suggested.

"Right, here goes! Hunter, look! That big rock over there just rolled and opened up the tunnel we are looking for. What do we do now?" Izzy asked.

"Do you need to ask? I'm going down the tunnel way and see where it leads. Are you coming?"

"I'm scared, but I'm right behind you."

"Okay, good. Bring the map and the scrolls, and I'll get our flashlights," I said.

"What happens if we get stuck down here?" Izzy asked, concerned.

"Remember that Galaxy knows where we are and what everything we are doing. I'm sure that what we are doing is just what we are supposed to be doing. Even if we never get out of here, we have each other," I said teasingly.

"Hunter, please! What are you saying?" Izzy shouted.

"Nothing, Izzy. Let's go."

We started down the tunnel about fifty feet and went down a couple of steps. The rock rolled back and closed the opening to the tunnel.

"The rock rolled back," Izzy announced.

"Just stay close to me. We'll be all right," I comforted her.

"It would be really nice if you knew what you were talking about," Izzy replied.

"What do you want me to say? That we are stuck under a rock? We can't do anything about it, so let's keep moving forward. Bring the map over here, and let's see if it says anything about this tunnel," I suggested. Izzy brought the map over to me. "Look, here is the cave and the tunnel, and it looks like there is another way out of here."

"Well, that makes me feel better. Even if we are going to spend the rest of our lives together, I'm glad it is not down here," Izzy declared.

"What are *you* saying, Izzy?" I stated.

"I'm just saying that if we get mad at each other, I wouldn't be able to say, 'Get out,' but now that we know that there's a way out, everything's cool," Izzy said with a nervous laugh.

Izzy and I followed the map to where it showed the other way out, and Galaxy was waiting there.

"Galaxy, it would be nice if you could have told us that there was another way out of the cave," I grumbled.

"Hunter, I keep telling you that I can't help you or tell you anything other than clues. You must figure everything out yourselves, remember?"

"Yeah, yeah I know. That's getting old. So now what do we do, Galaxy?" I asked.

"The map, Hunter. Keep following the map," Galaxy said.

"Why are we following the map? Oh, yes, I forgot—you can't tell us. Let's just see where it takes us. There's got to be a reason," I concluded. I turned around to look at Galaxy, but she was gone.

We were out of the cave and came up to what looked like was a trail going into some woods.

"Well, this is much better now that we're out of that cave, I must say. Does the map show the woods up ahead there?" Izzy asked.

"Actually, it does."

"So now what do we do?"

"I guess keep moving down the trail to see where it goes," I instructed.

"Does the map show anything at the end that we are supposed to see or find?" Izzy asked.

"The map just keeps going like there isn't any end to it," I explained.

We walked to the woods and stood there for a minute.

"What if something scary or alive is in those woods?" Izzy asked.

"I doubt there is anything in there. Let's start walking through and see where it takes us," I said.

Time passed as we walked through the woods. We finally came to the other side of the woods, and it opened up into a field. We could see Bonefairy Castle in the distance.

"Hunter, do you know where we are?" Izzy asked.

"I think I do. If Bonefairy Castle is there, then the town has to be over there to the left of us," I stated.

"I don't understand what's going on. Galaxy said that there were clues that we need to follow so we could find whatever we are supposed to find, but we don't know what that is. I think we should just be glad that we know where we are for now, call it a day, and head back toward town," Izzy said.

"We can take a little time and figure out everything that has happened Maybe look at the map some more. I know we can figure out the clues," I suggested.

"We haven't had anything to eat, and I'm getting hungry, so let's stop for today and get some rest, okay?" Izzy pleaded.

"All right, Izzy. We have been going at this pretty hard ever since we got back. It's not going anywhere, so let's head for home," I agreed.

CHAPTER 20

Izzy and I took our time and walked back toward town. We needed to think about everything that had happened to us over the past few weeks. After reaching town and being back at the tavern, it was time for some rest and good food. Victoria was there and had just come back from buying some food and putting away a few things when we arrived.

"Hi, guys. You look like you have been playing in a dirt pile again," Victoria said.

"I think we have. What a day we've had, and right now we are starving," Izzy confirmed.

"All right, well, let's see what we can cook up in the next few minutes. I'll do that while you guys go get changed and washed up," Victoria offered.

"Thanks, Victoria. That works for us. See you in a few minutes, but don't get carried away; we just want a sandwich and maybe some soup. That will be good enough," Izzy stated.

After some hot soup and a sandwich, we decided to get a little rest before talking about what had happened. Victoria said that she would clean up and for us to not worry about the mess.

After about an hour of rest, Izzy and I wanted to talk a little and look at the map and scrolls again.

"Hunter, we really didn't find anything back in that last cave that we were in, and I don't understand why we were even there," Izzy said.

"Izzy, Galaxy said that we needed to follow the map so we could find something that was important," I clarified.

"I know, but we didn't find anything," Izzy declared.

"That doesn't mean that there isn't something there. I really think that we are going to have to go back to try again."

"What if those men come back again?" she said with a concerned look.

"I think if we go back where we were when we came out of the cave, we will be better off and can continue from that point."

"All right, but let's look at the map some more and see if we can figure out any more cluses," Izzy said.

"Okay, look, here's where we came out of the cave. There's the woods, and the trail that winds around. I think if we go back to that trail, we won't run into those men again," I recommended.

"What does the scroll say?" Izzy asked.

"The scroll says that there was a dragon back in the first cave that we were in, right?" I replied.

"Yes, and we found all that gold and stones, right?"

"We know the map says we are to go down through the barn out by Sir Hunter's cabin, across the lake, and through the cave. We have done that, but we didn't keep following it, so I guess that's what we need to do. Let's go back and follow it to see where it will take us," I suggested.

"But we have done everything already," Izzy said, confused.

"Galaxy said that we need to do this, so I'm going to do it!" I proclaimed.

The next day, Izzy and I went back to the place that we were last at.

"All right, Hunter, we're here. Now what?"

"Let's follow the trail. I'm sure we'll find something. At least it's a nice day for a walk," I said with a smile.

I started down the trail as it wound back and forth. Then all of the sudden, we saw a large rock that was in the shape of the head of a dragon. It looked like it was another cave of some sort, and the mouth of the dragon was an entrance.

"Hunter, look over there!" Izzy shouted.

"Wow! I don't believe it. There are some vines covering the head of the dragon, but I think that if we cut a few of them, we will be able to go into the head through the mouth. Come on, help me."

"This is so cool."

We pulled and cut away some of the vines, and then we entered the head of the dragon through the mouth. It was much bigger on this inside compared to how it looked on the outside. After we got inside the head, we walked up to the center, which looked like a very large nest. Right in the middle was a large egg covered with mud.

"It looks like some kind of an egg," Izzy stated.

"Yes, I know, but what kind? Maybe this is what Galaxy wanted us to find," I concluded.

"Why would Galaxy want us to find this egg?"

"I have no idea."

"Okay, now that we have found this egg, what are we going to do with it?" Izzy asked.

"I'm not sure. I wonder how long it's been here? Let's take it back with us and see what we can figure out," I suggested.

"Do you think you can carry the egg? It looks a little heavy!"

"This has to be the largest egg I've ever seen."

"Well, what are we going to do with it?"

"I think Galaxy may know something, so we'll ask," I recommended.

"We should cover the egg back up, go back home, and get a wagon so we can get the egg and not damage it. If we try to carry it and drop it, then we don't have anything," Izzy suggested.

"Yeah, I think that is probably a good idea. Let's go," I admitted.

I covered the egg back up with mud the best I could, and we headed back to town to get a wagon. Once back in town, we went to the store to buy a wagon and that is when we saw the men again that were in the cave.

The men came over to talk to us. One of the men asked, "What are you two doing, and where are you going with that wagon?"

"Why don't you leave us alone? We're not doing anything," I said.

"We just need to make sure you're not doing anything. You two have been under suspicion for some time now," the man said.

"Hey, we just have some wood to move that was behind the tavern, not that it is any of your business," Izzy said.

"Okay, well, we will be keeping our eye on you," the man replied.

I was getting angry about all this. We got the wagon and left.

"Izzy, we should wait until the tomorrow before we go back, just in case the men are around," I said. I put the wagon behind the tavern and out of sight, and then went inside the tavern for a beer.

Once inside, Izzy said, "I think those men are going to be a problem. They have been watching every move we've made."

"Yes, I know, but they don't know what we're doing, and that is why they're watching," I commented.

"Okay, I agree. So we need to make a plan on what we're going to do with the egg once we have it," Izzy suggested.

"Well, I think that once we have the egg, we're going to have to hide it so no one knows we have it. Then we contact the right people who may know about eggs. Maybe if we look for a person who knows about prehistoric things, that will help. Maybe at a college? There should be someone there who can help us, or at least point us in the right direction, don't you think?" I offered.

"I guess so, but first we have to get the egg without anyone knowing about it," Izzy reiterated.

"I know. We simply have to be careful with the egg and then do our homework. I'm going to have another beer. Then we can figure out how we're going to do this stuff tomorrow. I think that once we get back to that egg, I'm going to ask for Galaxy to help us. Galaxy has always been true to us and has helped us make the right moves, so if we talk to Galaxy, we should be okay," I recommended.

"I'm not convinced that Galaxy will help us, but if you say so. All she keeps saying is we have to figure it out ourselves. But all right, Hunter, if that's the plan. Here's your beer. I'm going to get a few things done before going to bed. I think we're going to have a pretty big day tomorrow, so I want to get some rest."

"Thanks, Izzy. You've been with me through all this crazy stuff ever since we met. I don't know how I'd be able to do the things that we've done so far, if I hadn't met you that first day," I said.

Izzy smiled. "You're right—you are lucky, and now you can't get rid of me."

I looked up from his beer with a smile and said, "Good night, Izzy."

The next morning, Victoria was up early and had breakfast just about ready when we came down.

"Good morning, Victoria. Something smells good," I announced.

"Thanks, Hunter. You and Izzy get washed up, and I'll bring the food over for you guys. It looks like it's going to be a nice day, and you guys are going to need a good breakfast with how busy you're going to be," Victoria replied.

"Yeah, you're probably right," I answered.

After breakfast, Izzy and I started putting a few things in the wagon for the trip back to get the egg.

"Izzy, do you have an extra old blanket we can take with us so we can cover the egg up, and no one will be able to see it?" I asked.

"No, I don't, but there are a couple of old tarps out back that are used to cover the wood piles. Those will work, I think," Izzy offered.

"Okay, great. Yeah, that's probably better anyway," I replied.

"I'll grab one of those."

"Victoria, breakfast was great and did the job. Izzy and I want to thank you for all the trouble you went through," I complimented.

"No problem, Hunter. You and Izzy need to be careful going after that egg today. Watch out for any problems," Victoria stated.

"Thanks, Victoria, we will."

We went out the back door to where the wagon was. I thought it might be a good idea if we used a horse to help us pull the wagon.

"Izzy, do you know where we can get a horse?" I asked.

"No, not really, but I know where we can get a four-wheeler that I can borrow. They're friends of mine. Will that work?" Izzy offered.

"Yeah, that's even better. Let's give your friends a call and see if it's all right to use it for the day," I concurred.

"Hunter, I know it's okay. I've used it before, and they hardly use it anymore," Izzy replied.

"Okay, cool. Why don't you go see if you can use it? I'll finish folding up one of the tarps."

"I'll be right back. We'll probably have to stop and get gas so we don't run out today."

"Good idea, Izzy. See you in a little bit. I'm going to go back inside and see if Victoria has anything that we can make a sandwich out of, so we have something for later."

Izzy left to get the four-wheeler while I finished getting a few things ready for the day.

Back in town, Izzy ran into the men she was worried about. They drove their car right up to where she was, got out, and started asking questions about where I was. Izzy really didn't want anything to do with the men and tried to leave without talking to them. Izzy was afraid to even go after the four-wheeler because she knew they would be watching, and that would create be more trouble. She simply went to her friends' house and stayed there for a while, and talked to them about borrowing the four-wheeler. She then called me to tell me that the men were outside, and she thought that she had better stay where she was for a little bit until the men left. I agreed and went on with what I was doing until Izzy could return.

It wasn't long until Izzy showed up with the four-wheeler, and I hooked it up to the wagon. Then we were off. Knowing that at any time the men could show up, we took our time, making sure that we weren't followed.

We finally made it back to where the egg was, and we had to figure out how to get it loaded.

"Hunter, how are we going to get the egg on the wagon?" Izzy asked.

"Well, I believe that we will figure that out somehow, and I think I know what we can do. Let's dig a hole right in front of the egg. Make the hole big enough that we can back the wagon down in the hole and still be able to get the wagon back out once we have the egg loaded on the wagon. We simply have to be smart about this. After we get the wagon backed into the hole, we can start to dig under the egg and around it a little, until the egg rolls on to the wagon."

"That's a great idea. I didn't realize you were that smart," Izzy teased.

I laughed. "Izzy, it just came to me, and it does make for a good idea, doesn't it?"

"It does sound like a great idea, and besides, what other plans do we have?" Izzy commented.

"Right, so let's get the shovels out and start digging in front of the egg. It looks like the egg will just fit on the wagon. We need to get the wagon unloaded so when we are ready, we can back the wagon into the hole."

About two hours passed and the hole was finally big enough for the wagon to be backed in.

"Izzy, can you try to back the wagon in the hole, and I'll watch?" I asked.

"Sure, no problem," Izzy replied.

Izzy got in and started to back up.

"Okay, nice and easy. Not so fast," I stated.

Izzy kept backing up slowly.

"Okay, stop there. Let me dig around the egg a little and move some of the dirt."

I dug a little more of the dirt and moved it out of the way to make the hole bigger. It was hard to tell how much I had to dig without the wagon being closer to the egg.

"All right, Izzy, back the wagon up a little bit more."

Izzy did so.

"Okay, stop! I've got to dig a little bit more right here, and then I think you can back up almost right under it. It's not going to take much once we get the wagon in place." I began digging some more. "Okay, back up a little more," I instructed.

Izzy backed up a few inches.

"That's good. Now, if I dig a little bit here, maybe the egg will start to move."

"Easy, Hunter, and be careful," Izzy said.

"Just keep the wagon backed up as close as you can, because once the egg starts to move, I think we'll be fine. All right, here it comes. It's starting to move. Now back up—hurry, quick, Izzy!"

Izzy backed up, and the egg rolled right on to the wagon.

"Yes, yes! Izzy, we did it!. We got it on the wagon. Wow! I don't believe we did it. That was close, but I think we're okay. All right, Izzy, go ahead and pull the wagon back out of the hole."

"Hunter, you are so lucky when it comes to getting things done," Izzy complimented.

"I just try to use a little common sense. And besides, I wouldn't have been able to do it if you weren't here helping me with the wagon. Let's take a break and eat a sandwich that Victoria made us before we do anything else."

"Sounds like a good idea. I'm getting hungry, anyway," Izzy stated.

"You're always hungry," I said.

"I can't help it. All this adrenaline burns it off, so I get hungry again."

"Yeah, I know what you mean. All of this is so exciting. My adrenaline is very high too," I agreed.

After we finished our sandwich, it was time to load the wagon back up and cover the egg so no one would be able to see it.

"Izzy, I think we have everything now, so let's get out of here before we encounter any issues," I said.

"Once we get back to the house, we will have to think about what we're going to do with the egg and how to hide it," Izzy suggested.

"I think I know what we can do with the egg, and nobody will ever know about it. We can take it back out to the cabin, put it in the barn, and cover it up under with some tarps until we decide what we are going to do with it."

CHAPTER 21

W e secured the egg.

"Izzy, I think that we need to think about what we're going to do going forward," I said.

"What do you mean?" she asked.

"I think we need to ask about the cabin and the land that it's on, and see if my ancestors still own it before we get too far ahead of what we're doing," I suggested.

"Well, as far as I know, we'll have to go to the county and look up some of the records there."

"So, where's the county office?"

"I'm not sure. I haven't ever had to go there for anything."

"Okay, well, we'll find it. We can go there tomorrow, if that's all right," I stated.

"Sure, we can do that," Izzy responded.

We arrived at the county office the next morning.

"Hello, is this where a person comes to find out about land and who owns it, or if it is for sale?" I asked.

"Yes. What piece of land are you interested in?" the county clerk replied.

"Is there a map that I can look up the location to get the exact area?" I asked.

"There's a room over there with all the maps and descriptions of all properties. If you can tell me where it is, I can help you look for it," the county clerk explained.

"I was told by my family that my ancestors owned some land hundreds of years ago," I described. I tried to give the clerk as much as I know of where the land was. It took a little while, but the county clerk found the right map and told us that the government owned it now because there were taxes placed on the land, and no one ever paid.

"If I paid the taxes, would I be able to get the land back?" I asked.

The clerk looked up the records and found that I was related, and it would still be my ancestors' land if the taxes had been paid with everything brought up to date. I told the clerk that I would come back in a few days.

Izzy and I left the county office and drove back to Izzy's tavern to talk and make plans to get the money for the land. I was very excited and knew that with all the gold and precious stones that we had found in the cave, we'd be able the get the land back and in good standing. It would take a little doing to get money in exchange for the gold and precious stones, but I knew that there was enough to get the job done.

We did just that. We exchanged what needed and went back to the county office to do all the paperwork and get the land put in my name. While we were there, I asked the county clerk just how much land my ancestors had back then, and how much it would be worth today. The county clerk checked the records and told me that if I paid the back taxes that were owed, which was nearly $1.5 million, I would own 750 acres. I was very excited, and so was Izzy, as we paid the money and gathered all the paperwork proving that I owned it and could do whatever I wanted with the land. The county clerk gave me a map so I could see exactly what the land looked like and what the zoning was. According to the map, there was a small cabin on it, along with a lake and a mountain, but nothing else. I could see where the cabin was because I had been there with Izzy, along with the lake and the mountain. It was starting to fall into place and make sense with everything that we had been through. The map also showed that right next to the land that I now owned was the land of Bonefairy Castle.

We were so excited when we left the county office that we wanted to go back to the tavern to celebrate.

I said, "Izzy, I don't believe what has happened. I have the land back that my ancestors once owned! This is so fantastic, and I just can't believe it."

"Well, sit yourself down, and I'll get us a couple of beers," Izzy offered.

"Do you know what all this could mean to us?"

"What do you mean when you say *us*?" Izzy asked.

"I know that I now own that land, but none of this would have happened if it wasn't for you showing me everything and helping me, so you are a part of this as far as I'm concerned," I explained.

"Then we will have to do some more talking about all this later, but for now let's drink some beers and celebrate. This is a day I'll remember for the rest of my life," Izzy replied.

As the day continued and so did the beers, it wasn't long before we had too much to drink, but the celebrating was coming to an end. Izzy told me that she had to stop drinking and lie down for a while.

"I think that's a good idea, with all the excitement. I think I'm going to do the same thing," I declared.

The next day, things were moving kind of slow, but I wanted to go back out to the cabin and do some more looking around. Izzy had a few things to do around the tavern and told me to go ahead; she'd be out later. I agreed and left for the cabin. Once I was back out at the cabin, I went straight to the barn to make sure that the egg was still there, and it was. Then I cleaned up the cabin because it was bad inside, with old stuff and dirty things that had been there for so long. I needed to do a good cleaning so Izzy wouldn't mind staying here if I asked her. I had to do some repairs on the roof, where a tree had fallen and created a hole. It was going to take a while to get the cabin back in good shape, but it was a place where I wanted to be able to stay because I owned it now.

I started taking all the old things that were left long ago and going through everything. I took out things that needed to be burned or thrown away. It didn't take very long to empty out the cabin because it had just the one room. I built a fire in the fireplace and started throwing things into it to burn, along with anything that wasn't wanted. There wasn't any electricity in the cabin, just one small room with a fireplace and table. I wanted to get a bed and maybe a small dresser. I needed to get electricity installed and be able to close up the place with a lock on the front door. There were several old pots that were used in the past for cooking, and some could still be used for boiling water when a fire was in the fireplace.

A few hours passed before Izzy showed up and saw what I was

trying to do with the cabin. "Wow, Hunter, you've been busy. Can I help?" she inquired.

"Anything you can do or want to do is more than helpful. I wanted to clean up the place and make it livable again. I'm going to get a generator when I go back into town so we can have some lights until I can get some electric installed. I think once it's all cleaned up, and with some lights and a bed, it won't be so bad to stay here once in a while, instead of always having to go back to town all the time. I have this hole in the roof that needs fixing, but that shouldn't take very long. Then once everything is repaired, I can start thinking about other things. I checked on the egg when I came out this morning, and everything is good."

"So what are you going to do with the egg?"

"Well, I want to talk to someone who knows a little bit more about what kind of egg it is before I make any decisions."

"We don't even know if it's real, do we?"

I said, "If you remember, Galaxy is the one who wanted us to find it, so there has to be a reason."

"That's true enough. And if it is real, then what?" Izzy asked.

"You're asking things that I don't have an answer to. When we get back into town, I'll make some calls and see if I can get any answers to our questions," I stated.

"We don't even know how old the egg is," Izzy replied.

"All I know about eggs is that you either eat them or hatch them, and that is way too much to eat."

"That's gross. I don't even want to think of that. So I guess we're going to hatch it?" Izzy inquired.

"Maybe the reason it never hatched was because it was cold. Eggs need to be warm to hatch, if I remember right. That's why you always see the eggs covered up by whatever laid them."

"So are you telling me that if we cover up the egg and keep it warm, it could hatch?" Izzy asked.

"Well, maybe. I don't know."

"We don't even know what it is inside the egg," Izzy pointed out.

"Whatever comes out of that egg is going to be big, and I don't think I want to be around when it happens," I declared.

"You can stay and be its mama," Izzy teased.

"Izzy, let's not go jumping to conclusions. We don't know anything for sure right now," I clarified.

"I know, but I'm just saying."

"Okay, let's finish what we're doing and then go out to the barn to do a few things out there. There's so much that has happened since I've met you, and so many things we've been through. I can't even imagine what else could happen in the next few weeks," I said.

"I know, Hunter. It's been pretty wild for me too. So what do you want to do here in the barn?" Izzy inquired.

"I think we should hide the egg better until we can ask someone what we should do with it. Then we can clean up some of the horse stalls. I wouldn't mind having a few horses out here, because we have all this land now."

"What are you talking about?"

"This cabin and land are ours, or should I say mine, and this really changes a few things. We really don't need to go back to America for a while, or at all. We have money to live on, and you have the tavern. With this cabin and land, I think that we should try to do something here and go back to America only to visit once in a while," I said.

"Okay, well for now, let's clean a little here, hide the egg, and go back to town to do some planning," Izzy responded.

"I really want to do something out here, Izzy!"

"I know, and I think with the right plan, the sky is the limit, right?"

"Right. Hey, I think that maybe a big tractor would fit over there in the corner. What do you think?"

"If we are going to be out here, we probably will need a tractor," Izzy agreed.

"Well, all right then. We'll get a tractor!" I shouted. "Come on. let's finish up here and head for town, or the tavern. I could use a beer and a sandwich."

I closed the barn doors and locked them so no one could simply walk in, and I did the same with the cabin.

"There, that should do it until I can get something better. I just can't get everything done as fast as I'd like," I stated.

"I know, but we have plenty of time. Maybe we should think about getting someone to help us!" Izzy recommended.

"You know, that's not a bad idea. Do you know anybody?" I asked.

"No, not really, but we can ask around in town when we back, if you want," she offered.

"There's something else that I think we should get," I said.

"What's that, Hunter?" Izzy inquired.

"I want to get some signs made up so I can post them around the property. This way, people will now know that someone owns the place now, and will stay away," I responded.

"We can get the signs when we get back. They have signs already made up for that," Izzy advised.

"Okay, cool", I said.

CHAPTER 22

We had lunch and left the tavern to head into town so we could put the word out that we wanted to hire someone to help us. We put an ad in the paper and posted a few fliers in some store windows. We then went to look at some tractors. After finding out how much a tractor would cost, we decided that we needed to get some of the gold exchanged again so we would be able to buy the tractor and do the things we had planned.

We went back to the tavern and started to make some phone calls to get some of the gold exchanged. While at the tavern, a truck drove up out front, and an older man got out and came into the tavern.

Izzy asked, "Can I help you?"

The man said, "I'm looking for someone who posted a sign in the store in town asking for someone to do some work."

"Hunter, I think you may want to talk to this guy, because you know what you're looking for. I've got a few other things to get done," Izzy announced.

I looked at the man and saw that he may be just the kind of guy we were looking for. "We're looking for someone who is good at just about anything. We have about 750 acres outside of town, and we need a man who can do some hard work, like using a tractor and moving trees and brush, along with some building skills,"

The man smiled. "Yes, I think I can handle all of that, and I have this truck that is in pretty good shape."

"Where are you from?" I asked.

"I am just traveling around from different places and was looking for some work," the man said.

"Where are you staying?" I asked.

"I just got into town, and I don't have a place yet."

"Okay, what is your name?"

"I go by the name of Logger," he answered.

"Well, Logger, I don't know many people around this town either, so I'm going to give you a try. Maybe we can get a few things done. I have a cabin that is in need of some repairs. If you want, you can stay there while you do work on the projects I'll have for you. How's that sound?"

"That sounds great. When do you want me to start?" Logger asked.

I looked at Izzy, smiled, and said, "You can start as soon as you want, I guess."

"Where is the cabin?" Logger asked.

"I will take you out to the cabin right now, if you'd like. We need to get a few things before going back to the cabin, because there isn't anything there but the cabin. Why don't you meet me here tomorrow at about 9:00 a.m., and we'll go buy a few things to take back to the cabin when we go?" I offered.

Logger agreed and thanked me for the chance to work and a place to stay. He said that he would see them tomorrow.

"Well, Hunter, it looks like things are moving right along with us now having someone to help," noted Izzy.

"I agree, and he didn't look like he would be too much trouble, because he didn't look like he had anything but that truck. Tomorrow when Logger gets here, I'll have him go with me into town, and I'll buy a generator that we can have at the cabin. He can stay there and work on the cabin, and hopefully everything will start looking better around there."

"What are we going to do about the egg?"

"Well, that's in the barn and out of sight, and if he doesn't know about it, he won't be looking for it. I'll have to figure something out. I'll have him go somewhere and do something when we decide what we are going to do with the egg. I think that once I learn I can trust him, he'll be able to help us move it when we need to. In the meantime, we need to contact the university and see whom we can talk to about the egg. I'll take some pictures to the university and see what they say about it. Izzy, why don't you call the university after Logger and I go out to the cabin tomorrow, and see if you can make an appointment with someone?"

"Okay, I'll see what I can do," Izzy confirmed.

The next day, Logger was at the tavern right at 9:00 a.m.

"Good morning, Logger. Are you ready to get started?" I asked.

"Yes, sir, whenever you are!" Logger said excitedly.

"Okay, let me tell Izzy that we are going to leave so she knows what's going on. Then we can go into town and get a few things. We will probably be able to fill the back of your truck with some lumber and a generator for starters, along with some gas and whatever else we can think of. After we pick up the stuff in town, it is only a few miles outside of town to the cabin."

Izzy made some phone calls to the university and found out whom to talk to about the egg. The professor asked her what kind of egg it was and where it came from. Izzy couldn't answer any of the questions that the professor was asking, but she said she would get back in touch when she could.

Logger and I were finished at the store. We got all we could and were already at the cabin, so we started planning our day's work. I started a fire so we could burn some old things that needed to be thrown away, and I started making the cabin livable again. In the meantime, I went out to the barn to check on the egg, and saw that it was still okay. There was some old equipment that was left in the barn and also needed to be thrown out, along with cleaning out the stalls. I remembered that there was a hidden door in the floor of one of the stalls that we found, and I wanted to put a lock on the door and cover it up so it couldn't be seen.

Izzy arrived at the cabin and saw that Logger and I were into our day's work. Logger had a lot of the cabin cleaned up, which made the inside of the cabin look larger.

I was moving things around in the barn when Izzy walked in and asked, "What's going on?"

"Oh, we are just trying to clean up the cabin and the barn so we can start using it," I answered.

"It is looking like things are starting to shape up and look pretty good, Hunter. I called the university and talked to a professor about the egg. He had a few questions that I couldn't answer, like what kind of egg and where it came from," Izzy relayed.

"I think we're going to have to take some pictures of it and then go to the professor to show him what we have. Then we'll see what we should do. Do you have a camera?" I asked.

"Yes, I've got one in the car. I'll go get it!" Izzy stated.

"I'll go check on Logger and see how's he doing."

"I'll be right back," Izzy commented.

Izzy went to the car to get the camera, and I headed for the cabin.

"Wow, Logger, you really cleaned up the place," I complimented.

"Well, it's not so hard when everything is not worth keeping, so I'm just burning everything. Then we can determine what to repair," Logger declared.

"I know that the floor and the roof are going to need some repair."

"Yes, I can see that, but it doesn't look like that will take too long once we can get started."

"Well, Logger, you can stay here starting tonight, if you want," I offered.

"I really would like that," Logger said politely.

"Okay, not a problem. I hear Izzy calling me, so I'm going back out to the barn. She's got a camera that we're going to use to take a few pictures."

"Okay, let me know if you need me for anything," Logger offered.

"Thanks, I will," I said.

I yelled out to Izzy, who was in the barn, to tell her I was on my way.

"Okay, Izzy, I'll roll the egg out so we can get a few good pictures of it for the professor."

"How many pictures do you want me to take?" Izzy asked.

"Oh, just two or three should be good enough. We can take the pictures to the university, find the professor in a few days, and see what he says. In the meantime, we need to cover this egg back up so it can't be seen." I covered the egg back up with dirt and the tarp. "There, that should do it for now. Let's go back up to the cabin and see how Logger's doing. I told him that he could start staying out here if he wanted, and as long as he is fixing up the place, I'm not going to charge him rent or anything."

"Well, that sounds fair, and later, if he still wants to work for us, we can talk about room and board for additional work he can do," Izzy suggested.

We walked back to the cabin.

"Hey, Logger, let's get the generator out of the truck and put it out behind the cabin. I'm going to want to build a cabinet around it to keep it out of the weather. Let's try to get that done today so tonight when you fire it up, you'll have some lights and electricity," I instructed.

"Okay, Hunter, that shouldn't be too hard to do," Logger replied.

"I'll make some phone calls tomorrow and see about getting some electricity installed out here. It'll probably take a while, maybe even a week. I don't know, depending on how busy they are," I said.

"That's all right. I've roughed it before. You don't need to worry about me. I'm just happy we met and I've got a place to stay for a while," Logger said.

"Well, I'm glad you came along when you did. As you can see, there are plenty of things that need done and repaired. If you can do it, you can stay as long as you want. Izzy and I are going to head back into town in a little bit, so you can work when you want, and we'll be back tomorrow. I'll see about the electricity and also about a small refrigerator so you can have it for food and water. I'll also see about getting a bed for you," I stated.

"Thanks, Hunter, I really do appreciate what you're doing," Logger said.

"I wanted to get the place livable anyway. I just didn't think that it was going to be quite this fast! But that doesn't matter. We'll see you tomorrow, Logger," I said as Izzy and I walked out the door.

Izzy and I left for town and wanted to get the pictures developed as soon as we can. Once we had the pictures, we could book an appointment with the professor. We dropped off the film and asked to have them back tomorrow.

Back at the tavern, it was time for a beer, some food, and then rest. Tomorrow was going to be a pretty busy day for us. Victoria had some food ready, and Izzy and I didn't waste any time eating it.

"Victoria, this food tastes really good. I'm starving," I complimented.

Victoria replied, "I'm glad you like it. Just slow down a little and enjoy it; it's not going anywhere. I'll get you and Izzy another beer, so relax."

I was just pumped up from the way things were starting to go for me that I could hardly sit still.

"Izzy, what do you think about everything that has been happening?" I asked.

"Well, all I can say is that it's been very exciting since you first showed up here. I would have never believed what has happened if I wasn't there to see it," Izzy responded.

CHAPTER 23

T he next morning, we wanted to get the day started early, because we could hardly wait to see the pictures.

"Izzy, let's have a little breakfast and then go get the pictures," I suggested.

"All right. I know you want to see them," Izzy agreed.

"If they are good enough, we can make a phone call and see if we can see the professor."

We went to the diner to have some breakfast. We didn't want to eat too much so we could get done quicker and get the pictures. We finished eating and left. As we pulled up to photo mart, the men who had been bothering us before were sitting on a bench in front of the photo mart. We tried to not pay any attention and walked past them without saying anything. The men recognized us and were watching us as we went into the photo mart. We asked for our pictures and didn't take time to look at them there.

"Izzy, we need to get out of here before those men want something. Hide the pictures in your purse," I suggested.

As Izzy and I walked out of the photo mart, the men got into their car. We didn't waste any time getting into our own car. I backed the car out and turned to go toward Izzy's tavern, and so did the men. Once we reached the tavern, the men kept going by and didn't stop.

"Izzy, I think we're going to have to be really careful when we do anything, because those guys are going to be watching us every time we do something," I concluded.

"I agree, but they went on by, so let's go inside the tavern, look at the pictures, and see what we have," Izzy stated.

Once inside, we sat down at a table and began looking at the pictures. The pictures came out great, and we felt we had enough to make an appointment with the university professor.

"Izzy, these turned out pretty good, don't you think?"

"Yes, I think that we should call and make an appointment!" she said excitedly.

"Okay, I'll call now."

"After you make the call, I think if we have time, we should go back out to the cabin and check on Logger," Izzy suggested.

"Yes, that's a good idea. I'm sure we'll have time. We probably won't be able to see anyone at the university for a few days anyway," I said.

I tried calling the university.

"I couldn't get hold of anyone. It didn't even let me leave a message. I'll try again tomorrow, so let's make a few sandwiches and go back out to the cabin. I'm sure Logger is hungry and probably has a few questions by now," I offered.

Izzy made some sandwiches, and we packed up to head back to the cabin. As we drove up, we could see that Logger had a fire going in the fireplace.

"Looks like Logger is busy doing something," Izzy announced.

"I hope that he works out and stays with us for a while, so we can get this place looking good again," I confessed.

"I'm sure everything will be all right. He seems to like it here and is willing to work hard. Let's see what he's doing," Izzy said.

We walked in the cabin, but Logger was nowhere to be found.

"Hey, where's he at?" Izzy asked.

"Maybe he's in the barn doing something. I'll check it out," I suggested, and I went out to the barn.

"Hey, Logger, are you out there?" I hollered. "Oh, there you are. How's everything going? Izzy and I just got here and brought you and a sandwich. We thought that maybe the three of us could get a few things done today."

"Everything's fine. I've gotten a lot of cleaning up done. I'm up for anything you need me to do," Logger replied.

"Okay, well, let's have a sandwich first, and then we can decide what we're going to do. Logger, why don't you go ahead and get washed up a little, and I'll meet you in a little bit? I've got something to do in the barn, and then I'll be right up."

Logger did what he was told and headed for the cabin. I looked back to see that Logger was heading for the cabin. Once Logger was out of sight, I went straight to where the egg was hidden, and just when I saw that the egg was all right, Galaxy appeared.

I jumped. "Oh, wow, Galaxy, you surprised me."

"Yes, I know, but I have been watching you and Izzy and thought that now would be a good time for me to talk to you for a few minutes."

"All right, I'm sure you wouldn't be here if you didn't think that it was necessary, so what can I do for you?" I asked.

"Hunter, I know that you and Izzy are trying to get in to see someone at the university about the egg. What you need to know is that once you show up with the egg, there will be many people with a lot of questions about where you got the egg and what it is from. Have you and Izzy thought about that?" Galaxy challenged.

"We took some pictures to take with us to the university to show them what it looks like, so we didn't have to take the egg with us," I informed her.

"I know about the pictures, and that is very smart of you and Izzy to do that, but once they see the pictures, the questions are going to start. Do you know how you are going to answer them?" Galaxy asked.

"I don't know what the questions will be, but Izzy and I will try to make sure that no one will be able to find it until we have all the answers," I assured Galaxy.

"I do know what you need to know. I know about the egg, what kind it is, and where it came from. Unfortunately, I can't tell you. I can, however, appear quickly when you encounter any trouble," Galaxy stated.

"Yeah, that is unfortunate because it certainly would help us. We appreciate that you'll make sure that nothing happens to Izzy and me, along with the egg. I'd better get back to the cabin now before they come out looking for me," I said.

"You will always be watched, because the future is depending on how you and Izzy make it," Galaxy confirmed. And just as quickly as Galaxy appeared, she disappeared.

I started walking back to the cabin when Izzy walked out and said, "I was starting to wonder what was going on and what was keeping you."

"I'll tell you later. Let's talk to Logger and enjoy a sandwich," I suggested.

We walked into the cabin. "Hey, Logger, it's starting to look a little bit better in here now," I praised.

"Well, anything is better than it was," Logger commented.

"You have a good point. Once the cabin is cleaned up and the roof has been repaired, it shouldn't be so bad to stay out here, right?"

"I will be very happy to stay here. I don't need much," Logger replied.

"That's a good thing, because there isn't much here," I joked.

"Izzy, I do want to thank you and Hunter for the food that you brought. I was getting a little hungry," Logger confessed.

"Well, it's not much, and we'll bring out some more later. We need to bring out a refrigerator the next time, especially now that we have the generator outside. Maybe you can do a little wiring so we can get some lights in here too," I said.

"Yes, sir. If you bring the supplies, I'll sure try to get everything done that you want," Logger said.

"Izzy, before we head back into town, I want to get a few things that are in the barn," I commented.

"Okay, Hunter, go ahead. I'll stay here with Logger. Are you going to be long?" Izzy asked.

"No, I'll be just a few minutes. Just need to get something," I responded.

I headed for the barn while Izzy and Logger waited. Once in the barn, I went straight to the egg. I knew that I would need to get the size of the egg so I could tell the university. I measured the egg, and it was twenty-five inches wide by twelve inches high. After I got the measurements, I covered the egg back up so it could not be seen and went back to the cabin.

"Okay, Izzy, I'm ready to head back into town," I announced.

"Sure, Hunter. Just waiting on you," she replied.

"Logger, we'll see you in a while. We'll try to get back today if we can get a refrigerator, but if not, we'll be back tomorrow," I explained.

"I'll be here!" Logger assured us.

We left for town and wanted to contact the university again, to set up an appointment. Once back at the tavern, I made a call to the university and talked to a professor named Sovine. This professor had a PhD in oology, which was a branch of ornithology, and I came to learn it was a study of eggs. The professor said that he was available after 4:00 p.m. any weekday, and I could stop by.

"Izzy, I've made the appointment at the university with Professor Sovine for tomorrow at 4:30. After that, we can get a refrigerator, if we have the time," I concluded.

"All right, Hunter, that sounds good."

CHAPTER 24

The next day, Izzy and I were anxious to get to the university and see Professor Sovine. Professor Sovine only knew that we wanted to meet with him and had questions about an egg. We entered Professor Sovine's office, and he asked, "What can I do for you?"

"We appreciate you meeting with us, Professor Sovine. My name is Hunter, and this is my friend Izzy. We have some pictures of a large egg that we found, and we want you to look at them," I explained. I slid the pictures across the professor's desk. "We took the pictures a few days ago. Do you know what kind it is?"

"Well, let me take a better look at these," Professor Sovine said while putting a magnifying glass to the pictures. He started examining the pictures very closely. "It is really hard to tell by these pictures. If I could see it in person, I might be able to have a better look. Where is this egg now?"

"We have it hidden away until we get some answers," I answered.

"Do you know how big it is?" the professor asked.

"Yes, Professor, I measured it. It's about two feet by one foot," I described.

"That's a pretty big egg, Hunter," the professor proclaimed.

"Yes, it certainly is. We don't want anyone to know about it yet," I stated.

"Well, where did you find this egg?" the professor inquired.

"We don't want to divulge that either, Professor," I confessed.

"Well, you and your lady friend are going to have to let me examine the egg before I can give you any answers. When can I see it?"

"Izzy and I will go get the egg and bring it back here to you in and few days, if that's all right?" I asked.

"Yes, Hunter, that will be fine. You are going to have to let me know when that will be, and maybe I can have a few of my colleagues join us to examine it, if that's okay?"

"We don't have any problem with that," I stated, even though I was a little skeptical. "We'll call you when we are ready with the egg."

We left the university and went to buy a refrigerator for the cabin, along with some other supplies. I realized that I wouldn't be able to take the refrigerator to the cabin without a truck, so I'd need to go back to the cabin and get Logger and his truck so we could move the refrigerator. I bought the refrigerator and told the salesman I'd be back with a truck to pick it up. After buying the refrigerator, I took Izzy back to the tavern so she could pack up a few things to take back to the cabin while I went out to get Logger and his truck.

Once I was back at the cabin, I decided to just have Logger go back in town, pick up the refrigerator, and then stop and pick Izzy up at the tavern. While Logger was gone, I could go to the barn and see what I would have to do to get the egg ready to take to the university.

When I walked into the barn, suddenly Galaxy appeared. "Galaxy, you surprised me again. What made you decide to show up?"

"I know what you are planning to do with the egg. I'm going to tell you that you need to think about taking the egg to the university before you do it," Galaxy said.

"We are just trying to get some answers about the egg," I explained.

"Hunter, I know, but I will tell you now what you need to know before you make the mistake of taking it to the university. Once you take the egg to the university and they have it, you'll never get it back. They will keep it, and you'll never see it again. So what you need to do right now is listen to what I'm going to tell you, and what you need to do with the egg. You know that the egg is very old, but what you don't know is that it is still a good egg. The egg has been in a cold, dark cave for many years, as you know, and that is why it has never hatched. Eggs need to be kept warm before they can hatch. Hunter, I'm telling you to take the egg and put it in a bed of hay over there in the corner of the barn. Get some heating lamps from town to keep it warm, and you will see what will happen."

I did what Galaxy said. I put the egg in a corner of the barn and covered it up with hay. "Will the egg be all right if I leave it here and go back in town to get some lights?"

"Yes, it will be fine. Nothing will happen until the lights are set up to start warming it," Galaxy stated.

I left to go back to town and get some lights. I wanted to get back before Logger and Izzy showed up with the refrigerator. After I bought some heat lamps, I saw Logger's truck at the tavern, and I decided to stop.

"Hey, guys, I'm glad that I ran into you. I had to get a few things in town, and after that, a beer here at the tavern sounds pretty good. I see that you got the refrigerator, so that's good. Maybe we should take some beer with us and put it in the refrigerator for later," I suggested.

"I like that idea, but we have to get it working before we can start putting stuff in it," Izzy said.

"The generator will do that until we get some electricity put in place," I pointed out.

"All right, then, we'll take some beer! Do you guys want something to eat before we head back out to the cabin? I'll see what I can put together real fast here in the kitchen," Izzy offered.

"Izzy, don't get carried away now. Just a couple of sandwiches will be good enough. We've got a lot to get done at the cabin," I declared.

"Yes, Hunter, I know. I promise not to get carried away."

Izzy rode with me, and Logger followed behind with the refrigerator in the back of his truck. Once back out at the cabin, I helped Logger take the refrigerator off the truck and move it into the cabin.

"This is going to be nice now that we have this refrigerator here," I stated.

"Yes, it is. Now, go start the generator so it will start getting cold," Izzy suggested.

"I will, I will. Come on, Logger. Let's see if we can get it started. Remind me, Logger, when we go back into town to get some extra gas for the generator. With it running all the time now, we will be going through a lot of gas." I started up the generator. "Now, Logger, you stay here and help Izzy. I've got to take care of something in the barn, and I'll be right back."

I headed for the barn with the heat lamps. When I got to the barn,

I realized that the heat lamps weren't any good without electricity and had to store the lamps until I could get someone out to install some electricity for the cabin and the barn. I went back to the cabin with a sad look on my face.

"What's wrong, Hunter?" Izzy asked.

"Oh, nothing. I wanted to do something in the barn and realized I wasn't going to be able to do anything without electricity," I informed her.

"Well, what were you trying to do?" Izzy asked.

"Nothing, it's not important. It can wait."

"Well, I guess it will have to because there isn't any electricity," Izzy commented.

"I'll make a call and put an order in tomorrow to have someone out to install electric in the cabin and the barn. That will make everything much easier," I stated.

We left the cabin and headed back to Izzy's place for the night. We had a lot on our minds and were both exhausted, so we went to bed early.

The next day, I had a few phone calls to make, and one of them was to the university to tell the professor that something had come up, so we wouldn't be able to keep our appointment with him. After talking to Galaxy, I realized that what she had said about the university was true: they would keep the egg, and I wouldn't be able to do anything about it because of the rare find. I decided to wait, talk to Galaxy again, and keep the egg safe. The only problem was how to keep the egg hidden and out of sight. Now that the university knew about the egg, there was a possibility people would try to find it.

I made a call to have the electricity installed at the cabin and barn, and then I headed back out to the cabin, where Logger was. He was in the barn repairing some of the stalls so I could have a couple of horses. As I drove up, I shouted, "Hey, Logger, how is it going with the stalls? It looks like you'll have this barn in pretty good shape before long."

"I don't think the horses will complain any," Logger said.

"I am having the electricity installed in a few days, and that will make a big difference around here. Logger, as soon as the stalls are repaired, I'm going to see about getting a few horses to keep. There's a lot of land here, and it will be easier to move around and look at it on a horse. Also, a horse will come in handy to pull a wagon around when I need it," I described.

"I understand. That sounds really nice. I agree that a horse will make it easier. I'll do anything I can do to help."

"Have you ridden a horse before?" I asked.

"Oh, yes, many times. My parents owned a farm, and I helped my dad with the plowing of the fields."

"Is there anything you can't do?"

"Well, I'm not sure. I've done just about everything," Logger said with a grin.

CHAPTER 25

A couple of days passed. I got a call from the electric company stating they would be out to install electricity in the cabin and in the barn. I met them out there.

"I'm sure glad they're installing the electricity today, Logger," I stated.

"Yes, that should make things a little better," Logger agreed.

"I know Izzy will be a lot happier when she is out here. I also want to have a tractor out here that we can keep in the barn. Logger, if you are going to be around here for a while and are willing to stay, a tractor will help with many things that we have to do."

"I don't have any plans on leaving, so let's find a tractor, and we can start to make things better around here. We can also make the road a little nicer."

The electricity was installed in the cabin and the barn by the end of the day. I had the cabin bright inside.

"It's nice to be able to see in here now, isn't it?" I asked.

"That's for sure!" Logger agreed.

"Now that we have electricity, I think we may want to think about adding a couple of rooms on to the cabin. This one big room is okay, but a bedroom and maybe a bathroom are in order. We'll need to get with Izzy and see what she thinks about the idea."

"I think Izzy would love the idea," Logger commented.

"Okay, we'll work on it," I concluded.

I headed back into town and wanted to see Izzy to tell her how well everything was going out at the cabin.

"Hi, Izzy. I just left Logger at the cabin. The electricity is now working out there, so now we don't have to have that generator running all the time. Logger and I are thinking about adding a bedroom and maybe a bathroom to the cabin. What do you think?" I asked.

"That would be great if you guys think that you can do all that," Izzy stated.

"I know that it would really make it nicer."

"Yes, it definitely would. It would make it more of a house instead of just a room for one person."

"We will work on getting that done. I also want to get a tractor to keep out there in the barn as well," I announced.

"It sounds like you're going to be busy out there for a while," Izzy said.

"I just want it to be nicer than it is."

"I understand, but what have you decided on the egg?" Izzy asked.

"I need to talk to Galaxy again before anyone else knows about it. If I can get with Galaxy tomorrow, I'll ask."

The next day, I went into town, and after having breakfast with Izzy, I started looking for a tractor to buy. I really didn't know too much about tractors, but I wanted one big enough that would pull a wagon. I found a couple used ones and then started looking at new ones. The tractor dealership made it easy for me by explaining that the tractors they had would work for just about anything I wanted. The salesman also said they could deliver it to the cabin. I bought one and told them where to have it delivered. I then went back to Izzy at the tavern and told her I had bought a tractor, and it was being delivered to the cabin tomorrow.

"Izzy, I'm going to eat a little something and then go back out to the cabin to see if I can find Galaxy. I've got to talk with her so I know what to do with the egg."

"Okay. I'll come out later after I finish a few things around here," Izzy stated.

I ate, then loaded up the car with some extra water and food for the cabin, headed back. Logger had a fire going outside the cabin. He was burning some of the weeds and brush that had grown everywhere.

"Hey, Logger, how's it going?" I asked.

"I've been clearing out this area, as you can see. It has really cleaned up the area a lot, hasn't it?"

"Yes, it looks great. Good job! I bought a tractor and am having it delivered tomorrow, so we need to make sure there's a space big enough for it in the barn."

"Okay, I'll make sure," Logger assured me.

"I see that you're going to be here with the fire for a while, so I'm going to do a little straightening up in the barn. That's where I'll be if you need me."

I headed for the barn and left Logger with what he was doing. I wanted to contact Galaxy, and she knew it. Right when I got inside the barn, she appeared.

"Galaxy, I'm so glad that you're here. I need to know what to do with the egg," I said.

"I know that you want help with the egg, and I know that without my help, you'll never know. So here's what I want you to do! Now that you have electricity here in the barn, you're going to have to use your heat lamps to warm the egg, so it will hatch," Galaxy instructed.

"What am I going to do with what comes out of the egg?" I asked.

"Hunter, the egg is a dragon egg. For many hundreds of years, there were dragons. When the dragon hatches, it is going to see you. The queen and all the fairies have been waiting for this to happen, and now that you're here, it can hatch," Galaxy explained.

"But I don't know what to do with a dragon!" I said, shocked.

"We understand, and we'll make sure you know what to do. The dragon will take care of itself, and it will take care of you. You will be the very first living thing that it sees. You'll be able to tell the dragon what to do, and it will listen. This is why only you can know about this egg. The dragon will stay here in the barn and will hide when someone comes, unless it's you. Then the dragon will come out and come to you. It's going to get very big, very fast, and it will be able to fly after it is fully grown. That is when you'll have to go back to the cave and reopen it, so that the dragon can stay there."

I stood there in shock. Then I started to pace. "What am I going to do with a dragon? This is a lot to take in," I stated.

"I know it is a lot, but you will come to know why you were the chosen one," Galaxy said.

"What do I call this dragon?" I asked.

"There have been many dragons over the years, and there will be many more, but for now we want you to name it. What do you think a good name would be?" she asked.

"I have no idea, but I guess I can think of something. Galaxy, how long do you think it will take before the egg hatches?" I asked.

"I will make sure that you're here when it happens, because the most important thing is that the dragon sees you first before anything else. That's what gives you the control and the power over the dragon," she explained.

"Galaxy, I have many questions," I said in a panic. "How long do dragons live, and will I be around long enough to make a difference?"

"Hunter, dragons live a very long time, and you don't have to worry about that now. Remember, the queen and all the fairies know the future, including how everything will happen. We've been waiting for you to arrive so we could tell you. Remember, the queen wrote a lot in her scrolls, and she has chosen you to make her scrolls known to the world. Everything must be put in place first before that can happen. So for now, we need to take care of the egg. Cover it up in one of the stalls to keep it hidden. I think next week, we'll try to hatch the egg. Hunter, you may want to have Logger go somewhere or do a job for you in the fields, so he isn't around. Remember, only you are to be here." Then poof—she was gone.

"Great, now how am I going to take care of a dragon?" I stood there, still in shock. Then I looked down at the egg and covered it up to keep it out of site.

CHAPTER 26

The tractor arrived the next day, and I was anxious to try it out. I had Logger hook up the wagon, and we headed for the fields. I had so much that I wanted to do.

"Logger, I want us to work on getting a fence up across the back of this field, so when I get a few horses, they won't get out," I described.

"I understand. That will take a while, but I have nothing but time, so I can get started on it right away. I just need to know where to start and where to stop," Logger informed me.

"There's a river in the back of the field. We can start there, I guess. I don't have any horses yet, so there's no real hurry, but I just want everything set before I get some."

"You have 750 acres, which is a lot of land to put a fence on," Logger replied.

"Yes, I know, but we have to start somewhere," I stated.

As the days went on, Logger kept putting fence posts on the wagon and placing them with specific spacing for the fence to be added. The days were long, and the work was hard but satisfying.

After a week in the fields, Galaxy wanted to hatch the egg.

"Logger, I'm not going to be able to help you for a few days, because something has come up, so you'll be on your own," I said.

Logger said, "No problem. Go ahead; I can handle it."

The following day, I went to the barn, and Galaxy was waiting. I turned on the heat lamps and put them around the egg. Izzy was at the tavern working and Logger was in the field, so it was a good time.

Galaxy assured me that everything was going to be all right and said, "Just be patient, and the egg should hatch in a few hours."

While I waited, I worked on cleaning up some more in the other stalls. After a few hours passed, Galaxy reappeared, and the egg started to move a little. It startled me. Galaxy said, "It is just about time now."

The egg started to crack and move some more. Then a piece of the egg broke open and came apart. Galaxy told me that everything was normal, so I should not be afraid. A few minutes later, the egg broke open, and out came a slimy little creature about twelve inches long with a tail. I jumped back and didn't know what to do.

Galaxy said, "Don't worry. This baby dragon is new to this world and everything in it. The baby dragon won't hurt you; it is simply curious. Hunter, make a place for the dragon to stay here in the stall and close it off. You won't have to worry about the dragon, because I will make sure it is safe and no one will find it. You won't have to feed it or do anything. That will be my job. The baby dragon grows fast and will become very large in just a few days, and it will be fully grown in about a month. After that time, the dragon will not stay here and will move on. The dragon will always be around, if you call for it. As the dragon grows, I will be opening up the cave again with some of the other fairies, so the dragon can live there. This dragon is here to protect you and do what you want it to do. Remember, you are the first person that it will see, and that is why I said you need to be that person. The dragon has only one master, and you are it.

"For now, the baby dragon will stay here in the stall until it gets big enough that the stall will not hold it. After a week, the dragon will move out of the barn, and it knows to go to the cave. The cave will be reopened when it arrives, and that is where you will always find it. As time goes by, there will be occasions when people will see this dragon, and by then it will be able to fly. No one will ever know that you are its master. Hunter, you are very important to the queen, and you will be very important to the world and humanity in the years to come. This is why we have told you about the queen, the cave, the scrolls, the gold, and the fairies. The scrolls are what the world is waiting for but doesn't even know it yet. Now that the egg has hatched and the dragon knows you are its master, you will be able to go back to what you have been doing. Simply wait for a little time to pass. You can close up the barn now. I'll stay with the baby, and you can tell Izzy what has happened, if you want. Also, you may want to decide what name you're going to give the dragon so when you call for it, it will know to come."

I didn't know what to say. She had just given me a lot of information that was very shocking. "Galaxy, everything has been moving so fast since I came to this country. It's very hard for me to comprehend it all, but I will do as you say and close up the barn for now. I'll go back into town and talk to Izzy about what all has happened and what we should do going forward."

I walked out of the barn and closed it up. I wanted to go out to where Logger was before going back into town. Logger didn't know about the dragon and didn't know that the barn was going to be off-limits for a while. I left to find Logger and tell him to stay away from the barn. Once that was done, I headed back to the tavern.

"Izzy, we need to talk. I've been at the barn with Galaxy, and she showed me what to do with the egg. The egg has hatched, and a baby dragon has come out of the egg! Galaxy told me to close up the barn and not let anyone in the barn for a while. Galaxy said that the baby dragon will grow very fast, and when it is big enough, it will leave the barn on its own and head toward the cave in the mountain. Galaxy said when that happens, she and the rest of the fairies will reopen the cave so the dragon can live there again. In the meantime, we need to come up with a name for the dragon, so I can call to it when I want it."

Izzy's jaw dropped open; she was stunned. At first, she thought I was kidding, but with all we had seen lately, she thought twice about saying, *"You're kidding me, right?"* Instead, she asked, "Did you see the baby dragon?"

"Yes, I did, and it was kind of wild. I think that it thought I was its mother or something. Galaxy said that I had to be the first one the baby would see, because that way it would listen only to me when I called for it. I really don't know what to think about everything that is happening, but Galaxy will always be around to talk to me and tell me what to do. So for now, we need to come up with a name for the dragon. What do you think?"

"Hunter, you are asking me to name something that I have no idea or anything about," Izzy said.

"Okay, you're right. Give me a beer; I need one. I left Logger in the field putting fence poles in the ground, and I told him to stay away from the barn. He agreed without any questions, so that should be good. Have you heard anything back from the university yet?"

"No, they haven't called. What do you want me to tell them if they do?" Izzy asked.

"Well, let's just wait and see if they call. If they don't, let's forget about it. We'll have to make up some kind of excuse when they do."

"All right, so what now?" Izzy asked.

"I'm going to go back to help Logger in the field for now, and we can talk some more later when I get back," I informed her.

CHAPTER 27

L ogger was still digging holes in the ground for the fence poles when I showed back up.

"Logger, how are you doing?" I asked.

"Oh, I'm getting it done. It's just going to take a while," Logger stated.

"Yeah, I can see that, but it will be worth all the hard work in the end," I proclaimed.

"Yes, it will," Logger agreed.

"I'm going to take the wagon back to the cabin and get some more poles. I'll be back in a while."

"Okay, Hunter. I'll be here."

I left to the cabin with the tractor and the wagon. I looked toward the cabin and could see that there were a couple of cars waiting there. It looked like the FBI. I was getting nervous as I got closer to the cars. I approached the cabin, and the FBI agents were standing there, waiting.

"Can I help you guys?" I asked.

"Hunter, we know that you and your lady friend have been back out to Bonefairy Castle. With the castle belonging to the government now, we have to make sure that your visits don't happen anymore," one of the agents stated.

"Well, fellas, like I told you before, we just wanted to see the castle. I don't think we'll be going back anymore," I explained.

"Let us make sure you understand. If you do and don't ask before you arrive on the premises, we will arrest you both," one of the agents threatened.

"I understand! We will stay away from Bonefairy Castle."

The FBI started leaving but first asked, "This place has been sitting empty for a long time. How'd you get it?"

"It belonged to one of my ancestors. I just recently was able to pay the taxes on the place, so now it is mine. I'm starting to fix the place up."

"Well, it looks like you've got a pretty big job ahead of you, Hunter," the agent commented.

"Yes, I know, but it's home for me now, and I've got plenty of time. Thanks for stopping by," I said.

The FBI agents got back in their cars and left.

I wanted to go back to the barn and check on the dragon after the FBI was gone. When I opened the barn door up again, I could see that the dragon had already started getting bigger. Galaxy appeared and said, "Everything is going to be all right. You don't need to worry about anything."

"I want to name the dragon Dweller, because the dragon is going to live in the cave," I said.

Galaxy agreed and said, "That is a good name. The dragon will know its name immediately and will come to you when you call."

I smiled and said, "I want to head back into town. I'll be back tomorrow." I said goodbye to Galaxy and Dweller, closed the barn back up, and left for town.

Once back in town, I wanted to relax. I walked into the tavern, and Izzy asked, "Is everything al; right?"

"It's been a long day. I'm glad that it is almost over."

"Did you go see the dragon again?"

"Yes, and I've decided to call it Dweller."

"I like the sound of that," she replied as she gave me a beer.

"Thanks, Izzy. A beer really sounds pretty good right now."

"Well, I think you deserve it. It looks like you have things going pretty well right now," Izzy praised.

"I think so too. I guess the next thing we need to think about is what else is in the scrolls. Galaxy keeps telling me that the scrolls have something written about the future involving humankind, and that I need to keep figuring out the clues. Maybe I'll take a little time tomorrow and look at the scrolls some more to see if I can figure out anything before I go out and check on Logger. I could take the scrolls with me when I head to the cabin tomorrow to talk to Galaxy. Galaxy wants me to know what is in the scrolls, so maybe she will help me with the clues."

The next morning, I put the scrolls in my car and headed out to the cabin. As I arrived, Logger was loading up the wagon with some more poles to take into the field.

"Hey, Logger, how are you doing?" I asked.

"I'm doing all right. I just need to put a few more poles here on the wagon, and I'll be heading back out to the field."

"Okay. I'll help with the poles now and then be out to help you in a while. Is there anything you need?"

"No, I'm good. I've got everything I need for now, but thanks. I'll see you in a while," he replied.

After Logger left, I headed for the barn. When I opened it up, Dweller was standing right there in the door way.

"Wow, Dweller, you have really grown overnight. Galaxy, are you here?" I called out.

Poof! "Yes, Hunter, I'm right here," she replied.

"When you said that Dweller was going to grow very fast, you weren't kidding."

"In just a few more days, Dweller won't be able to stay in the barn. He will outgrow it. That's why he'll live in the cave," Galaxy explained.

"Do I need to lock the barn when I leave?" I asked.

"Dweller can break through the door now if he wanted to. Don't worry about locking the door. Simply close it, and when the time comes for Dweller to leave, he will. I know that you brought the scrolls with you today. Because there isn't anyone around, why don't we go into the cabin? Logger won't be back for a while, and I know that you want some clues answered," Galaxy suggested. I agreed, and we headed for the cabin with the scrolls.

Once inside the cabin, I opened up the scrolls, placed them on the table, and said, "Well, here they are. Now what?"

"If you remember, the queen asked Sir Hunter to always bring her pieces of the men who had been killed in battle, like pieces of clothing, hair, or body parts. When Sir Hunter did this, he would take what he brought back and give it to the queen in Bonefairy Castle. The queen would then take everything and disappear in her private quarters. The queen wrote down in the scrolls what she did so there was a record of each person's DNA," Galaxy explained.

"Galaxy, what exactly is DNA?" I asked.

Galaxy explained, "The queen had powers that could produce what she called the DNA of a person. A person's body is made up of many different chemical elements and molecule types, such as DNA, that are essential for all known forms of life. This hasn't been discovered yet, but it will be, and this is why the queen wants you to know: so you can make it known to all of humanity. The queen had trust in Sir Hunter back then, and because you are his ancestor, she knew that she would be able to trust you. That is what she has been waiting for you to show up. Now that you are here, the queen wants you to know everything."

"What do you mean, everything?"

"Hunter, you were supposed to come to Bonefairy Castle. You were supposed to find the scrolls. You were supposed to find the gold. With the gold, you were supposed to start a company that discovers how to get DNA from a person. You have used some of the gold to buy back the land that Sir Hunter had, and the cabin. You will also be able to buy some of your grandparents' land in America for your company. Hunter, the scrolls are here to guide you through everything the queen wants you to know, but not until you get your company started. You have a lot to do here with the cabin and land before starting your company in America. Go ahead and put the scrolls away for now, until you are ready."

"This is a lot of responsibility you dropped on me. How do I know I can fulfill it all?"

"Not to worry, Hunter. I know it sounds like a lot, but it will all fall into place, and I will be with you through it all," Galaxy said.

"Okay, Galaxy, I understand. There's time after I get this place fixed up, right?" I replied.

"Exactly, Hunter. I'm going to leave you now, but I will always be around if you need me. Just call," Galaxy explained. Then she was gone.

CHAPTER 28

I decided to go back into town and tell Izzy what had happened.

"Hi, Izzy. I just left the cabin and was talking to Galaxy. She told me a lot about the scrolls. She also said to not worry about them for a while and to finish what I wanted to do with the cabin, such as finish putting up the fence on the property, so I guess that's what I'm going to do. Logger is still out there putting fence poles in the ground, so after I get a little something to eat, I'll go back out and help him."

"What are you planning to do after that?" Izzy asked.

"I think I want to make the cabin real nice, so it will be enjoyable to stay there."

"Okay, and what is the latest on the dragon?"

I smiled. "Oh, you mean Dweller?"

"Oh, that's right, you named it."

"Yes. I thought of it when I was told by Galaxy that the dragon will eventually be living in the cave once it has grown. So the dragon is going to be dwelling in the cave. Get it?" I asked.

"Oh, I see how you came up with the name now." She giggled.

"Well, I had to come up with something. I don't know too many dragons, so that will have to do. Galaxy said that it will know its name immediately. Cool, huh?"

Izzy replied, "That is cool for sure. I wonder how that's possible?"

"I imagine Galaxy has something to do with it. Just like the cave will be reopened to allow the dragon to go live there."

I finished eating with Izzy and said that I'd be back later. Then I headed back out to the cabin to see Logger. When I drove up to the cabin, I saw that the barn door was open and that Dweller was nowhere to be found. *Great, now what?* I headed for the field to find Logger.

"Hey, Logger, where are you?" I hollered.

"Hunter, I'm over here. I'm just taking a little break and having a sandwich," Logger answered.

"Okay, how's it going?" I asked.

"Well, I think that maybe by the end of the day, I can have all the holes dug for the poles and have most of the poles in. Then I will start on installing the fence."

"That's great!

"What else is happening, Hunter?" Logger asked.

"Well, not much. I'm just doing a lot of running around, going back and forth into town. Logger, I know you have your hands full with the fence and stuff, but I also want to get somethings done around the cabin."

"Well, we can do both, can't we?" he asked.

"Yes, I guess we can. I'll start getting some material for the cabin and have it delivered out here in a few days."

"Hunter, look! What is that going across the field way over there?" Logger yelled.

"Where? I don't see anything."

"Over there by those trees!" Logger pointed.

"I don't see anything. What did you see?" I asked.

"I don't know. It looked like some big creature."

I laughed. "Logger, I think you've been out here in the sun too long."

"No, really, Hunter! I saw something by those trees, and it wasn't something little." Logger was exasperated.

"All right, I'll head over there in a minute and see if something's there," I assured him.

"Take the tractor. It'll be easier to get over there," Logger suggested.

"That's a good idea."

"What if it is some kind of creature?" he asked with wonder.

"I don't know, Logger. I'll just have to wait until I get over there. If there is something there, I'll stay back and not get to close until I can figure out what it is," I decided.

"Do you want me to go with you?"

I replied, "No, I want you to keep doing what you're doing, so we can get the fence up."

"Okay, but be careful," Logger said, concerned.

I started the tractor and said that I would be back in a little while. I knew it was Dweller in the area, so I was not too worried about what I was going to see. Dweller was moving across the field and heading in the direction of the cave. As I got closer, I hollered at Dweller, and it stopped. Dweller had grown to be very large and had wings now, just like Galaxy said would happen. I wasn't afraid because of what Galaxy had told him. I knew that once the cave was opened up again, that would be where I could always find Dweller. What Galaxy didn't tell me was that I could talk to Dweller like a person, Dweller would understand what I said. I had a new friend and was very excited about telling Izzy when I saw her. I stood there looking at Dweller, and he looked at me as if we'd known each other forever. I said goodbye to Dweller and let him continue on toward the cave. I then turned the tractor back toward where Logger was.

"Logger, I'm back!" I announced.

"Did you see anything, Hunter?" Logger asked.

"No. By the time I got over to those trees, whatever it was had gone, and I didn't see anything," I fibbed.

"Well, I know that I saw something," Logger said, confused.

"It's okay. We'll worry about it if you see it again. I'm going to head back to town now for the rest of the day and take care of a few things, unless you need me here," I stated.

"No problem, Hunter. I'll be okay," Logger replied.

"All right, then, I'll see you tomorrow."

I wanted to see Izzy to tell her what was happening and what I had seen.

"Hey, Izzy, how's it going?" I said after walking into the tavern.

"It's just going, you know," Izzy replied.

"Logger is getting the poles in the ground, and he's doing a great job. I told him that I'd see him tomorrow, but you'll never guess what we saw out there in the field. Logger saw it first!"

"What was it?"

"It was Dweller walking across the other side of the field. I knew when I saw him, but Logger didn't know anything about Dweller and thought that it was some kind of big creature. Anyway, I went over to where Dweller was, and you'll never believe how big he has grown. He has wings now, so he will be able to fly. Oh, and he can also understand what I say to him."

"How is that possible?" Izzy asked.

"I don't know. Not much was said, but I can tell he knows what I'm thinking."

"So what happened?"

I explained, "Nothing happened. Dweller is supposed to go the cave and live, so that is where he was heading. I said goodbye, and he left."

"What did you tell Logger when you got back?"

"I didn't tell him anything. I simply said whatever it was that he thought he saw was gone, so he should not worry about."

"Wow! It sounds like you've had quite a day."

"Well, yes, I guess you could say that," I agreed.

"So what else do you have planned?" she asked.

"Well, because Dweller is going to the cave to stay, I guess Logger and I will continue with the fence and then the cabin. Once we have the cabin nice inside, I'm going to want to talk to Galaxy again and find out a little more about the scrolls. Izzy, it's like every time I talk to Galaxy, I'm learning something different about the queen, what she wrote in the scrolls, and what she wants me to do," I explained.

"We want to know all that Galaxy has to say, right?"

"Yes, I think you're right," I agreed.

CHAPTER 29

The following day, I went to order some material for the cabin. The roof and the floor both needed some wood replaced, along with updating the rest of the cabin. I had the material scheduled to be delivered in a few days, along with some more fencing. Once that was done, I decided I wanted a well put in so we could have running water. Hundreds of years ago, back when Sir Hunter first built the cabin, there was only water from the river that was available. This would be a nice addition for the cabin.

After a few weeks passed, the fencing was completed, and the cabin was close to being done. I was out in the barn when Galaxy appeared and said, "Hunter, the queen wants you to find out what it will take for you to buy Bonefairy Castle from the government. It is going to take a lot of money, but with all the gold that the queen has given to you, it shouldn't be a problem. You simply need to know the amount. The queen and her fairies still live at the castle, but no one knows about it."

I said, "I will do whatever is requested of me, and I will find out when I go back in town what I will need to do to buy Bonefairy Castle. Oh, by the way, Dweller has gone back to the cave."

Galaxy said, "Yes, I know. Once Dweller was fully grown, that was what the queen intended. Dweller will be guarding the castle now that he is fully grown, and he will only trust you, Hunter. This is why you will need to buy the castle."

I said that I understood and would go back into town to see about the castle. I closed up the barn and thought that I had better check on Logger in the field before heading back to town, to see how he was doing and ask if he needed anything.

"Hey, Logger, how's it going?"

"I think that I'll be finished out here sometime today," Logger stated.

"Hey, that's great. When you're done, just head on back into town, and I'll meet you at the tavern and buy you a good meal. How's that sound?" I offered.

"Anytime you want to buy me a good meal, I won't complain!" Logger smiled.

"All right, I'll see you back in town, then."

I left Logger and said that I would see him later. I stopped by the tavern and told Izzy, "Logger is going to be coming in for a meal, and I'm hoping you can do something special for him. He hasn't had a good meal in a while."

Izzy asked, "Did Logger finish the fence?"

"Yes, he did, and that's why I want him to have a good meal."

"All right, I'll make him something special. Are you going to be here to eat too?" Izzy asked.

"Yes, I will be, but I'm heading to the county building right now to find out about how much Bonefairy Castle costs to buy it from the government," I explained.

"Hunter, why do you want to do that?" she asked.

"When I was back in the barn, Galaxy showed up and said that the queen wanted me to take some of the gold and buy the castle. What am I supposed to say? No? We wouldn't even have any of the gold if it wasn't for the queen, right?"

"Did Galaxy say why the queen wanted you to buy it?"

"Galaxy said that the queen and the fairies have always lived there, and now that I'm here, they're going to be around. The queen didn't want the government to always be there. Galaxy said that there are many things that we need to know about Bonefairy Castle. The castle can be restored back to what it once was," I informed her.

"I understand. So are you going to do this today?" Izzy inquired.

"If Galaxy says that I need to do this, I guess that I should go right away," I concluded.

"All right, well, I guess you'd better go!"

I headed for the county building and didn't know what I would have to do to buy the castle. With the government owning it, there would have to be a lot of paperwork to fill out before it could be purchased.

I walked into the building and approached one of the county clerks. "Hi, I would like to find out about Bonefairy Castle," I announced.

"Sir, what do you want to know?" the clerk asked.

"Well, I was told that the government owns it. Is this right?"

"Yes, that is correct."

"Well, how do I find out about buying it from the government?"

The clerk was confused. "Really, sir? What are you saying?"

"I'm saying that I want to know what I have to do to buy Bonefairy Castle," I explained.

"Well, government land and property can be bought, but there is paperwork that must be filled out before we continue."

"Yes, I understand. That is why I'm here, so I can do this and get started now. I figured there was going to be a process that needed to be done before I could buy it."

"Sir, I'll go get the paperwork so you can start filling it out—if you really are serious?"

"Yes, I'm really serious," I concurred.

"Okay, well, I'll be right back."

A few minutes later, the clerk came back with some papers and said, "You can start with these papers, and I'll see if there is a purchase price. I can't believe that you really want to buy Bonefairy Castle. The castle has been there for hundreds of years, and now you want to buy it? Wow! Can I ask you what you are planning on doing with it if you get it?"

"Well, yes, I want to update everything and restore whatever needs to be done. You see, my ancestors lived around there a long time ago, and they even worked inside and served the queen. So it's something that I want to do," I explained.

"If you have that much money, I guess you can buy it," the clerk replied.

"I know that it's not going to be cheap."

"That's an understatement. Sir, I'll be right back. I'm going to go check to see if I can get the price." The clerk left and soon returned with paperwork. "Well, I found out that if you are going to update and restore it, the government wants the castle to continue to be here, because it's a landmark and is very special as far as history is concerned. The price really isn't as bad as I thought it would be. If you're going to do what you say you're going to do, are willing to put everything in writing, and fill out all the proper paperwork, you can buy it for just two million dollars. Then if you want to add some of the land that goes with it, that will be more depending on how much land you want."

"I understand. Let's work on getting the castle for now, and I'll have to do some figuring on how much land I will want. Do you know how much land is available to buy?"

"It says here that the castle sits on five thousand acres," the clerk responded.

"Wow, that's a lot of land."

I took the paper, and sat down at a table to fill it out. I had no idea how much it was going to take. There were a lot of papers. It took me a while to read through everything. I was no lawyer, and some of the legal jargon was difficult to follow, but as I read it carefully, it was as if it became clear to me. It made me wonder whether Galaxy's powers had anything to do with it.

I said, "Here's the paperwork all filled out, so you can get everything started. I know that something this big is important to the town, so I'm sure it will take some time. I'll check back in a few days, if that's all right?"

The clerk nodded. "Yes, that will be fine. We should have everything all set by then."

CHAPTER 30

I headed back to the tavern to see Izzy. She was waiting on a few people who were there to eat. Bonefairy House that was now just a tavern, but it always had good food, and many of the townspeople came here. I looked around and headed for the kitchen, wanting to talk to Izzy and tell her what I had found out about purchasing the castle. Izzy had a big pot of homemade soup warming on the stove, and it smelled good.

At about that time, Izzy walked into the kitchen and said, "Hi. So what's happening?"

"I found out what it's going to take to buy Bonefairy Castle, and it's not as bad as I thought it would be," I announced.

"Really? How much?"

"Can you believe it's only two million dollars?"

"Only? You're kidding, right? That's still a lot of money. But I guess for what you're buying, it isn't that much," she responded.

"No, I'm not kidding. I thought it was going to be a lot more than that. Also, it's sitting on five thousand acres that are also available. We need to talk to Galaxy and find out just what I'm supposed to do and how much of the land I'm supposed to buy," I said.

"My relief should be coming in to work in a few minutes. If you want, we can go out to the cabin and see if Galaxy will show up so we can talk to her," Izzy suggested.

"That sounds good, but I think I'm going to have some of that soup you made before I do anything." My mouth was salivating.

"Yes, it does smell pretty good, doesn't it?"

"And how does it taste?" I asked.

"Well, you are going to have to tell me. I made a lot, but many of the customers have been asking for it, so it's going pretty fast."

"Okay, give me some over here at the table. I'm starving!"

I finished the soup, and Izzy did a little cleaning so we could head for the cabin. Logger was working around the cabin cutting weeds when we drove up.

"Hey, Logger, how's it going? It's starting to look pretty good," I said.

"Yeah, it's coming along. What have you guys been up to?" Logger asked.

"We're doing a little bit of everything. Hey, Izzy made some really good homemade soup, and we thought you may want some, so we brought you a container from the tavern," I offered.

"Thank you so much. I was trying to think what I was going to eat later," Logger replied.

"Well, there you go. Now you don't have to think about it. We're going to head to the barn to start moving a few things around," I announced.

"All right. Do you want some help?" Logger offered.

"No, that's okay. If we need you, I'll holler."

We headed for the barn, and Logger returned to cutting weeds. Once in the barn, it was just a few minutes before Galaxy appeared.

"I've been waiting for you, Hunter! I know what you are about to tell me about Bonefairy Castle, and I know what you are going to ask. The queen wants you to buy the castle and all the land around it, or at least you should be able to use the land if you don't buy it. Once the castle is purchased, you and Izzy can come and go as you please, and no one will be able to stop you. That is when the queen will show up and tell you about what she wants done, as well as what is in the scrolls that you will need to know. Let's leave everything as it is until you get the castle purchased, and then we will meet up in the castle and talk about what needs to be done."

"Okay, Galaxy. I told the clerk at the county building that I'd be back in a few days," I said.

"Yes, I know, and that will be just fine. We will have time to take some of the gold and change it money so you can purchase the castle. Remember that we already know what's going to happen."

"Yeah, I keep forgetting. How am I going to explain where all the money came from?" I asked.

"That is not for you to worry about. The money will be available in an account in your name with the bank, and it will appear as if the money has been there all along. There will be a spell to prevent anyone from making any inquiries about it," Galaxy explained.

We left the barn after talking to Galaxy and waved at Logger as we got into our car. I hollered at Logger and said that we would be back later. Logger waved as our car drove away. I wanted to go into town so I could exchange some of the gold to use for purchasing the castle. When we arrived back into town, the same van that we had seen at Bonefairy Castle was following us.

"Hunter, why do you think they're following us again?" Izzy asked.

I stated, "I don't know, but I'm afraid that we will know before long. Here they come. They are gesturing for me to pull over."

"Well, we'd better pull over, then. They can't know what we are doing!"

"Let's see what they want. Maybe it's nothing. Here they come." I said to the men, "Can I help you? Why did you want us to stop? We haven't done anything!"

"Sir, I've been instructed to have you follow us to our headquarters. We have a few questions we need answered. Please, follow us," the man replied. The men got back in their car.

"Great. I guess we'd better do what we're told," I decided.

"Hunter, they can't know anything," Izzy said.

"Maybe that's the problem. They're trying to find out what we're doing."

"Well, we can't say that Galaxy has told us to buy the castle, right?"

"Yeah, right. We're going to say that a fairy asked us to buy the castle. Get real. Of course we can't say that! So, let's just wait and see what they want," I suggested.

"No need to get snippy!" Izzy said, making a face.

CHAPTER 31

When we arrived at the county headquarters, we were told to follow the men into the building. The federal agents instructed us to go into a room where a team was waiting.

One of the agents said, "I know you guys are wondering what's going on and have some questions, but let me say this first: you haven't done anything wrong."

"We know that we didn't, or at least we aren't trying to do anything wrong. So why are we here?" I asked.

"We have you here to ask a few questions. We have been watching you, Hunter. Is it okay if we call you Hunter?" the agent asked.

"That's my name."

"Hunter, we've been watching you for a little while. We've been watching you and your lady friend going to Bonefairy Castle. You've been going back and forth to the castle more than the average person, and we are wondering why."

"Izzy and I just like castles. That's all," I informed him.

"You know that Bonefairy Castle is owned by the government, right?"

"Yes, we were told that," I responded.

"Well, anything that the government owns, we watch really close. You guys have been there even when we said that you couldn't go in or come back. So why are you breaking in?"

"We felt that we were being harassed. We simply wanted to look around, and suddenly we weren't allowed to go inside. We didn't break in. We went through a different way. The back door wasn't locked," I explained.

"Well, Hunter, when we told you that you can't go into the castle, that means you don't have permission, so that's breaking the law. That is why you are here today. So before we do anything, we have decided to ask a few questions and see what kind of answers you are going to give. We know that you are not from around here, right?"

"Yes, that's correct. I'm from America," I replied.

"Okay, then. Why break the law and get into trouble?" the agent inquired.

"I traveled all this way to look at the castle because of my ancestors. I've already told you that they were in the castle, and I wanted to learn more about my family history. I am not hurting anyone. But I promise you that I won't go back to the castle anymore without permission."

"We know that, because if you do, we will pick you up and charge you with breaking and entering, and I know you don't want that," the agent threatened.

"Yes, of course not."

"You said you found gemstones in the castle. Did you find any more? Whatever happened to them?"

"I still have them. I did not find any more, or anything else in the castle," I lied.

"We're going to want those gemstones because they're the property of the government," the agent said.

"Okay, I can get them and bring them to you. Where do you want to meet so I can bring them to you?" I asked.

"We'll be in touch. We know how to get hold of you. Okay, you guys can go now. I don't expect to see you at the castle anymore!" the agent stated.

"Thank you, sir," I said, and we left the building. "Izzy, let's get out of here! We've got things to do before we get into trouble. Once we have the deed to Bonefairy Castle and it belongs to us, we won't get into any more trouble, and they can't tell us what to do. Then we can do whatever we want!"

"Hunter, I've got to say that you sure do make a girl's life interesting," Izzy noted.

"Hey, I try."

"Are you going to give them some of the gemstones?" Izzy asked.

"I think we can spare a couple to keep them satisfied and out of our way."

"You're probably right. We can give them a couple of small ones. They can't prove how much we found, or even the size."

"That is exactly what I was thinking. Boy, are we a team!" I proclaimed.

We were pretty pumped up but nervous about having to talk with those agents, but we had to move on and continue with our lives. Logger and I continued to work on the cabin, and Izzy worked at the diner and the tavern.

I had to give the courthouse Izzy's phone number for them to call me when the paperwork was done for my purchase of Bonefairy Castle. I didn't have a phone hooked up yet, but I was working on it.

About a week went by, and Izzy got a phone call from the courthouse. When I drove into town for some lunch at the diner, she told me they had called.

"Oh, great. I will call them back," I said.

I used the pay phone at the diner and called the number Izzy gave me. The call didn't last long and I came back to my table and Izzy was standing there tapping her foot on the floor with her hands on her hips.

"Well, what did they say?" Izzy asked impatiently.

"The clerk said that everything is set, and we can come in anytime to sign the paperwork and purchase Bonefairy Castle. We simply need to have a bank check," I explained.

"Great! I'm starting to get excited."

"Yeah, it's really kind of cool, isn't it?"

"Heck, yeah!" Izzy said.

"Not everyone can say that they own a castle. Okay, we'll go to the bank first and then head to the county building to buy a castle!"

"Then to the tavern to celebrate," Izzy agreed.

"That's for sure!" I responded.

We headed for the bank. Even though Galaxy said we wouldn't have any issues getting the money for the purchase, it still seemed weird to simply walk in and ask for a bank check for that much money. But when we got to the bank and asked the teller for the bank check, she didn't even blink an eye. She informed us that due to the large amount, it would have to be approved by her manager. We waited while the bank teller went to get her manager. A few minutes later, the manager came out and approved the bank check. I shook the manager's hand, put the check in my pocket, and left the bank. We then headed for the county building headquarters.

We arrived at the county building, walked in, and asked the county clerk for the papers to buy Bonefairy Castle.

The clerk smiled and said, "Really? You're here to sign some papers to buy Bonefairy Castle?"

I replied, "Yes, that's right. We were here a few days ago, talked to a different clerk, and filled out some papers to get it started. Now we're here to close the deal. I was told then that it was going to take a few days to get everything in order and that I would get a phone call when everything was ready. Well, I got the call, so now here we are to do whatever we have to do to finalize everything."

"Okay, I'll be right back," said the county clerk.

I looked at Izzy and smiled. "I guess it does sound a bit crazy buying a castle, so it makes sense that we get some crazy looks."

As the clerk came back with the papers, she said, "I will need for you to follow me to an office to complete the paperwork."

"Okay, that's fine," I said.

We followed the county clerk to an office. After filling out everything and giving the bank check, we were told that it was going to take a few more days before the deed was available. I said that I understood there was a lot to go through before it could be finalized, and I would check back in a few days. We left the county building and got in our car.

"Okay, Izzy, let's head for the tavern. I need something to eat, and all this running around has got me a little tired," I suggested.

"I agree, but it's going to be well worth it in the end," she concurred.

CHAPTER 32

A few days later, we got a call from the county courthouse that the deed was ready, so we went back to the county building and picked up the deed for Bonefairy Castle. While there, I asked if I was going to have any trouble getting in the castle. The county clerk advised me to keep a copy of the deed and title on me to prove that I was now the owner. Also, anyone could check back at the county building for proof. I said thanks, and we headed back to the tavern.

"How does it feel to be a proud owner of the famous Bonefairy Castle?" Izzy asked.

"It hasn't really sunk in yet, but I'm sure it will once I'm able to go back there and walk in without any issues. I think I'm going to go see what Logger is doing. If he isn't in the middle of anything, I want to take him to Bonefairy Castle to see what he can start working on as far as repairs."

"Okay, but I think we need to see if we can talk to Galaxy before we do anything. After all, Galaxy is the one who knows what's really going to happen, right?" Izzy asked.

"Yes, I guess you're right. Do you want me to wait until you are able to go out to the cabin?"

"Yes, I think that would be nice. I do want to know what's happening," Izzy replied.

"All right, how long before you can leave?"

"How about thirty minutes?"

"Okay that's cool!" I concurred. I sat down at a table, and Izzy brought me a beer.

She was soon finishing up with cleaning, and I told I'd meet her in the car. Izzy soon walked out and got in the car.

"I can hardly wait to get back out to the cabin to talk to Galaxy," I said.

"I'm interested in knowing what's next myself," Izzy agreed.

As we drove up to the cabin, we saw Logger sitting out on the porch and drinking some coffee. He waved as we drove up.

"Hey, how's everything going?" I asked.

"Oh, just fine, I guess. Is everything okay with you guys?" he replied.

"Yes, everything couldn't be better."

"Well, that's good. So what's up?"

"We have been a little busy in town for the last few days, and we just now got a little time to see what you have been doing."

"I've been clearing some of the weeds around the place here, trying to make it look a little nicer," Logger replied.

"Izzy and I think that you've done a great job, and it looks a lot better. Logger, have you got any more of that coffee made?"

"No, I'm sorry, I just drank the last cup. But I can make some more, if you want me to," Logger offered.

"That would be great. Izzy and I want to do something in the barn, and we'll be back in a little bit," I announced.

"That's no problem. See you guys in a little bit, then," Logger said.

We headed for the barn as Logger went into the cabin to make some more coffee.

"I hope Galaxy shows up," I said anxiously.

"Remember that Galaxy knows what's happening, and I'm sure that it won't be long before she appears," Izzy stated.

We reached the barn and started to open the barn doors up, and suddenly there was Galaxy.

"Hey, Galaxy, I was hoping to talk to you," I said.

"Yes, I know. I know that the deed to Bonefairy Castle is now in your name. I also know that you want to know what is going to happen next. If you remember, I told you once Bonefairy Castle is yours, the queen will appear and will want to talk to you. She has been waiting a long time for this to happen. When you go back to the castle, she'll appear. I can also tell you that you'll need to bring the scrolls with you when you go to Bonefairy Castle. The queen is going to go through them with you. There is a lot of important information written in the scrolls that she'll show you and explain to you. Make sure to bring them, because if you forget, the queen will not appear. The scrolls are the key to everything going forward."

"Okay, Galaxy, I won't forget," I assured her.

Logger hollered that the coffee was ready, and I hollered back that we'd be there in a minute.

"Hunter, try to go to Bonefairy Castle tomorrow—and bring the scrolls," said Galaxy.

"All right, Galaxy, I will. We'll see you tomorrow." And just like that, Galaxy was gone.

We closed up the barn and headed for the cabin for some coffee.

"Hey, Hunter, can I ask what's going on in the barn?" Logger inquired.

"I'll fill you in on everything when it's time. I can't right now," I replied.

"Oh, okay. I didn't mean to intrude. I was just curious, because you go out there a lot."

"The coffee smells good," I praised.

"Go ahead and help yourselves. I need to get back doing a few things before the daylight is gone," Logger announced.

"Oh, sure. We don't want to keep you, Logger. Izzy and I will drink our coffee and enjoy ourselves. We'll let you know when we're going to leave," I said.

"That's fine," Logger answered.

Logger headed out the door to finish getting rid of the weeds. We stayed inside drinking our coffee, and we wanted to try to figure out what we were going to do now that they could go to Bonefairy Castle.

"Hunter, we need to think about everything that we're going to want to do at the castle," Izzy stated.

"I know, but I have a feeling that we need to wait to talk with the queen, because if we make plans, they could end up getting changed due to what she wants us do," I decided.

"Yeah, you're probably right."

"Let's wait and see what's going to happen tomorrow when we talk to the queen. I want to make sure that I don't forget the scrolls," I said.

"We can finish our coffee and let Logger know that we're going back into town. We'll see him later," Izzy said.

We gave Logger a wave as we left for town and said that we would see him later.

CHAPTER 33

Once back at the tavern, I wanted to look at the scrolls again. I wanted to make sure we were ready for the queen at Bonefairy Castle. I did not know what she would say, and my mind kept swirling with thoughts.

"Izzy, I'm not going to be able to do much of anything the rest of the day, because all I can think about is tomorrow and the queen," I informed her.

"Why don't you relax a little? Tomorrow will come before you know it," Izzy suggested.

"I know, but I'm trying to think of what the queen is going to tell us. I can't imagine what's next. I know Galaxy keeps telling me that there is information in the scrolls, and the queen will share it with me. All of this is still too weird and hard to comprehend. I am so anxious"

"I'm sure that whatever the queen has to say is going to be something that is very important. She chose you, Hunter. That does seem like a lot of pressure, but so far Galaxy is making it easy for you."

"You're right. But I can't help wonder what it is and what the queen has in store for me."

"We will just have to wait and see."

The night seemed to drag. Then the next day finally came. I didn't sleep very well and was up most of the night, pacing.

"Hunter, what's going on? You are up kind of early," Izzy noted.

"I've been up most of the night, thinking about everything," I replied.

"Well, sit down and let me make us some breakfast, so at least we will have something in our stomachs before heading to Bonefairy Castle," Izzy offered.

"Okay, yeah, we may be there for a while, so that's a good idea," I agreed.

"Just take it easy, and we'll get there," Izzy assured me.

"I know. I'm just anxious."

"Yeah, I can see that. I have to clean up a little after we eat, and then we can go. Hunter, why don't you put some water bottles for us in the car, along with the scrolls, and then I should be ready."

"Yes, I can do that," I concurred.

We closed up the tavern and headed for Bonefairy Castle. As we drove up to the main gate, we saw that there was a lock on the gate, and we didn't have any keys for it.

"Hunter, what are we going to do about the lock? I don't remember there being a lock before," Izzy said.

"I don't know. I guess I can call the county office and ask."

"Well, if you ask me, I think that the lock is part of Bonefairy Castle now, and you should be able to do whatever you want with it," Izzy replied.

"Hey, I think you're right. It's on my gate, so I should be able to remove it anyway I want, right?"

"That's right. So break it open!"

I got out of the car, opened the trunk, and got a tire iron. As I was about to hit the lock with tire iron, the lock simply opened.

"Izzy, did you see what just happened?" I said, rubbing my eyes.

"Yes, I think so," Izzy responded.

"Maybe the lock wasn't really locked. Maybe it was there just for looks, so people would think they couldn't get in," I stated.

"Well, whatever. Let's go in"

"Right. I'll pull the car in through the gate and put the lock back on the gate, so it looks like nobody can get in," I announced.

"That is a good idea."

We pulled up to the castle and got out of the car. As we walked up to the main doors of the castle, we saw that the doors were open a little bit, and we walked in.

"Well, here we are!" I announced loudly.

"I still can't get over how huge this place is," Izzy exclaimed.

"Yeah, I know. I love it! So now all we have to do is wait for the queen to appear."

"Why don't we go look around a little while we wait?" Izzy said.

"Yeah, all right. Maybe we can find something that we didn't see before," I replied.

"I think the queen will show us everything that we're going to want to know."

We started moving through the castle, and it wasn't very long before Galaxy appeared.

"Hey, Galaxy, where's the queen?" I asked.

"The queen will appear when she is ready. Did you bring the scrolls?" Galaxy asked.

"Yes, we have them," I answered.

"You'll need to go to the queen's private quarters and wait. I will take you and Izzy there. The queen will then appear," Galaxy instructed.

We followed her with the scrolls and headed for the queen's private quarters. Once inside the queen's private quarters, a bright light shined in our eyes, and then suddenly the queen appeared. The light was so bright that it was hard for us to look at her directly. As the queen came closer, the bright light became a dim hue. We were able to see the queen then. She was very beautiful and had very wide, white feather wings and a long, flowing gown. Her hair was very long and golden and moved as if she was standing in front of a fan.

The queen said, "Hello, Hunter. I've been waiting for you for a long time. As you know, Bonefairy Castle has been here for hundreds of years, and so have I. There are many things that I've been waiting to tell you about the castle and the scrolls. I know that you have been through the castle and have seen many things, but there are a few other things that you do not know yet. There are many tunnels that were built under the castle that take you in many different directions away from the castle. In these tunnels, there are also secret rooms that only my fairies know about. Hunter, you have met only Galaxy. She is in charge of all the other fairies, and they live in these rooms that are hidden in the tunnels. This is why the tunnels go in different directions away from the castle, so the fairies can come and go. Galaxy will show you these tunnels and the secret rooms a different time, so you will know where they are.

"Galaxy has told you that the scrolls you have are important, and I will explain them to you so you can understand them. You are to use the information to build your company so the rest of the world can benefit. In the scrolls, you'll see that I have entered a way to get a person's DNA, which is the hereditary material in humans and almost all other organisms. Nearly every cell in a person's body has deoxyribonucleic acid. We want you to create your company to build a technique to identify all information about a person's DNA. This will not be something that will be available to just anyone. You may have wondered why this castle was called Bonefairy Castle. Well, the name Bonefairy was given by the people who once lived in the town next to the castle. The townspeople knew that I lived in the castle and did things with human bones or objects with human cells on them. No one ever saw what was done with the bones, but they knew that it strengthened my powers, so that is where *Bone* came from. The fairies would bring the bones to me and made sure to clean up any mess, so *fairy* became the rest of the word, to make *Bonefairy*."

"Hunter, your company is going to be able to scientifically extract DNA from any person so they can determine what the unique identity is. That is going to be very important to the rest of the world going forward. I have written in the scrolls everything that is needed to get a person's DNA, and only you will know how that is done. Your ancestor, Sir Hunter, was very loyal to me, and I trusted him. I know many years have passed, but you are the one I will trust with my scrolls and all the important information in them. The scrolls must remain here at Bonefairy Castle now that you own it. They can be hidden here behind a secret wall. I will always be here, along with Galaxy and the other fairies. We'll be able to help you when it comes to your company and the knowledge that you have to know about DNA."

CHAPTER 34

After spending most of the day with the queen and Galaxy at the castle, I said that Izzy and I were going to go back into town because we had a lot to think about and were tired. We went through a lot of details regarding what the queen wanted me to do with the scrolls and different parts of the castle. I said that we would be back tomorrow. We said our goodbyes to the queen and Galaxy and headed back into town.

"Hunter, we sure have a lot to think about now. What do you want to do?" Izzy asked.

"I'm not sure of anything right now. I didn't expect all this when I first came here. I just wanted to learn about my ancestors. I had no clue that I'd be buying a castle and starting a company," I stated.

"It sounds like you have a lot to consider."

"Yes, I know."

"You now own a castle and have the money to do just about anything that needs to be done to it. You just happen to have the best people—or should I say fairies—working for you, so how can you fail?" Izzy pointed out.

"Yeah, I know. I have to keep reminding myself that they will be there to help me so I won't fail," I said.

"Besides that, you have me. I love everything that has been happening. You even have a dragon. Ever since you got here, my days have been filled with new and exciting things," Izzy said, beaming.

"Hey, I think you'd better get used to crazy stuff for a while."

"Well, I'm ready!" Izzy said excitedly.

"I hope I am!" I looked puzzled.

"Let's have a beer and relax," Izzy suggested.

"Better make it two. All of this is just too good to be true. You know, speaking of the dragon, that's something else I need to be thinking about. I probably need to talk to the queen about Dweller. I forgot to even ask her about it."

"I hope it's all right and not in any trouble," Izzy said worriedly.

"I'm sure it's fine, but you're right. We had better find out what it's been up to. Maybe we can check on it tomorrow before we go back to Bonefairy Castle."

"You mean go to the cave? It's been a few days since we last saw the dragon. It could be anywhere," Izzy said.

"I know, but I think that we should check anyway," I replied.

"Yeah, and then what do we do?"

"Well, we can head for Bonefairy Castle."

"What about Logger?" she inquired.

"We can check on him too," I said.

"Hey, speaking of Logger, look who just walked in," Izzy said.

I said, "Hey, Logger, we were just talking about you. We were going check on you tomorrow out at the cabin. What brings you to town?"

"You guys aren't going to believe this, but I saw some big creature walking around out by the fence," he said, out of breath.

I looked at Izzy, and we both had that *uh-oh* look. I knew I had to eventually tell Logger about Dweller, but I was hoping for some more time with all the Bonefairy Castle stuff going on. "Logger, sit down and have a beer. You're going to need one after what I'm about to tell you," I said.

"All right, I'll have one. So what are you going to tell me? Do you know something about what is out there in the field?"

"Logger, what you saw out there walking around is a dragon. I didn't tell you because I didn't think that you would take me seriously," I explained.

"Well, I take you seriously now. Do you know how big that thing is?" He was exasperated.

"Actually, I haven't seen it for a couple of weeks, so I don't know how big it is. But I do know it's still growing. Hey, just wait until it starts flying!" I said.

"Say what? Did you say flying?" Logger asked.

"Logger, you remember me going out to the barn a lot a few weeks ago?"

"Yeah, I remember. I didn't know what was going on," Logger admitted.

"Well, that was when the dragon was still in an egg and hadn't hatched yet. It recently hatched and grew quickly. I have called it Dweller because it dwells in the cave up on mountain. Dweller knows me and isn't afraid of me. I was there when it first came out of the shell, so it kind of thinks I'm its mama or something," I explained.

"Well, Hunter, let me tell you: when Dweller comes around, I won't be around. It is just too big for me," Logger decided.

"I understand. I'll make sure that you know if it's coming. Since you are here and we're talking, I might as well tell you that I bought Bonefairy Castle yesterday. If you ever want to help me with some repairs there, I'll have plenty of work for you," I offered.

Logger looked shocked. "Wow, really? You really bought the castle?"

"Yes, I really did. I wasn't going to say anything for a while, but now that you know, I guess it's all right."

"Hunter, what are you going to do with a castle?" Logger asked, confused.

"I'm not really sure, but I had the chance to buy it, and I couldn't pass it up. I do know that I want to do a lot of updating and repairs, so you should have plenty of work, if you want it."

"That sounds like something I would like to do," Logger agreed.

"That's good! We'll get into all that in a few days, but for now have another beer," I offered.

The next day, I prepared to go back to Bonefairy Castle and see the queen. After breakfast, I grabbed the scrolls, and Izzy and I left for the castle. Once there, we went inside and started looking around waiting for someone to appear. I had the scrolls under my arm as we headed toward the queen's hidden quarters.

Suddenly Galaxy appeared. I said, "Oh, hi, Galaxy. We're just getting here and wanted to talk to the queen, if that's possible."

"Yes, Hunter, I know—and so does the queen. She is waiting

for you in her private quarters. Once you're in her quarters, she will appear," Galaxy instructed.

"Okay, great! I can't imagine what she wants to say about the scrolls."

"Hunter, you have to remember that she has been waiting a long time for you to show up. Why don't you take the scrolls, go over to that table over there, and roll the scrolls out across the table?" Galaxy instructed.

"Your Highness, you're here!" I hollered.

"Yes, Hunter, I am. I'm always around. Now, we need to talk about the scrolls and what are in them. You already know about the gold and precious stones. Those will be yours to use for what you need to do regarding what has been written in the scrolls. Back when your ancestor was here with me, I had him bring me bones from men who died in battle. The fairies and I took the substance from the bones in order to get the information needed to put in the scrolls. Once all the bones were recorded in the scrolls, the fairies would burn the bones to get rid of them. That is where all the black smoke came from, which the people in town saw. The scrolls are very sacred and need to be saved forever. Regarding all the writing that I have put in the scrolls, you'll be able to share it with governments and scientists. Many people will want to know how you have all this information and where it came from. This is something that you cannot tell anyone. The scrolls must never be available for anyone to see or examine. Even if by chance people get their hands on the scrolls, they won't be able to see the writing, because it will appear and be available only to you. I will always know where the scrolls are and who has them. If you happen to be with someone, and they look at the scrolls at the same time, you won't see any writing either. You will not be able to explain anything."

"This castle that you just bought was made available for you after you arrived here. You didn't know any of this, but I did, and so did the fairies. We have been waiting for you for a long time, and now that you're here, there is much for you to learn. I know that Izzy is a friend whom you have met here when you came to find your ancestors, but what you're going to learn about the scrolls, the castle, and the future is going to be made available only to you. Izzy is here with you, and we will show you many things here at Bonefairy Castle with her, but when it comes to the scrolls, she cannot be here. I will wait until the time comes and will explain it then. Remember that only you will know what's in the scrolls, and you will be able to see the writing and understand the writing that I will make available to you. The next time, you must come alone. We understand that Izzy will want to be here, but she cannot be here when I make the writings in the scrolls known to you. This is the way it must be. We'll know when you'll be by yourself. For now, let us go to another part of the castle. The castle is very big, as you know, but there are places in the castle that you don't know about. Down under the castle is where the fairies live, and that is why most people never see them. Passageways and tunnels to rooms are there for the fairies. This too is written in the scrolls."

"Your Highness, I understand what you've explained to me, but I would like to ask you about Dweller, the dragon who lives in the cave now. Can you tell me anything?" I asked.

"Hunter, Dweller will be yours for your protection and will be here for as long as you live. Dweller isn't a pet! I can have Dweller do many things, and I do so will when necessary. When you learn what is in the scrolls, you'll understand everything. Why don't we figure on you coming back here tomorrow by yourself, and then we can begin?" the queen instructed.

"Okay, Your Highness," I answered.

"For now, we can show you and Izzy the castle and answer any questions that you have," the queen offered.

"Well, Your Highness, can you tell me how many fairies you have?"

"Hunter, there are many, and Galaxy is in charge of them. Galaxy will always be around for you to call upon. She knows what is in the scrolls but isn't allowed to tell you. As for how many fairies I have, let me say that I have all I want or will ever need."

We started walking through the castle. The queen took us below the castle.

"Down here under the castle, as you can see, there is water that comes in from the river. The castle was built here for that reason, so water would always be available. You will want to use the water that comes in here in the future. Over there are the hidden rooms in which

223

the fairies live. You can see them only as long as Galaxy is here with you, or when I allow it. Once you know the information in the scrolls, you'll know about the fairies, where they are, and where they live. The fairies are here to do everything that I and Galaxy need done. The fairies can change into different things and do things that you'll never be able to explain to anybody. They get their powers from me. Things will also be made known to you once you learn the scrolls," the queen explained.

We walked through the tunnels under the castle. There were so many, and every once in a while, I'd see something move in one of the tunnels or passageways.

"Are those the fairies I keep seeing?" I asked.

"Yes, Hunter. They are busy at work with cleaning and getting the castle ready for you," the queen replied. "I think that is enough for today. You both can go back home. Hunter, you come back tomorrow alone."

"Okay, Izzy, let's go, and then I'll come back tomorrow."

Izzy smiled. "Yes, Hunter, I understand what is happening, and I realize that this is the only way the scrolls are going to be known to you. I'll wait in town until you come back and tell me what's happened."

"Izzy, I appreciate you being so understanding. I'm so glad that you are here and are a part of this," I replied.

We left the castle and headed back to the tavern.

"Hunter, I know that you're going to be learning a lot from the queen and Galaxy, and you won't be able to tell me everything, so I won't even be able to understand what you're trying to say," Izzy said.

"I keep thinking all of this is a dream, and I'll wake up and it will be gone," I admitted.

"I know what you mean. When this all started, I thought none of this could be true. It is really out there," Izzy replied.

"No one believes me back at home in America," I said.

"Speaking of that, what are you going to say to you parents?" Izzy asked.

"I haven't gotten that far yet, but I'm sure I'm going to have to tell them sooner or later.".

We sat there at the table for a while. Victoria brought us over a beer. I sat there and stared at the mug. I felt numb.

The next day, I told Izzy, "I'll be back as soon as I can."

"I know. Be careful, please. You really don't know what is going to happen," Izzy replied.

"I know, but I will know in a little bit." I smiled and waved goodbye.

I drove straight to Bonefairy Castle and didn't want to waste any time. As I drove back, I couldn't help but think, *I must be really nuts. It seems the queen is really depending on me. I can't imagine what on earth she is going to share with me.* Once I got back to the Bonefairy Castle, I went directly to the queen's private quarters.

Galaxy and the queen were there, waiting. "Your Highness, I came back as soon as I could," I said.

"I know, and I appreciate it. Galaxy is going to have you do something. I don't want you to be concerned, but you will need to do what you are told," the queen instructed.

"Okay, Your Highness, I understand. So, Galaxy, what am I supposed to do?" I asked.

"Hunter, you are to come over here to the table. There is a small vile of magical potion for you to drink. This is only here for you. The queen has created this magical potion that will put you in a deep sleep for about an hour. When you come out of your sleep, you will know everything that is in the scrolls. The magical potion will enlarge your brain and transfer all the information in the scrolls to the front of your brain, which is the parietal lobe in the hidden part of your brain. You'll not be able to tell anyone what has happened or explain it to anyone. This is why it must be done while you're sleeping. You'll know what has happened, but you can't explain it."

"Will I feel any pain? I am not really fond of pain."

"No, Hunter, you will not feel any pain. You will feel different, but in a good way," the queen explained.

"This is all very impressive. I feel honored you've chosen me. So you want me to go ahead and drink the magical potion now?" I asked.

"Yes, Hunter, drink it now!" Galaxy ordered.

I picked up the vile and examined it in. Galaxy and the queen watched me with anticipation. I slowly lifted the vile to my mouth and said, "Well, here it goes."

I drank the magic potion like I was told, and in a few minutes the potion started to take effect. I was facing the queen and Galaxy, and they started to look blurry. I reached out to them as if I was hallucinating, and then I could feel my eyes get heavy. I tried to keep my eyes open, but then I put my head down on the table and fell into a deep sleep.

An hour later, I came out of my sleep and looked around the room. The queen was gone, and only Galaxy was there.

"Galaxy, what happened to me?" I asked.

"You fell asleep, as I told you would happen. Now you know what is written in the scrolls, and only you will be able to look at them. The scrolls will have to remain here in the queen's private quarters at Bonefairy Castle. They can never be seen again by anyone but you. You will use the information that was transferred from the scrolls to your mind, to build your company," Galaxy explained.

"I don't feel like I've been asleep that long. I don't feel any different," I admitted.

"That is understandable. It won't really take effect until you realize the knowledge you've gained. When that happens, it will be as if it all comes naturally to you. People will be astonished at how much you know, but they will certainly appreciate your knowledge."

"I'm very excited for this new endeavor that the queen has given me. I feel like Sir Hunter did back when he served the queen."

"Yes, Hunter. Be assured that I will always be with you as you develop what you've learned from *The Scrolls of Bonefairy Castle*, and I'd like to emphasize that you remember my name, because the future of humankind depends on it," Galaxy said as she flew straight up. Then poof—she was gone.

The queen of Bonefairy

Sir Hunter, royal servant to the queen of Bonefairy

The mean ogre

The werewolf

The tormenting toad

The mermaid

The fierce dragon

Galaxy, the leader of the fairies, who serves the queen of Bonefairy